BETTER OFF DEAD

No Longer The Property
Of Security Public Library

Also by HP Mallory:

THE JOLIE WILKINS SERIES:

Fire Burn and Cauldron Bubble
Toil and Trouble
Be Witched (Novella
Witchful Thinking
The Witch Is Back
Something Witchy This Way Comes
Stay Tuned For The Jolie Wilkins Spinoff Series!

THE DULCIE O'NEIL SERIES:

To Kill A Warlock
A Tale Of Two Goblins
Great Hexpectations
Wuthering Frights
Malice In Wonderland
For Whom The Spell Tolls

THE LILY HARPER SERIES:

Better Off Dead

BETTER OFF DEAD

Book 1 of the Lily Harper series

HP MALLORY

BETTER OFF DEAD
by
H.P. Mallory

Copyright © 2013 by H.P. Mallory

All rights reserved. Without limiting the rights under copyright reserved above, no part of this publication may be reproduced, stored in or introduced into a retrieval system, or transmitted, in any form, or by any means (electronic, mechanical, photocopying, recording, or otherwise) without the prior written permission of both the copyright owner and the above publisher of this book.

This is a work of fiction. Names, characters, places, brands, media, and incidents are either the product of the author's imagination or are used fictitiously. The author acknowledges the trademarked status and trademark owners of various products referenced in this work of fiction, which have been used without permission. The publication/use of these trademarks is not authorized, associated with, or sponsored by the trademark owners.

For One Of My Readers, Amanda Mulkey:

Your courage is awe inspiring.

I'm so grateful my books brought you into my life.

Much love,

HP

Acknowledgements:

To my family: Thank you for everything.

To Sherita Eaton: Thank you so much for entering my "Become a character in my next book" contest. I hope you enjoy seeing yourself in print!

To my beta readers: Evie Amaro and the Eaton sisters: Thank you so much for all your help!

To my editor, Teri, at www.editingfairy.com: thank you for an excellent job, as always.

"Midway upon the journey of our life, I found myself within a forest dark, For the straight foreward pathway had been lost."
— Dante's *Inferno*

ONE

The rain pelted the windshield relentlessly. Drops like little daggers assaulted the glass, only to be swept away by the frantic motion of the wipers. The scenery outside my window melted into dripping blobs of color through a screen of gray. I took my foot off the accelerator and slowed to forty miles an hour, focusing on the blurry yellow lines in the road.

Lightning stabbed the gray skies. A roar of thunder followed and the rain came down heavier, as if having been reprimanded for not falling hard enough.

"This rain is gonna keep on comin', folks," the radio meteorologist announced. Annoyed, I changed the station and resettled myself into my seat to the sound of Vivaldi's "Four Seasons, Summer." *Ha, Summer ...*

The rain morphed into hail. The visibility was slightly better, but now I was under a barrage of machine-gunned ice. I took a deep breath and tried to imagine myself on a sunny beach, sipping a strawberry margarita with a well-endowed man wearing nothing but a banana hammock and a smile.

In reality, I was as far as possible from a cocktail on a sunny beach with Sven, the lust god, as possible. Nope, I was trapped in Colorado Springs in the middle of winter. If that weren't bad enough, I was late to work. To make matters worse? Today was not only my yearly review but I also had to give a presentation to the CEO, defending my decision to move forward with a risky and expensive marketing campaign. So, yes, being late didn't exactly figure into my plans.

With a sigh, I turned on my seat heater and tried to enact the presentation in my head, tried to remember the slides from my PowerPoint and each of the topics I needed to broach. I held my chin up high and cleared my throat, reminding myself to look the CEO and the board of directors in the eyes and not to say "um."

"Choc-o-late cake," I said out loud, opening my mouth wide and then bringing my teeth together again in an exaggerated way. "Choc-o-late cake." It was a good way to warm up my voice and to remind myself to pronounce every syllable of every word. And, perhaps the most important point to keep in mind—not to rush.

This whole being late thing wasn't exactly good timing, considering I planned to ask for a raise. With my heart rate increasing, I remembered the words of Jack Canfield, one of the many motivational speakers whose advice I followed like the Bible.

"'When you've figured out what you want to ask for,' Lily, 'do it with certainty, boldness and confidence,'" I quoted, taking a deep breath and holding it for a count of three before I released it for another count of three. "Certainty, boldness and confidence," I repeated to myself. "Choc-o-late cake."

Feeling my heart rate decreasing, I focused on counting the stacks of chicken coops in the truck ahead of me—five up and four across. Each coop was maybe a foot by a foot, barely enough room for the chickens to breathe. White feathers decorated the wire and contrasted against the bright blue of a plastic tarp that covered the top layer of coops. The tarp was held in place by a brown rope that wove in and around the coops like spaghetti. I couldn't help but feel guilty about the chicken salad sandwich currently residing in my lunch sack but then I remembered I had more important things to think about.

"Choc-o-late cake."

The truck's brake lights suddenly flashed red. The chicken coops rattled against one another as the truck lurched to a stop. A vindictive gust of wind caught the edge of the blue tarp and tore it halfway off the coops. As if heading for certain slaughter wasn't bad enough, the chickens now had to freeze en route. My concern for the birds was suddenly interrupted by another flash of the truck's brake lights.

Then I heard the sound of my cell phone ringing from my purse, which happened to be behind my seat. I reached behind myself, while still trying to pay attention to the road, and felt around for my purse. I only ended up ramming my hand into the cardboard box which held my velvet and brocade gown. The dress had taken me two months to make and was as historically accurate to the gothic period of the middle ages as was possible.

I finally reached my purse and then fingered my cell phone, pulling it out as I noticed Miranda's name on the caller ID.

"Hi," I said.

"I'm just calling to make sure you didn't forget your dress," Miranda said in her high pitch, nasally voice which sounded like a five-year-old with a cold.

"Forget it?" I scoffed, shaking my head at the very idea. "Are you kidding? This is only one of the most important evenings of our lives!" Yes, tonight would mark the night that, if successful, Miranda and I would be allowed to move up the hierarchical chain of our medieval reenactment club. We'd started as lowly peasants and had worked our way up to the merchant class and now we sought to be allowed entrance into the world of the knights.

"Can you imagine finally being able to enter the class of the knights?" Miranda continued. Even though I obviously couldn't see her, I could just imagine her pushing her Coke-bottle glasses back up to the bridge of her nose as she gazed longingly at the empire-waisted, fur trimmed gown (also historically accurate!) that I'd made for her birthday present.

"Yeah, instead of burlap, we can wear silk!" I chirped as I nodded and thought about how expensive it was going to be to costume ourselves if we actually did get admitted into the class of the knights.

"And maybe Albert will finally want to talk to me," Miranda continued, again in that dreamy voice.

I didn't think becoming a knight's lady would make Albert any more likely to talk to Miranda, but I didn't say anything. If the truth be told, Albert was far more interested in the knights than he ever was in their ladies.

"Okay, Miranda, I gotta go. I'm almost at work," I said and then heard the beep on the other line which meant someone else was trying to call me. I pulled the phone away from my ear and after quickly glancing at the road, I tried to answer my other call. That was when I heard the sound of brakes screeching.

I felt like I was swimming in slow motion through the next few images—my phone bouncing off my lap as I dropped it, my hands gripping the wheel until my knuckles turned white, the pull of the car skidding on the slick asphalt, and the tail end of the truck, up close and personal. Time sped up and I braced myself for the inevitable impact.

Even though I had my seatbelt on, the jolt was immense. I was suddenly thrown forward only to be wrenched backwards again, as if by the invisible hands of some monstrous Titan. Tiny threads of anguish weaved up my spine until they became an aching symphony that spanned the back of my neck.

The sound of my windshield shattering pulled my thoughts from the pain. I opened my right eye—since the left appeared to be sealed shut—to find my face buried against the steering wheel.

I couldn't feel anything. The searing pain in my neck was soon a fading memory and nothing but the void of numbness reigned over the rest of my body. As if someone had turned on a switch in my ears, a sudden screeching met me like an enemy. The more I listened, the louder it got—a high-pitched wailing. It took me a second to realize it was the horn of my car.

My vision grew cloudy as I focused on the white of the feathers that danced through the air like winter fairies, only to land against the shattered windshield and drown in a deluge of red. Sunlight suddenly filtered through the car until it was so bright, I had to close my good eye.

And then there was nothing at all.

***

"Number three million, seven hundred fifty thousand forty-five."

I shook my head as I opened my eyes, blinking a few times as the scratchy voice droned in my ears. Not knowing where I was, or what was happening, I glanced around nervously, absorbing the nondescript beige of the walls. Plastic, multicolored chairs littered the room like discarded toys. What seemed like hundreds of people dotted the landscape of chairs in the stadium-sized room. Next to me, though, was only an old man. Glancing at me, he frowned. I fixed my attention on the snarly looking employees trapped inside multiple rows of cubicles. Choosing not to focus on them, I honed in on an electric board above me that read: *Number 3,750,045.*

The fluorescent green of the board flashed and twittered as if it had just zapped an unfortunate insect. I shook my head again, hoping to remember how the heck I'd gotten here. My last memory was in my car, driving in the rain as I chatted with Miranda. Then there was that truck with all the chickens. *An accident—I'd gotten into an accident.* After that, my thoughts blurred into each other. But nothing could explain why I was suddenly at the DMV.

Maybe I was dreaming. And it just happened to be the most lucid, real dream I'd ever had and the only time I'd ever realized I was dreaming while dreaming. *Hey, stranger things have happened, right?*

I glanced around again, taking in the low ceiling. There weren't any windows in the dreary room. Instead, posters with vibrant colors decorated the walls, looking like circus banners. The one closest to me read: *Smoking kills*. A picture of a skeleton in cowboy gear, atop an Appaloosa further emphasized the point. Someone had scribbled "ha ha" in the lower corner.

"Three million, seven hundred fifty thousand forty-five!"

Turning toward the voice, I realized it belonged to an old woman with orange hair, and 1950's-style rhinestone glasses on a string. A line of twelve or so porcelain cat statues, playing various instruments, decorated the ledge of her cubicle. What was it about old women and cats?

The cat lady scanned the room, peering over the ridiculous glasses and tapping her outlandishly long, red fingernails against the ledge. Her mouth was so tight, it swallowed her lips. As her narrowed gaze met mine, I flushed and averted my eyes to my lap, where I noticed a white piece of paper clutched in my right hand. I stared at the black numbers before the realization dawned on me.

Three million, seven hundred fifty thousand forty-five. She was calling my number! Without hesitation, I jumped up.

"That's me!" I announced, feeling embarrassed as the old man glared at me. "Sorry."

"Come on then," the woman interrupted. "I don't have all day."

Approaching her desk, I thought this dream couldn't get much weirder—I mean, I was number three million or something and yet there were only a few hundred people in the room? I handed the woman my ticket. She scowled at me, her scarlet lips so raw and wet that her mouth looked like a piece of talking sushi. She rolled the ticket into a little ball and flung it behind her. It landed squarely in her wastebasket, vanishing amid a sea of other white, scrunched paper balls.

"Name?" she asked as she worked a huge wad of pink gum between her clicking jaws.

"Um, Lily," I said with a pause, feigning interest in a cat playing a violin. It wore an obscene smile and appeared to be dancing, one chubby little leg lifted in the semblance of a jig. I touched the cold statue and ran the pad of my index finger along the ridges of his fur. I was beginning to think this might not be a dream, because I could clearly touch and feel things. But if this weren't a dream, how did I get here? It was like I'd just popped up out of nowhere.

"Last name?"

I faced the woman again. "Um, Harper."

The woman simply nodded, continuing to chomp on her gum like a cow chewing its cud. "Harper … Harper … Harper," she said as she stared at the computer screen in front of her.

"Um, could you, uh, tell me why I'm here?" My voice sounded weak and thin. I had to remind myself that I was the master of my own destiny and needed to act like it. And that was when I remembered my presentation. A feeling of complete panic overwhelmed me as I searched the wall for a clock so I could figure out how much time remained before I was due to convince a panel of mostly unenlightened penny-pinchers that we needed to invest nearly a quarter of a million in advertising. "What time is it?" I demanded.

"Time?" the woman repeated and then frowned at me. "Not my concern."

I felt my eyebrows knot in the middle as I glanced behind me, wondering if there was a clock to be found anywhere. The blank walls were answer enough. I faced forward again, now more nervous than before and still at a complete loss as to where I was or why. "Um, what am I doing here?" I repeated, not meaning to sound so … stupid.

The woman's wrinkled mouth stretched into a smile, which looked even scarier than all the grimaces she'd given me earlier. She turned to the computer and typed something, her talon-like fingernails covering the keyboard with exaggerated flourishes. She hit "enter" and turned the screen to face me.

"You're here because you're dead."

"What?" It was all I could say as I felt the bottom of my stomach give way, my figurative guts spilling all over my feet. "You're joking."

She wasn't laughing though. Instead, she sighed like I was taking up too much of her time. She flicked her computer screen with the long, scarlet fingernail of her index finger. The tap against the screen reverberated through my head like the blade of a dull axe.

"Watch."

With my heart pounding in my chest, I glanced at the screen, and saw what looked like the opening of a low-budget film. Rain spattered the camera lens, making it difficult to decipher the scene beyond. One thing I could make out was the bumper-to-bumper traffic. It appeared to be a traffic cam in real time.

"I don't know what this has to do …"

She chomped louder, her jaw clicking with the effort, sounding like it was mere seconds from breaking. "Just watch it."

I crossed my arms against my flat chest and stared at the screen again. An old, Chevy truck came rumbling down the freeway, stopping and starting as the traffic dictated. The camera angle panned toward the back of the truck. I recognized the load of chicken coops piled atop one another. Like déjà vu, the camera lens zoomed in on the blue tarp covering the chickens. It was just a matter of time before the wind would yank the tarp up and over the coops, leaving the chickens exposed to the elements.

Realization stirred in my gut like acid reflux. I dropped my arms and leaned closer to the screen, still wishing this was a dream, but somehow knowing it wasn't. The camera was now leaving the rear of the truck and it started panning behind the truck, to a white Volvo S40. *My white Volvo.*

My rational mind tried to reject the idea that this was happening—that I was about to see my car accident. Who the heck was filming? And moreover, where in the heck were they? This looked like it'd been filmed by more than one cameraman, with multiple angles, impossible for just one photographer.

I heard the sound of wheels squealing, knowing only too well what would happen next. I forced my attention back to the strange woman who was now curling her hair around her index finger, making the Cheeto-colored lock look edible.

"So someone videotaped my accident, what does that have to do with why I'm here?" I asked in an unsteady voice, afraid for her answer. "And you should also know that I'm incredibly late to work and I'm due to give a presentation not only to the CEO but also the board of directors."

She shook her head. "You really don't get it, do you?"

"I don't think *you* get it," I snapped. The woman grumbled something unintelligible and turned the computer monitor back towards her, then opened a manila file sitting on her desk. She rummaged through the papers until she found what she was looking for and started scanning the sheet, using her fingernail to guide her.

"Ah, no wonder," she said, snapping her wad of gum. She sighed as her triangular eyebrows reached for the ceiling. "He is not going to be happy."

I leaned on the counter, wishing I knew what was going on so I could get the heck out of here and on with my life. "No wonder what?"

She shook her head. "Not for me to explain. Gotta get the manager."

Picking up the phone, she punched in an extension, then turned around and spoke in a muffled tone. The fact that I wasn't privy to whatever she was discussing even though it involved me was annoying, to say the least. A few minutes later, she ended her cocooned conversation and pointed to the pastel chairs behind me.

"Have a seat. The manager will be with you in a minute."

"I don't have time for this," I said gruffly, trying to act out a charade of the fact that I *was* the master of my own destiny. "Didn't you hear me? I have to give a presentation!"

"The manager will be with you in a minute," she repeated in the same droll tone and then faced her screen again as if to say our conversation was over.

With hollow resignation, I threw my hands up in the air, but returned to the seat I'd hoped to vacate permanently. The plastic felt cold and unwelcoming. It creaked and groaned as if taunting me about my weight. I didn't need a stupid chair to remind me I was fat. I melted into the L-shaped seat and stretched my short legs out before me, trying to relax, and not to cry. I closed my eyes and breathed in for three seconds and out for three seconds.

Lily, stress is nothing more than a socially acceptable form of mental illness, I told myself, quoting one of my favorite self-help gurus, Richard Carlson. *And you aren't mentally ill, are you?*

No, but I might be dead! I railed back at myself. *But if you really were dead, why don't you feel like it?* I reached down to pinch myself, just to check if it would hurt and, what-do-you-know? It did ... *So, really, I can't be dead. And furthermore, if I were dead, where in the heck am I now? I can't imagine the DMV exists anywhere near heaven. If I'd gone south instead ... oh jeez ...*

Don't be ridiculous, Lily Harper! This is nothing more than some sort of bad dream, courtesy of your subconscious because you're nervous about your presentation and your review.

I closed my eyes and willed myself to stop thinking about the what ifs. I wasn't dead. It was a joke. Heck, the woman was weird—anyone with musician cat statues couldn't be all there. And once I met with this manager of hers, I'd be sure to express my dissatisfaction.

You are the master of your own destiny, I told myself again.

I opened my eyes and watched the woman click her fingernails against the keyboard. The sound of a door opening caught my attention and I glanced up to find a very tall, thin man coming toward the orange-haired demon. He glanced at me, then headed toward the woman, who leaned in and whispered something in his ear. His eyes went wide; then his eyebrows knitted in the middle.

It didn't look good.

He nodded three, four times then cleared his throat, ran his hands down his suit jacket and approached me.

"Ms. Harper," he started and I raised my head. "Will you please come with me?"

I stood up and the chair underneath me sighed with relief. I ignored it and followed the man through the maze of cubicles into his office.

"Please have a seat," he said, peering down his long nose at me. He closed the door behind us, and in two brief strides, reached his desk and took a seat.

I didn't say anything, but sat across from him. He reached a long, spindly finger toward his business card holder and produced a white, nondescript card. It read:

Jason Streethorn

Manager

AfterLife Enterprises

"We need to make this quick," I started. "I'm late to work and I have to give a presentation. Can we discuss whatever damages you want to collect from the insurance companies of the other vehicles involved in the accident over the phone?" I paused for a second as I recalled the accident. "Actually, I think I was at fault."

"I see," he said and then sighed.

I didn't know what to say, so I just looked at him dumbly, ramming the sharp corners of the business card into the fleshy part of my index finger until it left a purple indentation in my skin.

The man cleared his throat. He looked like a skeleton.

"Ms. Harper, it seems we're in a bit of a pickle."

"A pickle?"

Jason Streethorn nodded and diverted his eyes. That's when I knew I wasn't going to like whatever came out of his mouth next. It's never good when people refuse to make eye contact with you.

"Yes, as I learned from my secretary, Hilda, you don't know why you're here."

"Right. And just so you know, Hilda wasn't very helpful," I said purposefully.

"Yes, she preferred I handle this."

"Handle this?" I repeated, my voice cracking. "What's going on?"

He nodded again and then took a deep breath. "Well, you see, Ms. Harper, you died in a car accident this afternoon. But the problem is: you weren't supposed to."

I was quiet for exactly four seconds. "Is this some sort of joke?" I sputtered finally while still trying to regain my composure.

He shook his head and glanced at me. "I'm afraid not."

His shoulders slumped as another deep sigh escaped his lips. He seemed defeated, more exhausted than sad. Even though my inner soul was starting to believe him—that didn't mean my intellect was prepared to accept it. Then something occurred to me and I glanced up at him, irritated.

"If I'm going to be on some stupid reality show, and this whole thing is a setup, you better tell me now because I've had enough," I said, scouring the small office for some telltale sign of A/V equipment. Or failing that, Ashton Kutcher. "And, furthermore, my boss and the board of directors aren't going to react well at all." I took a deep breath.

"Ms. Harper, I know you're confused, but I assure you, this isn't a joke." He paused and inhaled as deeply as I just had. "I'm sure this is hard for you to conceptualize. Usually, when it's a person's time to go, their guardian angel walks them through the process and accompanies them toward the light. Sometimes a relative or two might even attend." His voice trailed until the air swallowed it entirely.

Somehow, the last hour of my life, which made no sense, was now making sense. I guess dying was a confusing experience.

He jumped up, as if the proverbial lightbulb had gone off over his head. Then, throwing himself back into his chair, he spun around, faced his computer and began to type. Sighing, I glanced around, taking in his office for the first time.

Like the waiting room, there weren't any windows, just white walls without a mark on them. The air was still and although there wasn't anything offensive about the odor, it was stagnant, like it wouldn't know what to do if it met fresh air. The furniture consisted of Jason's desk, his chair and the two chairs across from him, one of which I occupied. All the furniture appeared to be made of cheap pine, like what you'd find at IKEA. Other than the nondescript furniture, there was a computer and beside that, a long, plastic tube about nine inches in diameter, that disappeared into the ceiling. It looked like some sort of suction device.

With a self-satisfied smile, he faced me again. "We have your whole life in our database."

He pointed toward the computer screen. "My whole life in his database" amounted to a word document with a humble blue border and my name scrawled across the top in Monotype Corsiva. It looked like a fifth grader's book report.

He eyed the document and moved his head from right to left with such vigor, he reminded me of a cartoon character eating corn. Then I realized he was scanning through the Lily Harper book report. With an enthusiastic nod, he turned toward me.

"Looks like you lost your first tooth at age six. Um … In school, you were a year younger than everyone else, but smarter than the majority of your class. You double majored in English and Political Science. You were a director of marketing for a prestigious bank."

"'Were' is a fitting word because after this, I'm sure I'll be fired," I grumbled.

The man paused, his eyes still on his computer. "When you were eighteen, you had a crush on your best friend and when you tried to kiss him, he pushed you away and told you he was gay."

I stood up so fast, my chair bucked. "Okay, I've heard enough."

The part about Matt rebuffing my kiss was something I'd never told anyone. I'd been too mortified. Guess the Word document was better than I thought.

"It's all there," Jason said as he turned to regard me with something that resembled sympathy.

"I don't understand …" I started.

He nodded, as though satisfied we'd moved beyond the "you're dead" conversation and into the "why you're dead" conversation. He pulled open his top desk drawer and produced a spongy stress ball—the kind you work in your palm. The ball flattened and popped back into shape under the tensile strength of his skeletal fingers.

"I'm afraid your guardian angel wasn't doing his job. This was supposed to be a minor accident—just to teach you not to text and drive, especially in the rain."

"I wasn't texting," I ground out.

Jason shrugged as if whatever I *was* doing was trivial and beside the point. "Unfortunately, your angel was MIA and now here you are."

I leaned forward, not quite believing my ears. "I have an angel?"

Jason nodded. "Everyone does. Some are just a little better than others."

I shook my head, wondering if there was a limit to how much information my small brain could process before it went on overload. "So, let me understand this, not only do I have a guardian angel, but mine isn't a very good one?"

"That about sums it up. Your angel ..." He paused. "His name is Bill, by the way."

"Bill?"

"He's been on probation for ... failing to do his duties for you and a few others."

My hands tightened on the arms of my chair as I wondered at what point my non-comprehending brain would simply implode with all this ridiculousness. "Probation?"

He nodded. "Yes, it seems he's had a bit of trouble with alcohol recently."

"My angel is an alcoholic?" I slouched into my chair, the words "angel" and "alcoholic" swimming through the air as I began to doubt my sanity.

"Yes, I'm afraid so."

Jason parted his thin lips, but that exhausted look resurrected itself on his face. I was quick to interrupt, shock and anger suddenly warring within me until I couldn't contain them any longer. "This is the most ridiculous thing I've ever heard! Alcoholic angels? I didn't even know they could drink!"

"They can do everything humans can," he said in an affronted tone, like he was annoyed that I was annoyed.

I sat back into my chair, not feeling any better with the situation, but also figuring my outbursts were finished for the immediate future. Well, until I could come to terms with what was really going on. But flipping out wasn't going to do me any good. I needed to stay in control of myself and in control of my emotions. Wayne Dyer's words, "it makes no sense to worry about things you have no control over because there's nothing you can do about them," floated through my head as I tried to prepare myself for whatever I had coming.

Jason Streethorn, the office manager of death, folded his hands in his lap and leaned forward. "Since your angel, our employee, failed you, we do have an offer of restitution."

Apparently, this was where the business side of our conversation began. "Restitution?"

"Yes, because this oversight is our fault, I'd like to offer you the chance to live again."

I had to suspend my disbelief of being dead in the first place and just play along with him, figuring at some point I'd wake up and Jason Streethorn, the orange-haired woman and this DMV-like place would be nothing more than the aftermath of a cheese pizza and Coke eaten too close to bedtime. "Okay, that sounds good. What do I ..."

He rebuffed me with his raised hand. "However, if you accept this offer, you'll have to be employed by AfterLife Enterprises."

I sank back into my chair, suddenly wanting nothing more than to pull my hair out. "What does that mean?"

He sighed, as though the explanation would take a while. "Unfortunately, AfterLife Enterprises is a bit on the unorganized side of late. When the computer system switched from 1999 to 2000, we weren't prepared, and a computer glitch resulted in thousands of souls getting misplaced."

The fact that death relied on a computer system which wasn't even as good as Windows XP was too much. "The Y2K bug didn't affect anyone."

Jason worked the stress ball between his emaciated fingers, making multiple knuckles crack, the sound imbedding itself in my psyche. "On Earth, it didn't affect anything, but such was not the case with the AfterLife." He exhaled like he was trying to expel all the air from his lungs. "Unfortunately, we were affected and it's a problem we've been trying to sort out ever since." He paused and shook his head like it was a great, big shame. Then he apparently remembered he had the recently dead to contend with and faced me again. "As I said before, due to this glitch, we've had souls sent to the Kingdom who should've gone to the Underground City. And vice versa." He paused. "And some souls are locked on the earthly plane as well. It's been a big nightmare, to say the least."

My mouth was still hanging open. "The Kingdom and the Underground City? Is that like heaven and hell?" Why did I have the sudden feeling he was going to start the Dungeons and Dragons lingo?

"Similar."

I rubbed my tired eyes and let it all sink in. So, not only were there bad dead people in heaven, aka the Kingdom, but there were good dead people in hell, aka the Underground City? And to make things even more complicated, there were bad and good dead people stuck on Earth?

"Is that still happening now? Or did you fix the computer glitch?" I asked, wondering if maybe I'd been sent to the wrong place. I thought this place seemed like hell from the get-go. And though I was never a church-goer, I definitely wasn't destined for the South Pole.

"We fixed the glitch, but that doesn't change the fact that there are still thousands of misplaced souls. And the longer those souls who should be in the Kingdom are left in the Underground City, or on the earthly plain, the bigger the chances of lawsuits against AfterLife Enterprises. We've already had a host of them and we can't afford anymore."

I didn't have the wherewithal to contemplate AfterLife lawsuits, so I focused on the other details. "So how are you going to get all those people, er souls, back where they belong?"

"That's where you would come in, should you accept this job offer."

"I would bring the spirits back?" I asked, aghast. "I'd be a ghost hunter or something?"

He laughed; it was the first time he seemed warm and, well, alive. Funny what a laugh will do for you.

"Yes, your title would be 'Retriever' and we have hundreds who, like you, are currently retrieving souls."

An image of the Ghostbusters jumped into my mind and I had to shake it free. Whatever this job entailed, I doubted it included slaying Slimer. "And if I don't agree?"

Jason shrugged and turned to the computer again. After a few clicks, he faced me with a frown. "Looks like you'll be on the waiting list for the Kingdom."

"The waiting list?" I asked, shocked. "I think I've led a pretty decent life!"

He shook his head and faced the computer again. "I show three accounts of thievery—when you were six, nine and eleven."

"I was just a kid!"

He cleared his throat and returned his attention to the Word doc. "I also show multiple accounts of cheating when you were in university."

Affronted, I launched myself from the chair. "I've never cheated in my life!"

He frowned, looking anything but amused. "No, but you aided a certain Jordan Summers by giving him the answers in your Biology class and I show that happened over the course of the semester."

I sat back down and folded my arms against my chest. "I would think helping someone wouldn't slate me for a waiting list!"

"Cheating takes more than one form." He glanced at the screen again. "Shall I go on?"

"No." I frowned. "So how long will I be on the waiting list?"

He leaned back in his chair and resumed working the stress ball. "You're fairly close to the top of the list since your offenses are only minor. I'd say about one hundred years."

"One hundred years!" I bit my lip to keep it from quivering. When I felt I could rationally conduct myself again, I faced Jason. "So where would I be for the next one hundred years?"

"In Shade."

I frowned. "And what is that? Like Limbo?"

"Yes, close to it."

"What would I do there?"

He shrugged. "Nothing, really. Shade exists merely as a loading dock for those who are awaiting the Kingdom ... or the Underground City."

I didn't like the sound of that. "What's it like?"

"There is neither light nor dark, everything exists in gray. There's nothing good to look forward to, nor anything bad. You just exist."

"But if those people who are going to hell," I started.

"The Underground City," he corrected me. "Those destined for the Underground are kept separate from those destined for the Kingdom," he finished, answering my question before I even asked it.

I felt tears stinging my eyes. "Shade sounds like my idea of hell."

Jason shook his head while a wry chuckle escaped him. "Oh, no. The Underground City is much worse." He paused. "The good news is that if you do become a Retriever and you relocate ten souls, you can then go directly to the Kingdom and bypass Shade altogether."

"So I wouldn't have to go to Shade at all?"

"As long as you relocate ten souls, you bypass Shade," he repeated, nodding as if to make it obvious that this was the choice I should make.

"What does retrieving these souls mean?"

He started rolling the stress ball against his desk. "We'd start you with one assignment, or one soul. With the help of a guide, you'd go after that soul and retrieve it." He paused. "Are you interested?"

I exhaled. Did I want to die and live the next century in Shade? The short answer was no. Did I want to be a soul-retriever? Not really, but I guessed it was better than dying.

"Okay, I guess so."

"We could start you out and see how you do. You can always decide not to do it."

"But then I'd die?"

"I'm afraid that's the alternative."

"Why can't you let me go back to my old life?"

He shook his head. "It's not possible. Your soul has already left your body. Once the soul departs, the body goes bad within three seconds. Unfortunately, you are way past your three seconds. That and the coroners have already pronounced you dead and the newspapers are preparing your obituary. Your mother was notified, as well."

Mom has been notified ... Something hollow and dreadful stirred in my gut and started climbing up my throat. I gulped it down, hell-bent on not getting hysterical. Tears welled up in my eyes and I furiously batted them away.

"I never got to say good-bye," I managed as I tried to rack my brain to remember the last conversation I'd had with my mother, the only person (besides Miranda) with whom I was close. Truly, my mother and Miranda were my best friends. And right about now, both of them had to be traumatized.

Jason nodded, but it wasn't a nod that said he was sympathizing. It was a hurried nod. "I'm sorry; but you need to make a decision soon. Time is of the essence and Shade will be calling soon to find out if you're joining them."

I forced my tears aside and focused on his angular face, trying to ignore my grief so I could come to a decision which would completely change the course of my life ... or AfterLife. "So, if I take this job and choose to live, I can't do so in my own body?"

It wasn't like I was thrilled with my appearance: I was short, overweight and plain. I was the woman whom no one ever noticed—the one always behind the scenes. I'd had one major boyfriend in my life and that had lasted all of two months. Yep, anyway I looked at it, I was basically hopeless—a twenty-two-year-old workaholic virgin with nothing but the redundancy of a stress-inducing job to force me to wake up each morning. But, I was me, and the idea of coming back in another body left me cold. No pun intended.

"You would not be able to come back as yourself," Jason said. "You'd have to come back in another body."

I glanced down at myself. As far as I could tell, I still looked the same. "But, I'm in my body now."

"You're here in spirit only."

The phone on his desk rang and he faced me with impatience etched in his eyes and mouth. "That's probably Shade calling."

He picked up the phone. "Jason Streethorn, AfterLife Enterprises, how can I help you?

After a few nods, he glanced at me. "Yes, she's here. She's just deciding what she wants to do. Yes, I understand it's been over an hour."

He muffled the end of the phone with his palm and faced me again. "You need to decide now." He faced the phone again. "Yes, I've informed her. You're going to send someone over within the hour?"

"Wait," I interrupted. "Tell them I'll take the job. I want to live."

"So bitter is it, death is little more."
— Dante's *Inferno*

TWO

Jason Streethorn hung up the phone and gave me a big smile. I figured he wanted me to make this decision—to become an employee of AfterLife Enterprises. And me? Well, even though the words just sort of vomited from my mouth, I wasn't sure I'd made the right decision. Frankly, I'd just come to terms with the idea that I was dead, and this wasn't some prolonged and awful dream. And then there was the part about my mom having just been notified of her only child's demise.

More than anything else, I wanted to tell her how much I loved her. Reassure her that I was going to be fine …

I turned away from Jason, feeling tears welling in my eyes. I focused on the pristine white of the office walls, trying to talk my tears into retreating. The fact that there were no pictures, no smudges or spots of any kind to interrupt the milky white of the walls suddenly infuriated me. How could someone spend the majority of his time in a room that looked this unlived in? I scanned the wall, searching for some sort of flaw—an insect, a scratch, anything! But there was nothing.

Jason clapped his hands together and I begrudgingly faced him again.

"We have much to do," he said, spearing his tongue against his teeth a few times like he was trying to suck out something left over from lunch.

"Did you have a will?" he asked.

"No," I said with a shrug. "All I ever owned was my car." And I think I was overdrawn in my bank account. Overdraft charges? Ha! I got the last laugh on them.

Jason nodded. "Okay, then that makes things a bit easier. We'll just open you a new account."

"A new account?"

"Yep," he nodded emphatically. "This is the best part ... the benefits for working for AfterLife Enterprises. You'll get company housing, a company car, a company credit card and company allowance."

Wow, this wasn't sounding half bad ... well, if I could get past the being dead part.

"First things first, we need to find you a new name." He turned to his computer and started typing like a madman. I watched the screen as a database of names popped up. He moused through them so quickly, I felt like I was reading a book on fast forward.

"A new name? Why can't I ..." I didn't finish my sentence before realizing the answer. Lily Harper was dead. *Lily Harper was dead.*

I felt a pang of nausea churn my gut. *It makes no sense to worry about things you have no control over because there's nothing you can do about them,* I told myself, recalling Wayne Dyer's advice again. *There's nothing you can do about them ...*

"You can keep your first name, but as for your second..." Jason's voice grew quiet as he hit "enter" and the database stopped spinning. One name was highlighted among the rest.

"O'Shaughnessey," Jason announced.

"What? I'm Irish now?"

He laughed. "Well, your name is."

"Lily O'Shaughnessey," I said, trying out the flavor on my tongue. "I guess it sort of has a nice ring to it."

"Hilda will take care of your new legal documents while we finish up the rest of this. By the time we're done here, you'll have a new birth certificate, social security card, driver's license, passport and green card, if you require one." He paused and glanced at me. "But more on that later."

I'd never had a passport before. That was sort of cool. But as to the green card …

"Okay," Jason said, turning to face me again. "Now, where you're going to live … We have corporate housing all over the world."

"I want to live abroad," I said quickly, suddenly wanting this new life of mine to be totally new. If I was going to start fresh, I didn't want any reminders of my old life. I didn't think I had the emotional strength to handle it. Instead, I wanted to embark on a completely new voyage, leaving everything I knew far far behind.

"Okay," he said as he brought up what looked like a real estate multiple listings page.

"So, how does this corporate housing work? Do I have to pay rent?"

Jason didn't turn around, but continued searching through the listings. "No, we cover your room and board. We give you whatever you require, and in return, you work a few jobs during the year for us."

"A few jobs during the year?" I argued. "At that rate, it will take me years to relocate the ten souls!"

Jason shrugged. "So take on more jobs." Then he glanced over at me again. "Besides, you won't age."

I didn't know what to say to that, so chose not to respond, instead turning to other questions swarming my mind. "So I don't get a salary?"

He shook his head, still intently scanning through the house listings. "You'll get an allowance, but not a salary. The allowance is to cover things you can't use a credit card for. Just think of it as a bank account that maintains a high balance."

Hmm … a consistently full bank account didn't sound half bad. Sort of like repeatedly passing "Go" in Monopoly. "So, do I use a debit card?"

He nodded. "Yes, and you also get a corporate credit card. Whatever you need, you can use one or the other, though we prefer you use the credit card—it's easier to sort out any fraudulent charges." Jason stopped typing and turned back to me, shifting the screen so we both could view it. "Okay, looks like we've got several properties available. We've got a penthouse in Barcelona, Spain; a cabin in Quebec, Canada; and an elaborate apartment in Edinburgh, Scotland; just to list the first three ..." he started scrolling for more listings, but my mind froze on the apartment.

"This one in Scotland," I started.

Jason clicked and pulled up the listing. I'm not sure the word "apartment" did it justice. From what I could see, it was at the top of a four- or five-story brick building, overlooking a vast sea of green grass, scored by walking paths. Hugging both sides of the paths were mature and densely foliated trees that acted as umbrellas over the walkways.

"A charming apartment facing the Meadows of Edinburgh," Jason read. "Conveniently located near the city center, the Meadows is one of the nicer areas of Edinburgh. Enjoy free golf," he glanced up at me, adding, "apparently, you just bring your own clubs and balls." Then he looked at the listing again. "With views of the Edinburgh Castle and Arthur's Seat."

"What's Arthur's Seat?" I asked.

Jason shrugged and read through the rest of the listing himself before facing me again. "Apparently, it's a well-known mountain that you can also hike."

"Oh," I said as I started fidgeting. The weight of this decision suddenly dawned on me. Was I really going to move so far away? To another country? Granted, Scotland wouldn't be too bad a location—I mean, they did speak English there, and I had to admit I was fond of men in kilts. Plus, *Braveheart* was my all-time favorite movie ...

"As to the apartment, itself," Jason continued, "it is two bedrooms, two bathrooms, has a view of the Meadows;

and apparently, each unit has its own private garden. It features: wood floors, high ceilings with crown molding, fireplaces in the living room *and* the master bedroom, tile in the kitchen and bathrooms ..." He paused for a moment or two. "You know, you don't have to live in an apartment. We have homes available as well."

But I didn't need a lot of space. I had no interest in pomp and circumstance. "The apartment sounds perfect," I said in a small voice.

Jason glanced at me. "Want it?"

I nodded dumbly and he clicked a red button that said "reserve." Then he exited the webpage. He leaned back in his chair and gave me a smile, as if waiting for something. Suddenly, what sounded like a vacuum emanated from the top of the long, plastic tube beside his computer. Before I had time to take another breath, something metallic dropped down the tube, landing on Jason's desk.

"Two sets of house keys," he said, handing them to me.

I just stared at the gold keys in my open palm, wondering if I was going to wake up. This was just too ... unbelievable.

"Now, we have some corporate cars available, if you're interested. Or you can simply go out and buy your own."

"What have you got?" I asked, feeling more like I was asking what flavors of ice cream he had available, not what vehicles he had in his fleet.

He pulled up another webpage and pored through a long list. It looked like the pages of *Autotrader*. "We have quite a selection. What do you like?"

I shrugged as I remembered my reliable Volvo. If only it could see me now. "Maybe an Audi?" I shrugged, hoping it wasn't too much to ask for; then something dawned on me. "Don't they drive on the other side of the road in Scotland?"

Jason glanced at me quickly. "Yes, but it won't take you long to get used to it. Those damned roundabouts, though, now they're another story." Then he chuckled at his own joke, which wasn't funny at all.

"Okay," I said with a hesitant smile.

"We have eighty Audis on file with the steering wheel on the right-hand side. Can you be more exact as to which model you'd prefer?"

Hmm, I didn't know anything about cars. All I knew was Audis were nice, but as far as models? I was clueless. "Um, I don't really know. I'm not much of a car person."

He smiled and shook his head, like it was a shame. "Okay, SUV?"

I did like SUVs. They were big … and safe. And safety was suddenly more important to me now than it ever had been before. "Yeah, an SUV sounds perfect."

He hit "enter" and a list of SUVs popped up. "How about the first one?" Jason asked. "It's not too big to maneuver, and lots of women buy them."

Jason clicked and a silver Audi popped up. I read the headline: "Audi Q5" and paused to consider it. It wasn't too boxy or overpowering. "I like it."

He clicked "reserve" then waited for the keys to pop out of the plastic tube. Once they arrived, he handed them to me.

"Now comes the truly fun part," he said with a grin that reminded me of the Cheshire cat. "You get to choose your new body."

Despite Jason's apparent delight, this was the part I liked least—it just seemed so weird, to be picking someone else's body, to suddenly look like someone else.

"Now, this is going to be tougher than choosing the car or the house because you'll have exactly three seconds to make your decision."

"Three seconds?" I repeated, my voice laced with doubt. I'd never been good with deadlines.

Jason nodded. "Yes, all the pictures you're about to see are people who are going to die within seconds. The body, once the soul leaves it, remains inhabitable for about three seconds; so you'll have to act quickly. Then once you decide, we have about two seconds to give you the animation shot. After that, you'll be good to go."

"Okay, hold it," I started, my stomach feeling as if it just dropped to my toes. "The animation shot?"

Jason nodded. "Yes, when the body you choose dies, it has a couple of seconds before it arrives at our morgue unit here. We'll take your soul into a syringe and then inject it into the body before it starts to deteriorate."

I could feel my brain starting to pound ... sort of like an ice cream headache. "But the body is still on Earth, right?"

Jason nodded. "A clone. It would be a very difficult thing if the body disappeared from the scene of its death altogether. So we just replace the real body with a fake one—it looks exactly the same as the original, made of flesh and blood."

"You replace it? And no one suspects anything? Don't they see you replacing it?"

Jason shook his head. "No, they see nothing. It happens in a split second, like magic, I guess you could say."

I couldn't seem to get past the fact that my entire identity could be sucked up into a little vial. That, plus I was never good around needles. "Okay, let's go back to the part about sucking up my soul into a syringe and then injecting it into the new body ... You haven't ever screwed this part up in the past, I hope?" I could just see myself coming back as a chimp.

"It's virtually mistake-free. No need to worry," he said with what I hoped was a genuine smile. "Now, time's wasting. Let's see what bodies are available for you."

I shook my head and narrowed my gaze on his screen, trying not to quantify the words "virtually mistake-free."

"How tall do you want to be?"

Okay, so I could kinda, sorta see how he could describe this part as fun. I mean, when did you ever get to build the perfect you? I turned my thoughts to the height question, but didn't have to ponder it long. I was short, so I wanted to be tall. "Um, how about five foot eight, with long legs?"

"Okay, let's give you a thirty-two-inch inseam." He entered my desired height into the proper field and made a note about my inseam. "Great. Now, how much do you want to weigh?"

Well, not as much as I did now, that was for sure. But I also didn't want to be stick thin. "How about one hundred forty?"

Jason nodded. "Okay, what size breasts do you want?"

Where my bust was concerned, all I could think about was the fact that throughout high school, the boys called me Billy instead of Lily. I wanted some serious boobs. "How about a thirty-six, D?"

Jason gave me a smile. "Okay, done. What hair and eye color do you want?"

And suddenly it occurred to me that there had to be something about the new me that resembled the old me. "Let's do dark red hair and green eyes."

"And age?"

That was easy. I didn't want to be any older than I already was. "Twenty-two."

Jason entered my final specification and clicked "submit." Instantly, about three hundred thumbnail-sized photos of women sprouted up.

"Okay, now scan through these profiles and decide which one you like," he ordered.

He stood up and motioned for me to take his seat. I did so and grabbed the mouse with a trembling hand. "This is final, right? I mean, I can't change my mind later?"

He nodded and leaned against his desk. "Yeah, no changing your mind. And once you click on a profile, you have a few seconds to make your decision."

Phew. That was a lot of pressure.

"Okay," I said as I started scanning. Waves of faces danced before me and all I could do was quickly focus on each one, trying to decide if it was a face that I wanted to replace my own. If I hoped my specifications would only yield attractive people, I was wrong. I was introduced to buck teeth, wall-eyes, voluminous noses and ski-jump chins. I gulped, thinking I could end up less attractive than I already was.

That's when I saw a face that truly could have launched a thousand ships.

"Wow, she's beautiful," I whispered, even though the image on her profile only revealed her head and shoulders. She had long, dark red hair and large, round, green eyes with a fringe of thick, dark eyelashes. Her eyebrows, which appeared to be natural, were narrow and perfectly arched in the middle. Her nose was pert and upturned, like something you'd imagine finding on a pixie. She was smiling in the photo and her smile revealed pouty lips and perfectly white, straight teeth. I eyed the red "reserve" button up above her smiling face with apprehension.

There was no going back if I clicked that button.

"Two seconds remaining."

It was like slow motion as I moved the mouse to the red button and clicked.

Then, before I could register what was happening, the tiny pinch of a pin-prick stung my arm. I glanced down to find Jason stabbing me with a syringe. My heart sped up as I watched the five-inch vial fill with blood.

Suddenly I felt faint, really faint.

"You're going to be fine, Lily. This is all going to seem like a dream to you."

"How do I get out of here?" I started, bracing myself against the desk in an effort to stand. Suddenly, the room was spinning and the white walls seemed to be breathing, pushing out against me only to suck themselves back in again.

"Everything will be taken care of for you." Jason's voice sounded distant, like he was whispering.

I wanted to say something. I had so many questions swimming through my brain, but all I could think about was closing my eyes.

I was suddenly so tired.

***

Something cold and hard pressed against my cheek. I opened my eyes to find myself lying on a hardwood floor. Pushing up on my hands and knees, I focused on the lines in the floor, which were knotted and hinted at pine or rustic maple. Hmm, since my apartment in Colorado Springs was lavishly adorned with wall-to-wall, shaggy brown carpet, I couldn't have been home.

Wondering if I were still asleep, I glanced around myself. Apparently, my brain hadn't yet woken up, because I didn't feel any panic at the sight of an unfurnished room dominated by a brick fireplace. To my left was a bay window that revealed acres of verdant grassland, bisected by paths and tall trees.

I had the feeling I wasn't in Kansas anymore, much less Colorado.

Like a bitter aftertaste, images of a white office with cheap furniture kept haunting my mind. My heart started throbbing as I stood up: the blood rushing from my head and shooting stars in my eyes. I stumbled like a drunken college student and closed my eyes against another vision—that of a waiting room with an angry, old man.

Leaning against the whitewashed wall of the living room, my parched throat ached with the need for water. Glancing around, I spied the kitchen and made my way toward the sparkling marble countertops. My heart felt like it was climbing into my throat, and I had to swallow it down.

I turned on the faucet and cupped my hands under the ice blue flow, gulping the water like a thirsty dog. Then, hoping it might wake me up, I splashed my face with the freezing cold water. That was when I realized I didn't have a towel. Oh, well, my shirt would have to do.

Glancing down at myself, the image of white terry short-shorts, a pink tube top and black high-heeled sandals met my delirious eyes. I never wore pink, since it clashed with my naturally red hair. But what floored me even more than the pink top were my legs. They were as long as flagpoles, long and skinny. Not my legs at all.

I felt a scream rising from my throat and collapsed against the marble countertop, smearing it with my sweaty palms. Flashes of miniature cat statues with musical instruments bounced through my head until it was all I could do to squeeze my eyes shut and hope the images disappeared.

"Adopting the right attitude can convert a negative stress into a positive one," I said out loud, repeating Hans Selye's mantra.

I forced my eyes open again and noticed a large, padded manila envelope lying on the counter before me. In scrawled, cursive writing, my first name was displayed like it was an invitation to Prince Charming's ball. I tore into the package, hoping it held answers for me, hoping a conversation with a guy named Jason was merely the fabric of my dreams. I gripped the spine of what felt like a book, and pulling it out, noticed it was a copy of Dante's *Inferno*. Not knowing what to make of the book, I set it on the counter beside the envelope and thrust my hand inside the package again. This time, I felt the thin edges of a piece of paper. I pulled it out and read:

Dear Lily,

I hope you like your new home. Please feel free to furnish it anyway you wish. Also, I forgot to mention that any contact with relatives only leads to complications. It's for this reason that we strictly prohibit any of our employees from contacting former family members or close friends. As far as your previous possessions, they have all been surrendered to your former mother and your old apartment is empty.

As you have agreed to take up the position of Retriever for AfterLife Enterprises, I searched our databases for openings, and found we are in desperate need of Retrievers in the Underground City. Before you worry yourself unnecessarily, you will be provided with a guide who will not only lead you through the City, but will also act as your guard. I've included a handbook to the Underground City which you might find useful.

I glanced at Dante's Inferno and had the sudden heart-wrenching suspicion that Jason must have made a mistake and sent me the wrong book. My heart started palpitating at the very thought of becoming a Retriever in what basically amounted to hell; and now it seemed I was even missing the proper guidebook. I glanced at the letter again, hoping Jason left some form of contact information.

The handbook, as you will find, is Dante's Inferno. *AfterLife Enterprises hired Mr. Alighieri back in the fourteenth century to chart a guide to the Underground City. While you will find many of his references and his writing, in general, a bit outdated, the book should certainly help you navigate your way throughout the levels of the Underground City.*

Should you have any questions, please contact me at the number below. It was a pleasure meeting you and I am very happy to welcome you to the AfterLife Enterprises team. We're all pleased to have you on board.

Warm Regards,
Jason Streethorn
Manager, AfterLife Enterprises
111-111-1111

I dropped the letter as if it burned me.

So it was true! Everything that seemed like a disturbing dream was reality. And a reality that meant I couldn't ever see my mother or Miranda again. I'd already assumed such was the case, but to see it in writing drilled the fact home even more. I couldn't even contemplate the idea that I was going to be soul retrieving in hell. No, as soon as I could collect my wits, I was going to call Jason and demand he find me a more suitable, not to mention safer, career.

As for now, I wouldn't allow myself to wallow in my own grief—I wouldn't allow myself to worry over the fact that I was now in a foreign country and thousands of miles from Colorado Springs. No, I would not give myself a pity party. Not if this was going to be my new life.

My new life ... I lurched forward, in search of a full-length mirror. The hallway off the kitchen led into a bedroom and I galloped down the hall like a newly born foal, feeling completely unaccustomed to my legs. Losing my balance, I careened into the wall and paced myself the rest of the way.

Not finding a mirror in the bedroom, I continued into the en-suite and was rewarded with an expanse of mirror above the dual sinks. Anxiety waged a destructive path from my gut to my head as I beheld the image reflecting back at me.

I was beautiful. Approaching the mirror tentatively, I couldn't stop my hands from exploring my face like a blind person. Gone were my flared-nostrils and pig-like nose. In its place was something that would make Nicole Kidman envious. My once smallish eyes had become orbs of green, fringed by extraordinarily long, black lashes. My cheekbones looked like they'd been sculpted by Da Vinci himself. My face was undeniably beautiful, waves of natural auburn hair rippling around it, reaching the tops of my boobs. My boobs ... I pulled my tank top forward and glanced down. I couldn't help gasping. I finally had boobs and they were in a word ... exquisite. I squeezed them to ascertain if they were real, and when the tensile spring of true flesh met my fingers, I couldn't stop smiling.

But just as quickly, the smile dropped right off my lips as the gravity of everything I'd just been through—the accident; knowing I'd never see my mother again; dying ... mingled into a tempest and beat down on me. I couldn't bear to watch my tears falling from alien green eyes, coursing down a perfectly sculpted cheek. Instead, I collapsed into a heap on the floor.

I wanted to fight against the sadness, but I wasn't strong enough. I wasn't even me! The tears didn't let up and I rocked back and forth, huddled into a little ball, amid a vacuous room that offered no solace.

A melodic harmony interrupted my breakdown session and I cocked my head to my right side, trying to decipher where it was coming from. It repeated, sounding like notes being plucked on a harp. I stood up and glanced around, seeking the source. A strident knock at the front door alerted me that someone was outside. The symphony of notes? Just my doorbell.

On unstable legs, I reached the front door and opened it while castigating myself for not checking the peephole first.

"It's about freakin', deakin' time."

The little man frowned and strode inside as I stood there, gaping at him. He threw his hands on his hips—spinning around as he surveyed the room with blatant approval. He was maybe five foot five, with a circular little body that made him look like an animated apple. His hair was thick and dark brown and looked as if it hadn't seen a shampoo bottle in weeks. He faced me again, a smile on a face so round, you could've bounced it. He was maybe in his early thirties.

"Nice digs. Where's all your furniture, though ... yo?" His voice sounded much too deep for such a squat little thing—like Danny DeVito lip-synching Barry White. I did, however, manage to find some semblance of comfort in his

American accent. He was American, I was American. At least we had that in common.

A gust of cold, Scottish air wrapped itself around my legs, and I realized I hadn't shut the front door. Never taking my eyes off my pudgy guest, even though I couldn't say he seemed in the least bit alarming, I closed the door behind us.

"Um, who are you?" I asked, finally finding myself.

They were the first words I'd spoken since occupying my new body, and my voice wasn't familiar. It was lighter and more sing-song than my old voice could ever hope to sound.

The man nodded, as if my question were reasonable and extended a pudgy hand with fingers that looked like white baby carrots. "I'm Bill, your guardian angel."

"One ought to fear those things only that have power of doing harm, the others not, for they are not dreadful."
— Dante's *Inferno*

THREE

I couldn't stifle my shock. This stout little man definitely didn't look like an angel. Not that I expected white, feathery wings, but wasn't cleanliness next to godliness? This guy looked like he'd been plucked from the *Animal House* set and dropped unceremoniously into my living room.

I crossed my arms over my chest, uncomfortable because he was ogling my breasts as if they were his opponents in a staring contest. 'Course, the top of his head was about bust level so maybe he couldn't help it. "You're Bill, my angel?"

"Is a frog's ass water tight?" he answered with a smile.

I frowned. "I guess that means yes?"

"Yessiree, Bob," he said, smiling widely, his teeth too large for his face. "Bill's ma name and thrills are ma game." Then he winked. When I didn't respond to his offered hand, he wiped it on his gray T-shirt that had as many stains as he had freckles across the bridge of his nose. He looked like Howdy Doody's slovenly, overweight cousin.

"What are you doing here?" I asked, still unfamiliar with the melodic tone of my voice. How long would it take to get used to the new me?

Bill plopped himself down on the floor and started retying one of his shoelaces as he turned his beady eyes up to me. "I'm your guide." He said it like there should have been a "duh" at the end of the sentence. "And I'm here to take you on your first mission; so get ready, girly."

"My first mission?" I repeated in disbelief. I had no time to consider when my first mission might be, but I never imagined it would've been the very day I arrived in my new home. I mean, my house was still unfurnished!

"Yep, we got us an appointment with the blacksmith."

"The what?" I asked, feeling a headache beginning behind my eyes. Everything just seemed to be happening so suddenly—first the arrival of this ... angel, and then the assignment of my first mission, a mere few minutes later? Apparently, things in the AfterLife moved lots faster than they did in my previous one.

"Yeah, the blacksmith," Bill repeated, frowning at me. "He's the dude who's gonna set you up with your weapons. He's gotta fit you for your sword and shiznit."

"My sword?" I asked, my tone clearly relaying the fact that swords and Lily Harper, er, O'Shaughnessey, weren't exactly a household item.

"How else are you gonna slay demons?" he asked, shaking his head. "Hello, McFly! Anyone home?"

"Demons?!" I exclaimed as my stomach dropped to my toes. I squeezed my eyes shut, thinking I desperately needed to get in touch with Jason Streethorn and protest this was NOT what I signed up for.

"They ain't so bad," Bill said, dismissing my outburst with a wave of his pudgy fingers. "Anyways, we got us a long-ass drive, so we'd better make like a fugly one-night-stand and get the hell outta here."

Instead of following Bill to the door, I glanced around the room, looking for a phone. Of course, there wasn't one.

"Watcha lookin' for?" he asked, slapping his hands on his hips.

"A phone; do you have one?"

He nodded, fishing inside his pocket. He produced a black cell phone, covered in electrical tape from having apparently been dropped too many times. I glanced at the sheet of paper with Jason's phone number and punched the numbers into Bill's phone. It rang ... and rang. After five more rings, I didn't expect anyone to pick up and waited for the voice mail or the machine to come on. But nothing. Another three rings, and I hung up.

"Callin' AE?" Bill asked, his eyebrows raised in an expression of discouragement. I just nodded as he shook his head. "Good luck gettin' through."

"It just rang," I said, swallowing hard.

"Yep, that's about right."

"You mean no one ever answers?"

"Odds are that monkeys would sooner fly outta my ass."

I just stared at him, unable to come to terms with the fact that he was an angel, and more so, that he was mine.

"Let's get to the blacksmith's and you can try AE again later, although you ain't gonna have much better luck."

"Why is that?" I demanded, feeling my heart pounding with panic that started down deep in my gut. What had I signed up for? This job was nothing like Jason had described it!

"'Cause AE don't wanna hear from you," Bill said matter of factly. "Yep, you and AE are like unrequited besties."

"Unrequited what?"

He shook his head like I was slow. "Unrequited best friends. You think you and AfterLife Enterprises are tight, right?" he asked and smiled at me, the smile immediately dropping off his face seconds later. "Wrong! AE wants a whole lotta nothin' to do with you, girl, so it's time you got that into your thick little pretty head and realized you gotta paddle your own ship."

"Canoe," I corrected him but it didn't seem as if he'd even realized he'd gotten the phrase wrong in the first place. I shook my head, determined that I would get in touch with Jason and demand that he resign me from the position of soul-retriever in the Underground City. The more I thought about it, the more I realized it had to have been a mistake. I was just a novice! There was no way I'd be able to defend myself against demons! But then I remembered Jason's letter, and how clearly he'd defined my role as a soul-retriever and there was that whole part about Dante's *Inferno* being my guide. Maybe it hadn't been a mistake after all? Maybe AE approached this whole thing with the shotgun mentality? Perhaps it was a numbers game and they'd rather throw me in the deep end, not really caring if I sank or swam. There were probably thousands of retrievers just like me; and according to the laws of probability, a percentage of us would no doubt swim. That must have been what AE was betting on ...

"Where are we going?" I asked Bill, figuring I had no other options at this point.

Bill glanced down at his pocket and pulled out a wrinkled piece of paper with coffee stains all over it. "Some place called Peter ... head." Then he started laughing uncontrollably. "Peterhead! Like dickhead! Who the hell names a city that?" he smirked, his whole belly contorting with chuckles. "Hey, Slick, what should we name our new town?" he said in a deep voice. He held his head high as he ran his hand down his filthy shirt, fisting his fingers around the fake collar of a suit jacket. Then he dropped the persona of what I imagined was supposed to be a mayor, and said, "Shit, I dunno, Mayor Peter, let's name it after something we both like ... how about head?" Then he bent over and started bellowing again, slapping his knees in time with his chortles.

I suddenly wanted to cry.

"You're my angel?" I repeated again. This time, my tone was filled with anguished concern.

"Yep, girl, believe it 'cause it's the truth," he said, winking at me. "Be happy you didn't get stuck with one of them boring a-holes." He shook his head and grinned wide. "Me? I'm a piss-your-pants good time."

"Weren't you on probation?" It suddenly occurred to me that the reason I was in this whole mess in the first place was owing to this repugnant creature. "And, by the way, I have a bone to pick with you."

"She said bone!" he squawked, erupting into a new round of raucous laughter.

"Stop it! This isn't funny!" I screamed at him, feeling my anger suddenly surging out of control as my voice broke. "It's because of you that I'm in this mess to begin with!"

"CTFD," he said and held up his hands in a play of submission, but the smile never left his lips.

"What?"

"Calm the fuck down, baby," he said and then smiled even more broadly. "I want you to know that I'm real sorry about the whole accident mess ..." I shook my head, not about to believe him, but he interrupted me. "No, seriously, I really am." He even dropped the smile before starting to eye me up and down appreciatively. "But, come on ... really, I did you a favor. I mean, you're way hotter now."

"I don't care about that!" I said, throwing my hands up in frustration as tears burned my eyes. I clamped them shut tightly, knowing I had to regain control of myself. If I lost control now, there was no telling if I'd be able to pick up the pieces again.

"Aw, come on, little goob, don't start crying."

I opened my eyes to find him smiling up at me. For some reason, and I don't know why or how, it was reassuring. I wiped my arm across my eyes and forced a smile of my own, reminding myself that everything happened for a reason. It was time to make lemonade out of lemons. "Little goob?"

"Yeah, you know, like junior goober?" He smiled wider. "It's okay, cream puff. We're gonna work it all out together."

I shook my head and didn't know what else to say or think—Bill had a way of addling my brain with incoherent thoughts.

"Don't you worry your hot little ass cheeks about it, 'kay?"

I felt my jaw drop as the tears started again. *How could I have ended up in this predicament?* I would soon be headed toward the equivalent of hell, where I'd have to defend myself against God only knew what, and my only asset was ... Bill?

Treat everyone you meet as if they were going to be dead by midnight. Extend to them all the care, kindness and understanding you can muster, and do it with no thought of any reward, I said to myself, repeating Og Mandino's words. I focused on Bill and wondered if I had the stamina to make Mr. Mandino proud.

"And as to my probation, pah!" Bill continued, physically brushing away my concern with a chunky and indifferent hand. "You got nothin' to worry about, girl. I've been on best behavior for the last six months and my probationary period is nearly over."

"So if you're on probation, why were you assigned as my guide?"

He leaned against the wall with a heartfelt sigh. "I don't think Jason Skeletor-Horn could find anyone else on such short notice."

I sighed long, deep and hard before shaking my head against the insanity of everything I'd experienced in the last four hours; or at least, it felt like it couldn't have been more than four hours. "I'm not sure how I feel about any of this," I mumbled. And that was the naked truth. I was starting to think AfterLife Enterprises had placed me at the bottom of the totem pole.

"Everything is gonna be fine, sugar nipples," Bill said with another grin. Then he glanced at his watch and frowned. "I left the car running so we'd better get going. It's a pretty long drive to Dickhead."

Care, kindness and understanding ...

He started for the door, shaking his head as a new round of mirth seized him. I followed, only because I wasn't sure what else I should do. I wanted to call Jason and scream at him that this was not what I signed up for, but the phone was in Bill's pocket and he was convinced I wouldn't be able to get through to Jason anyway, so what was the point?

I shut the door behind me without locking it, since there wasn't anything inside to steal. Then I took the stairs two at a time, with Bill directly in front of me. At the bottom of the stairwell, halfway parked in the grass and half on the pavers of the driveway, was the Audi I'd chosen in Jason's office.

"How'd you get …?" I started.

"Someone had to deliver it to you," he answered with a shrug. "You wanna drive or what?"

I couldn't say I was in any shape to get behind the wheel. 'Course, there was that little part about Bill and his alcoholism. "Jason said you were an alcoholic."

"I haven't had a drink in six months, or something like that. I'm on the clean and sober path." He said it like he wasn't exactly thrilled about it. I frowned and he continued. "Hey, I drove it over here in the first place … give a brother a break, yo."

I didn't have the energy or the wherewithal to argue; and there were those British roundabouts Jason warned me about. "Fine."

Like a scheming gnome, Bill smiled and rubbed his hands together before opening the car door. He climbed up the running board and heaved himself into the seat. I wasn't much more graceful; after tripping over my foot, I stumbled into the passenger's seat.

"So about this mission to the blacksmith's, are we going to be gone long?" I asked after realizing I hadn't packed an overnight bag and furthermore, had nothing to pack. "I don't have any clothes if it's going to be more than one day."

Bill nodded as he backed out of the driveway, looking over his right shoulder before offering me an apologetic smile and looking over his left. "Skeletor took care of all that. There's a bag packed for you in the trunk, which makes me guess that this little trip might be longer than a day."

The bag in the back relieved me slightly, but it didn't address the mysterious mission we were undertaking. "So what's this about the blacksmith and my sword? Does Jason really expect me to battle demons?" I asked, my voice sinking at the last part.

"Yep, that's what lives in the Underground City, so unless you want to become the sexiest dinner one of them little shits has ever eaten, you gotta learn how to defend yourself."

"Are all angels like you?" I asked with a frown, wondering how my Sunday school teacher could have gotten angels so very wrong.

"Hellz no!" he shot back. "I'm an O-riginal."

Shaking my head, I decided to leave that conversation alone. "Have you ever done this sort of thing before?" Noting his confused expression, I continued. "I mean, have you ever retrieved a soul?"

He nodded, but it soon turned into head-shaking. "Well, not exactly, but I know lots of guides and I've had it explained to me pretty often, so I figured if they could do it, it couldn't be that hard, ya know? Besides, I read most of the Cliff's Notes of that Dante book, so it's all good in ma hood."

"You read most of the Cliff's Notes of the *Inferno*?" I sounded ... shocked. *The Cliff's Notes, for crying out loud?*

He frowned. "Okay, okay, I read like two chapters."

"You read two chapters?"

"Sure did. Pretty good ones too. There were dudes chewing on the backs of the heads of some other dudes." He paused for a second, narrowing his eyes. "I can't remember why, though. Maybe for giving it to the other dude's wives."

Care, kindness and understanding ...

I took a deep breath and sighed, wondering what I'd done in a past life to merit this one. "So neither of us knows what we're doing?" I asked in a shaky voice. If this wasn't cause for a crisis, I didn't know what was.

Bill shook his head. "Girl, readin' has never been my thing. An' just look how far I've gotten without it! I'm a jen-you-wine, bone-if-eyed angel and it's not like just anyone gets to wear that title." Before I could respond, he scratched his wrist and I noticed a flashing green bracelet on his arm.

"What's that?"

A blush passed over his pasty, dough-like skin and he suddenly seemed enthralled with the steering wheel. "Oh, that's my monitor."

"Which means?"

He shrugged. "If I do something I'm not supposed to ..."

"Like?"

"Like drink or get into a fight. The damn thing will go off and then I'll have to sit through another five-hour lecture from Skeletor. Then again, I might even get demoted to a junior angel, which would be totally sucksational."

I had a mind to set it off so I could rid myself of my unwanted guide. "So going back to this retrieving thing, if you've never been a guide before, how in the heck do you know what we're supposed to do?"

He reached inside his pocket and pulled out another piece of paper that looked like it had barely survived World War II. "I got all the four-one-one right here, honey mounds." He held the paper closer to his eyes, glancing every now and then at the road. Great, I'd already died in one car accident and now it looked like number two was just around the corner.

"What's that?" I demanded.

"Notes."

I ripped the paper from between his nubby fingers. Glancing down at it, I read aloud:

"Bring coins for Sharon, the chick who's going to take us across the River Sticks." I dropped the paper into my lap and faced Bill, a new sense of despondency erupting inside me. "You do realize the ferryman of the River Styx is exactly that, a man?" I started, remembering reading the *Inferno* from my English Lit class during my sophomore year at college. "And his name is Charon, not Sharon."

"Sharon, Charon, chick or fairy gay dude, whatevs. I'm not a homo-phobe but I do believe in gay buffering."

"What buffering?"

"You know, like when I'm out with a dude friend and we go to the movies or something—it's always good to leave an extra seat between us so we don't look gay."

I shook my head and returned to his notes. "Make sure nothing touches you." I glanced up at him for his confirmation.

"I'm an angel, we aren't supposed to get any of that Underground City shit on us."

"Why?"

He shrugged. "Angels aren't even supposed to go into the Underground because if anything there touches us ..." But his words suddenly faded on his tongue.

"Yes?"

He shrugged and I realized he had no idea what he was talking about. "I don't know what would happen, but it's not like it'd be good, you know? It'd probably be like that witch chick who melts." He glanced over at me and smiled. "I'm meeelltinng!"

I sighed, not even slightly entertained by his less than convincing rendition of the Wicked Witch of the West. "So if angels aren't supposed to go to the Underground City, why are we?"

"'Cause you were a dumbass and didn't read the fine print before you decided to become a supermodel and I'm on probation. It means I've gotta do whatever Skeletor-Horn tells me to, which basically means we're both SOL."

I decided to ignore the part about me being a dumbass and the fine print Jason had neglected to include during my orientation. Instead, I turned to the view outside my window. It was a crisp, beautifully clear day with a cornflower-blue sky peppered by wistful clouds. The grass of what I assumed was the Meadows appeared a lush, verdant green. If not for my companion, I might have considered it a nice afternoon.

"What is the Kingdom like?" I asked, hoping to find some level of polite conversation.

"Supes," he said, smiling.

"Excuse me?" I asked, at an obvious loss.

"Super, girl, super. Gotta keep up with ma lingo!" The car lurched forward as the light turned green and Bill gave me an apologetic smile. "Maybe when we're done with this mission, I can help you furnish that place."

"Does that mean you're going to be my roommate?" I asked, aghast at the very thought.

"Hellz no! Talk about putting the kibosh on my sex life," he spat out with a shrug. "Besides, I got fart-apnea."

"I have never met anyone like you," I said simply, shaking my head as I felt the gravity of my words drop all the way down to my feet.

"I told you, girl, I'm an O-riginal."

He turned on the radio, scanning through the stations with unconcealed amusement. At the sound of screeching and the heavy thunder of a bass guitar, he settled back into his seat.

"What's this?" I asked with audible annoyance.

"Winger! Hello!"

He dropped his hands from the wheel to play air guitar. I sighed, wondering how I was going to survive the next few hours or days with Bill for company.

That which doesn't kill you only makes you stronger, I reminded myself, swallowing down the sentiment.

I only hoped I could survive Bill the second time around.

***

It turned out that the drive to Peterhead wasn't such a long one at all—a mere two hours, although it felt more like six. Bill was, in a word ... exhausting, but I preferred his company to being alone with my depressing thoughts about missing my mother and Miranda. Instead, I turned to the scenery outside my window which was slowly growing gray as dark storm clouds trespassed the skies, throwing a cloak of drab shadows over the green hills and the blue ocean beside us.

"Looks like it's going to rain," I said softly. "Is the weather always this finicky in Scotland?"

Bill frowned at me. "Do I look like a friggin' weatherman?"

"Well I figured you were familiar with this place since you showed up on my doorstep?"

He shook his head. "Nope. I got the call from AE that I had to get my ass to Edinburgs and so I went. I've never been here before." He glanced out his window and sighed. "Why the hell you didn't choose a phat beach house in the Bahamas with nothin' but half naked chicks to stare at beats the shiznit outta me."

I said nothing more as he pulled onto a small street called Gadie Braes that bordered the cliffs of Peterhead and continued heading north. As far as I could tell, the area seemed pretty suburban with long blocks of houses surrounding vast stretches of green parks.

"Merge slightly right onto Ware Road," the polite English voice of the Audi's navigation rang out. Bill grumbled something unintelligible, but obeyed the instructions.

"Your destination is ahead on the right," the woman continued as both Bill and I leaned forward, seeing nothing more than a shack looming before us.

"What the …?" Bill started.

"You have reached your destination," the navigation finished before triumphantly turning itself off.

"Um, is this right?" I asked, glancing between Bill and the one-room shack that looked more like an outhouse than the residence of a blacksmith.

Bill shrugged and turned the car off, opening his door as a cold ocean wind whipped around him and chilled me. I shivered in my short-shorts and tube top, wishing the previous owner of my body resided in a cold climate at the time of her departure.

I watched Bill as he hopped down from the driver's seat and took a few paces forward. He turned around in a three-sixty and eyed his new environment with confusion, scratching his head in apparent wonder.

"It's gotta be right," he said. He started forward as I unbuckled myself and jumped down, shivering in the cold, Scottish wind. Freezing in my shorts and tube top, I decided to make a quick detour to the trunk of the car to investigate the bag Jason had given Bill. I opened the trunk and sorted through the bag, tossing aside thong underwear, lacy bras and a nightie that looked more like a negligee. There were two skimpy day dresses, more obscene short-shorts and blouses that were so small, they looked like they'd fit a cat. My fingers caught onto a pair of black leather pants, and pulling them out, I felt my jaw drop. Then I realized they were the only pants in the bag and, as such, I'd have to wear them or freeze.

"This is not funny, Jason Streethorn," I muttered as I stepped into the pants and worked them up my stork legs. They were skintight and barely fit. I zipped them up and buttoned them before diving into the bag again, this time looking for something that resembled a sweater. A second later, I found a red, long-sleeved cotton shirt that was just as tight as the pants. But it was warmer than the singlet I was currently wearing, so I wasn't going to complain.

"What the hell are you doing?" Bill railed out from beside the shack.

I threw the top over my head, pulled it down and noticing a pair of ankle-high, black boots, grabbed them before slamming the trunk closed. I walked back toward Bill, watching his eyes widen as he took in the leather pants and boots. "You look like that chick from that movie," then he pursed his lips together as he attempted to remember said movie. "You know the one," he continued and cleared his throat before he started singing "'we go together like ramming dingy dongs, bang bang bangy cha bangy cock!"

"*Grease*," I finished for him, shaking my head as my thoughts returned to my current wardrobe. "As soon as we're done here, we need to go shopping."

Bill didn't say anything, but started for the wooden door of the shack, so I followed him. The door was warped, discolored and generally had the look of something weathered and old, matching the rest of the lean-to. Bill shrugged and knocked on the door. No one answered, so he knocked again. When it seemed no one was home, I turned and started for the Audi again, eager to find the nearest department store. Then I heard the sound of the door opening. Turning back toward Bill, I watched him peer into the house before walking inside.

"Looks like no one's home," he called out.

I hurried up the walkway behind him, reaching the front door of the shack. I continued forward, intending to talk him out of breaking and entering. But as soon as I stepped over the threshold, I was suddenly blinded by a huge flare of light.

> "... and when he had moved on, I entered along the deep and savage road."
> — Dante's *Inferno*

FOUR

I gasped and opened my eyes, blinking a few times to clear my vision because something very strange had happened. The last thing I could remember was setting foot into the decrepit shack at the end of the road, and then being blinded by a bright light. And now? I gulped as I tried to make sense of what lay before me, rubbing my eyes in a vain attempt to clear what could only be a trick of my vision. Why? Because I now found myself in the midst of a forest. I glanced up at the impossibly tall pine trees, watching as the sun gleamed through the threadbare coverage of the needles. Snow covered the trees, weighing down the heavy boughs, and dotting the banks of grass and ferns below them. The grass and ferns were punctuated by the brown of dirt and rocks. A gentle wind shook the needles, dropping them onto my face as I shivered and wrapped my arms around myself to keep warm.

"Bill?" I asked, my voice reflecting the awe and fear in my gut. "What just happened?"

Bill was standing maybe two feet in front of me and wore the same expression of astonishment. Somehow the fact that he, a supernatural being, seemed just as dazed as I was didn't bode well for our situation.

"Where are we?" I continued, glancing around again.

Bill didn't say anything, but scratched his head, looking back at me with a dumbfounded stare. Then, as if something just dawned on him, he lifted his arm and studied his monitor. He even flicked it a few times, but when it apparently didn't do whatever it was supposed to, he simply dropped his arm and frowned, raising his eyebrows in question.

"Looks like I'm not drunk or high," he said plainly with a shrug. "*One pill makes you larger and one pill makes you small*," he semi-sang.

I didn't say anything since I didn't really get his gist. Instead, I watched as he walked head first into a huge spiderweb. He twirled around twice, like a hefty, uncoordinated ballerina. Then he clawed at his face as he tried to free himself from the gossamer strands.

"Damn spiders," he muttered, wiping the sticky remnants of the web on his pants and continuing forward. Not wanting to be left alone in Narnia, I followed.

How does this make any sense? I asked myself, shaking my head as I tried to piece together the puzzle. *You stepped into that house and then suddenly you're out here? In the wilderness? Maybe it was some sort of portal?*

My thoughts were interrupted by the sound of Bill clearing his throat. Actually he sounded more like someone attempting to start an old engine in the dead of winter. "Huhhh! Hreeeph! Hoogannitt!" he grunted, slamming his fist into his chest as if to help clear whatever needed clearing. "Think I swallowed that spider," he grumbled before leaning over and hawking up something foul in a nearby bush. Then he started clearing his throat again, a sound that was beginning to make my stomach queasy.

"So, what? We just keep walking?" I asked, wanting to concentrate on other, more important topics—such as what in the heck our plan was. I didn't think exploring this weird place was such a good idea. Instead, I was of the vote that we retrace our steps and try to find the cabin again so we could get the heck out of Dodge.

"You gotta better idea, Slick?" he grumbled and then paused. "Whhheeeck!" he finished, spitting up another mouthful.

I frowned, thinking I wanted nothing more than to turn around and go back rather than continue traipsing through some random forest, the location of which was still a complete question. "Aren't you in the least bit apprehensive as to where we're going? Or how we got here?"

"Pah!" Bill said, waving away my anxiety with his arm. Then he fished inside his mouth with his squat index finger and wiped away the debris on his pants. "It's no hair off my balls," he continued with a shrug. "The nav led us here, and I've never heard of an AE nav unit being wrong; so as far as I can figure, we must be where we're 'sposed to be."

"But ..." I started.

"Hey," he said, turning around to face me. He tucked his Oompa-Loompa-like arms across his wide chest. "If you wanna give yourself anxiarrhea, be my guest." He grunted something unintelligible while rubbing his belly. "Hopefully, Sherwood Forest's got some grub 'cause I am hungry like the wolf." Then he started humming "Rio" by Duran Duran but somehow I couldn't find it within me to correct him.

Instead, I took a deep breath and tried to calm my beating heart. *Fear has its use, but cowardice has none*, I repeated Gandhi's words in my head and acquired a new feeling of determination. I hastened my steps and caught up with Bill. A wind shook through the pines and a clump of snow fell onto my shoulder.

"You got snow-shitted on," Bill said with a hefty laugh, sweeping the wet flakes away with his short, chubby fingers. Then he simply went back to forging a path through the wilderness, taking us God only knew where. And not feeling brave enough to go it alone, I had no choice but to follow him.

The snow crunched underfoot as we trekked deeper into the forest. The scurry of woodland creatures rustled from the snowy ferns and bushes below the massive pines. The canopy of branches kept the forest in darkness, dappling the sunlight as it shone through in multiple, shimmering pockets.

Bill suddenly stopped walking mid-stride, and I nearly plowed right into him. He remained frozen and I wasn't sure if it was because he thought he heard something which gave him cause for pause, or if he were just setting the stage for a massive fart.

I figured it was most likely the latter.

"What?" I whispered.

"I got this funny feeling that ..." Then he cocked his head to the side and sighed only to shake his head and smile reassuringly." Nah, the feeling's gone ... I think it's all good." Then he slid his hand into his pocket and produced a small, green plastic box. He opened it as I glanced over his shoulder. Multicolored pills of various sizes and shapes— maybe twenty of them, lay inside. He fished out two oblong, yellow ones. Realizing what they were, a fire of rage began to ignite inside me accordingly.

"Drugs?" I snapped, immediately glancing at his monitor as I wondered if it would go off at the mere proximity of something illegal, or if Bill would have to swallow the pills first. "Your dependencies on alcohol and drugs are what got me killed in the first place!" I railed at him, my hands on my hips. "How dare you even think to start using again in front of me!"

"First of all, Nurse Ratched, these aren't drugs," Bill said curtly, enunciating each word, in a tone dripping with irritation. "So before you go run and tell that to Skeletor and make yourself look like an arch douche, pay attention." Then he handed one of the pills to me.

"What is it?" I asked, frowning. I made no attempt to accept it. "And what the heck is an arch douche?"

"Are you incapable of saying "hell,'" he spat back at me.

"I don't see the point," I started but he interrupted me.

"I refuse to hang out with you if you say 'what the heck' one more time. That's like nerd talk and then some." I frowned as he continued. "Come on, say it, h-e-l-l..."

I took a deep breath but gave in, not finding the wherewithal to argue with him about something so completely idiotic. "What the hell is an arch douche?"

He smiled. "That's better, reverse cowgirl," he said and smiled even wider. "An arch douche is someone high up the corporate ladder who's also a total and complete douche bag. Case in point? Skeletor. He's like the arch douche of arch douches."

I just shook my head.

"It's a good one if you want to borrow it sometime," Bill added.

"Thanks for that," I grumbled. "So were you going to get back to the point about what the heck, er hell, these pills are anyway?"

"These little guys are gonna help us see what the hell is out there," he barked back. "Now stop being an ask-hole and take the damn thing!"

I opened my palm with a frown, not appreciating the name calling. Bill dropped the pill into my palm as I inspected it with my index finger. I glanced up at him and sighed, still wondering if I should trust him or not.

"It's AE provided," he said, his eyebrow cocked. Then he tossed the pill into his mouth and made an exaggerated effort of swallowing it. "Bon appétit," he grinned.

I stared down at the nondescript pill in my hand, still reluctant to do anything more than that. I mean, Bill had a history of problems with illegal narcotics, so why wouldn't I expect him to pull a fast one over on me? And, furthermore, having never taken any illegal substances in my life, I wasn't about to start now.

"What do you want, a written invitation?" Bill asked, waving his little starfish hand as if to say, "Get on with it." With a sigh, I brought the pill to my mouth, plopped it on my tongue, and swallowed it. Then I just waited, anxious for the pill to do its stuff, but after a few seconds, I couldn't say I felt any different. I glanced at Bill, wondering why nothing seemed to be happening.

"Nothing's different?" I whispered, without realizing why I was whispering. "I don't think mine worked."

He frowned. "Look around."

So I did—first I glanced to my left and then to my right. The pine trees looked the same as they had a few minutes ago, and as far as I could tell, the snow on the ground hadn't really changed—except, perhaps it had melted just a bit more. I gazed at the trunks of the trees, my eyes moving upward to each great expanse of branches. A flurry of snow sailed through the sky and landed on my cheek. It felt like regular snow—just as cold.

"Maybe you gave me the wrong pill," I said, bringing my attention back to the ground. But the words froze on my tongue. Bright white lights suddenly appeared between the trees directly in front of me. The lights strobed and flittered, pausing for a few seconds, before disappearing right before my eyes. "Oh my gosh," I started, my jaw dropping.

"Spirits," Bill said in explanation.

I jerked my head toward him and gasped. Bill was completely bathed in white light. His skin was glowing like an ember. And it wasn't a light from without—as in shining a beam on him. This luminosity emanated from Bill; it glowed from somewhere deep within him, becoming so bright, I had to avert my eyes, eventually covering them with my hand.

"You're glowing," I said in awe.

"Control your girl wood," he said and shrugged. "I told you, I'm an angel. You're just seeing me in my natural state."

"Your natural state is blinding," I grumbled, finding it impossible to look directly at him.

"Yeah, I call it my bling. I can turn it down." Within a second, he no longer burned like the sun, but more like an eager nightlight.

"That's better." I dropped my hand and unshielded my eyes.

"Shit," he said and frowned, glancing around himself. "I just got that funny feelin' again."

"That what?" My heart lurched into my throat because his tone made it sound like it wasn't a *good* funny feeling.

"That something's not right," he said very slowly, turning to examine his surroundings as if whatever wasn't quite right was about to pop out of the shrubbery and ambush us.

I glanced around, noticing nothing beyond the tall pines that loomed as far as the eye could see over the powdery shrubs. But one thing did strike me. I couldn't hear the sounds of birds any longer. In fact, the entire forest had gone utterly, eerily quiet.

"It's too quiet," I whispered.

"Yep, no bueno."

He turned away and again, surveyed his surroundings. "Can't say that I see anything out of the ordinary, but you ain't sposed to ignore them bad feelings, ya know?"

"What kind of bad feeling was it? Like something might hurt us?" I asked with trepidation.

He just nodded and suddenly was off, moving much faster than he looked capable of. I chased him up a steep bank of snow-carpeted grass, huffing and puffing all the way. Guess my new body had adopted my previous body's lack of athleticism.

"Holy shit," Bill said as he dropped to the ground, peering into the shallow valley below us. He glanced up at me before grabbing my arm and pulling me down beside him. Before I could complain about the pain he'd just caused in my arm, my attention was diverted to his outstretched finger, which was pointing directly ahead of us.

There, maybe twenty feet away, were glowing orbs of red lights that circled one another. Little by little, the balls of light began to morph into the shapes of animals, well not exactly animals, more like ... monsters. I couldn't think of anything else to call them.

They were smallish, probably standing as high as my mid-thighs. But, though they weren't enormous, they were the most frightening things I'd ever seen. Each one, and there must have been at least six, radiated a bright scarlet light. They were all hunched over and misshapen. Shiny, rust-colored scales covered most of their bodies, while their limbs terminated into cloven hooves, making it look like someone had glued a goat's legs to an iguana. But their faces frightened me most—rows and rows of miniature razor teeth filled their snarling canine mouths. Steam blew from their muzzles as their eyes blazed with an unnatural red light.

They appeared to be taunting one another, circling and growling at each other. "Oh. My. God," I whispered. "What are they?"

"Grevels from the lower Underground," Bill answered, shaking his head in amazement. "I've only seen 'em in books."

"Then what are they doing here?" I started before something terrible occurred to me. "Oh no ... Does this mean we're already ... in the Underground City?"

"Keep your panties on, Dorothy," he said and shook his head. "We're still in Kansas far as I can tell. Well, one thing's fer sure—we're not in the Underground City."

"How do you know if you've never been there?" I demanded, my attention riveted on the Grevels.

"'Cause I've heard stories and seen pictures," he spat back. "There you go being an ask-hole again."

"So if we aren't in the Underground, then what are *they* doing here?" I demanded, ignoring my new nickname.

"Good freakin' question, yo," Bill said, shaking his head and sighing in what appeared to be confusion. "I got no clue how the hell demons escaped the Underground."

"Demons?" I hissed, feeling my heartbeat pound in my ears.

Bill threw me a glare. "Shhh. Shit girl, you trying to get us spotted?"

I glanced down at my shaking hands, and didn't know what to think, other than the obvious. "We need to get out of here, Bill. This isn't safe."

But Bill didn't respond. He was too busy gawking at me. Or at something looming behind me.

It felt like slow motion as I turned to find myself face-to-face with the blood-red muzzle of a demon. I didn't scream, I don't even think I gasped. Sometimes, you're just too scared to react.

"Get up very slowly," Bill whispered. I didn't take my eyes from the demon, but based on the proximity of Bills voice, I knew he was standing right behind me.

I did as he said, my eyes fastened on the creature. It did nothing but stare at me, appearing as curious about me as I was about it. Scratch that, I wasn't curious—I was terrified. As soon as I stood, it approached me, beginning to growl in a low, warning tone. Its loud hooves crunched against the snow as it got closer; and the steam from its mouth looked like tortured souls riding its breath.

"Walk backwards toward me," Bill ordered. "Real slow like."

I maybe took two steps before it pounced. I felt the air rush from my lungs as I hit the snow-packed hill—hard. I pushed my hands out before me on pure reflex, my body aware that I'd have to defend myself against the creature's attack. But all I did was slap my hands against the blubber of Bill's back. It took me a few seconds to regain my bearings and that's when I realized Bill had thrust himself in front of me, taking the brunt of the demon's attack.

Now Bill was flailing helplessly with the demon atop him, and the only sounds to shatter the otherwise still air was snorting—I wasn't sure whose—the creature's or Bill's. I attempted to emerge from behind him, feeling like I needed to do something to help him, but he shoved me behind him forcefully.

"Stay where you are, fuck nut!"

The demon attempted to secure Bill's arm with its mouth, but Bill jabbed it in the muzzle with his fist before it had the chance. I heard myself scream. Seconds later, I realized my mistake. The remaining demons now all turned their full attention toward us. They cocked their heads like curious dogs, not wasting any time in approaching us. Instantly recognizing their angry demon comrade, their muzzles peeled back to show hideous pointed teeth. Their piercing growls continued to clash with the quiet night air.

"Bill!" I screamed. "More are coming!"

The demon straddling Bill suddenly backed away, pawing the ground as it neared its clan. Turning back toward us, it began growling, just like the others.

"Back yourself up against that tree," Bill said between clenched teeth, motioning to a pine beside him.

I took the three necessary steps to find my back against the trunk while my heart thundered painfully. Bill walked backwards as well, never allowing his body to expose mine. Guess he wasn't such a bad guardian angel after all. Well, recently anyway ...

"What should we do?" I whispered, motioning toward the other demons who were now nearly on us.

"*We* are gonna do nothin', *I'm* gonna protect your ass like I was hired to do," he ground out, taking a deep breath as he swung his arms forward and then backward. He threw his butt into it too, as if he were about to attempt a long jump. And he did jump, but not exactly far. With the accompaniment of a banshee-like cry, he hopped about a foot or so forward, then threw his arms out to his sides, looking like he was in the process of being abducted by an alien spacecraft.

"You're about ta get some angel retaliation, bitches!" he yelled. He then proceeded to do five jumping-jacks in quick procession, uttering high-pitched yips and whoops until he sounded like the captions from a melee on the old *Batman* TV series.

The demons simply stared at him, stupefied.

"Woo!" Bill yelled as he pointed his fingers, holding them out before him like guns. "I'm about ta make yer day, douche faces!" he screamed, turning his glowing finger gun at the creature closest to him. "Woo!" he screamed again as he cocked his fingers back. A bright light shot off the end of his hand, combusting into a fireworks show right in front of the demon. The creature roared, doubling over on itself in an attempt to get away from the sparks of Bill's finger gun.

"Yeah, how you like them angel apples, you little turd monkey?" he called, suddenly spinning on his heel in a Michael Jackson move. "Oooo smack!" he sang, holding his fingers out before him while a flame of white light encircled him. The demons pulled back as he approached, baring their teeth, and trying to intimidate him.

"Yeah, that's right; smile, and say cheese, bitches," he laughed, sounding like he'd completely lost his mind. Throwing bursts of light into the sky, he continued raving like a mad man. "Give me some lip, you little demon farts!" Then he faced the Grevels again. "Yeah, you heard me, you smell like Satan's ass!"

One of the demons pawed the ground, snarling as Bill approached him. But Bill seemed unfazed and continued with his aerobic angel resistance tirade. He jumped up and threw out his leg like he was kickboxing. "Yeah, you want some more, you little gonad sucker?" The demon growled again, pulling its lips back and exposing rows of fierce, saber-sharp teeth. "That all you got, Rainbow Brite?" Bill asked, roaring at it, like he was attempting to impersonate The Lion King. The demon responded by further curling its lip back, to which Bill did the same, revealing his teeth that were about as intimidating as Mr. Ed's. "You wanna shit yer last chance undies, buddy?"

The Grevel pawed the ground again, erecting itself to its full height as it growled louder, steam filling its nostrils.

"Thoir do chasan leat!"

I heard the deep voice coming from behind me and turned so quickly, I gave myself whiplash. But the pain in my neck was a distant memory as words died in my throat. It was all I could do to stare at the stranger, fear already enveloping me. He was, in a word ... intimidating. He was huge—maybe bordering on seven feet tall—easily the tallest man I'd ever seen. And his build was just as threatening: incredibly broad shoulders, offset with bulky pecs, and abs that could have redefined "washboard." He wasn't wearing anything besides a black kilt and what looked like Gladiator sandals—leather straps that snaked up his muscular legs. In his right hand he held a sword with an incredibly long blade—the tip of which currently rested in the snow.

Even though his body seemed built for combat, I couldn't pry my eyes away from his face. It was a face that would be very difficult to forget—with chiseled and square lines that didn't seem at home in the category of "handsome." In fact, I'm not sure you could have termed this guy handsome because he was entirely too masculine for the word. His eyes, which were currently narrowed on me, were navy blue and hard, just like the rest of him. In fact, hard was a good description. There was a certain hard edge to the frown that contorted his full lips and the scar that bisected his cheek. It ran from the tip of one eyebrow and ended at his jaw line. His short, black hair and olive complexion gave him a certain Mediterranean air, but there was no question as to his ancestry. He was Scottish, born and bred. If his kilt didn't convince me, his Gaelic did.

The demons immediately stopped their advance on Bill and cowered behind the imposing man, making it pretty obvious that we had more to fear from him than from them.

"Bill?" I asked, turning to ensure my guardian angel was okay. As soon as I peeled my eyes from the stranger, I felt the air catch in my throat as he hurled himself against me. The blade of his sword was suddenly poised underneath my chin.

"Take it easy there, Conan," Bill said slowly, approaching us with his hands in the air in an appeal for surrender.

"Who are ye? An' what do ye want?" the man spat out in a deep Scottish brogue, his eyes never leaving mine.

"We came to see the blacksmith," Bill said slowly, continuing his advance, step-by-step.

"Ye can stop there," the man barked at Bill, glaring at him before he returned his eyes to me, pushing the blade deeper into my neck. "What business do ye have with the blacksmith?"

"She needs a sword," Bill answered, in a level and even tone.

I closed my eyes, trying to curb the panic that crested through me, and restrain the sudden sensation that I was going to pass out. I opened my eyes and found that icy, navy blue gaze studying me intently. There wasn't a trace of warmth in his eyes. The man said nothing, but continued studying me for a few seconds. I still couldn't find the wherewithal to even breathe, let alone talk.

"Yer name?" he ground out.

I forced myself to take a deep breath, suddenly feeling my heart pounding through my head. "Lily," I said softly.

"Surname?"

"Harper," I said automatically, before remembering that I was now O'Shaughnessey. I didn't correct myself.

The stranger said nothing more. In one quick move, he pulled away from me, dropping the tip of the sword back into the snow. I rubbed my neck, half wondering if he'd drawn blood. When I pulled my hand away to check, there wasn't any.

"Ye would know if Ah cut ye," he said in a deep tone, his eyes still narrowed with distrust.

"You know where can we find the blacksmith, He-Man?" Bill asked, inserting himself between the man and me. I had to admit I was impressed by his protective nature.

Maybe he was trying to make up for letting me get killed a few hours ago.

The man didn't say anything right away, but managed to unnerve me with the intensity of his glare. "Ye found him."

"You're the blacksmith?" Bill repeated, his eyebrows reaching for the sky. I wasn't sure why he was surprised. The more I thought about it, this guy probably could have created a weapon in his sleep. His ease while handling his sword only reiterated the fact.

"Och aye, though Ah am far more than ah mere blacksmith. Ah am ah bladesmith."

"Bladesmith, blacksmith, potato, potahto, balls, testies, gonads, nuts—what the hell's the difference?" Bill piped up.

The man glared at him in response. "Ah bladesmith is far more skilled than ah 'blacksmith,' who hammers oot or casts tools ah soft iron," (He said it "arne.") "Ah bladesmith has ta know how ta make ah sword from steel."

"File that under who gives a shit," Bill grumbled.

The man took a deep breath. "Ye got ah name, angel?"

It was Bill's turn to regard him suspiciously, but a moment or so later, he extended his hand. "No handshake rapin', either," he warned. "I'm Bill."

The man made no attempt to shake Bill's proffered hand, but simply turned on his heel and started walking away, calling back to us over his shoulder. "Mah name is Tallis Black, boot ye will call me Bladesmith."

"How hard a thing it is to say what was this forest savage, rough, and stern, which in the very thought renews the fear."
— Dante's *Inferno*

FIVE

"Dude!" Bill called at the bladesmith's retreating figure. "What the hell?" He even threw his arms up to act out his frustration. "Where are you going? We need a sword!"

But the man didn't stop walking, the mob of demons following him like ugly sheep. Bill faced me with a frown and then shrugged, shaking his head as he muttered, "So much for customer service."

"So, what now?" I started, glancing back at the bladesmith's figure as it got smaller and smaller the farther away he walked. Somehow, I got the idea that we needed to follow him.

"After you," Bill muttered, and we both jogged to catch up with the gigantic, taciturn man. When we finally managed to reach him, we were both huffing and puffing. He responded with a raised eyebrow and a frown.

"Hey, Hulk Hogan, didn't you hear me?" Bill asked between great gulps of air, seemingly grateful when the man eventually slowed his steps and paused. He turned to face the much shorter, more out of shape angel who now tried to stand, but remained bent over, his hands on his knees as he attempted to catch his breath.

"Aye."

"And, what? You don't like cash?" Bill asked, glaring at the demons. They growled at him as they menacingly circled their master protectively. "Don't tempt me again, bitches," he grumbled. One of the demons, presumably the one who'd given Bill the most attitude, started forward. The bladesmith rewarded it with a taste of his heel and it fell back in place among all the others.

"The sun is settin'. There will be nae forgin' ah blade this day."

I imagined he meant he only worked in the daylight—probably because it was too difficult to hammer a sword without any light. Before I could inquire, he resumed his inhuman pace again, deserting Bill and me in his wake.

"So what are we supposed to do? Come back later?" Bill called after the man's retreating figure.

"Nae. It wouldna be ah good idea ta trespass these woods alone," he called over his shoulder.

"Okay, so ..." Bill continued, his tone of voice becoming increasingly agitated as he hurried his steps. Eventually he broke into another jog, and I followed right alongside him.

The man stopped walking and faced Bill, his arms crossed against his massive chest—his tight lips just as unfriendly. "Ah will offer ye protection this night an' ye will be on yer way come the morrow."

Bill glanced at me, the frown apparently now a permanent set to his features. "What the fuck does that mean?"

"Tonight we're staying here with him, I guess," I answered, nervous because I couldn't predict how much more of Bill the bladesmith would willingly put up with. He didn't seem to be a patient man. And speaking of our less than friendly host, I wasn't certain I wholeheartedly liked this plan. In the first place, this man didn't exactly inspire my trust. But I had no idea what the forest might have in store for us, if we did decide to try and locate the car.

"And her sword?" Bill continued, motioning to me, but his eyes were still locked on the bladesmith.

The man glanced over at me, his eyes raking me from head to toe, but there didn't appear to be anything of a sexual nature in his gaze. It was more like he was taking stock of me—well, as far as I could tell anyway. It wasn't like I had much experience when it came to men and their lustful appetites. Strangely enough, when he didn't appear to regard "me" (well, the new-bodied me, anyway) in a sexual manner, I was somehow ... bothered by it. Maybe it wasn't so much that I was bothered by his lack of interest but more that I was floored by it? I just couldn't understand how any man wouldn't be attracted to the body I now inhabited. I mean, as far as I was concerned, when I'd picked it, this body was model perfect, model gorgeous ...

Maybe the blacksmith, aka Tallis Black was ... gay?

I had to figuratively slap myself, irritated that such ridiculous and useless thoughts were even occurring to me. Who cared if this man didn't find "me" attractive? Who cared if he was gay or wasn't gay? It wasn't like I wanted anything to do with him ... right? I mean, it wasn't as though he was a nice person, as far as I could tell ... I shook my head, even more convinced that I was acting like an absolute imbecile because Tallis Black didn't appear to be "nice" at all! Surly, abrupt and aloof seemed better adjectives to describe him. The truth of the matter was that this man was menacing and downright scary.

"Ahem," Bill continued when the bladesmith made no response.

The man finally nodded. "She will have her sword." Then he started walking forward again, the gaggle of demons trailing behind him.

Bill faced me and shrugged. "Looks like we ain't got much of a choice."

Figuring Bill had a point, I just nodded and took a few steps, noticing that the bladesmith maintained a good two-pace distance in front of us. Whenever we sped up, so did he. Obviously he wasn't one for conversation. "You think we're safe with him?" I whispered to Bill, watching the muscles in the man's legs ripple as the incline of the path steepened, the rocks and snow acting as obstacles.

Apparently noticing the heightened difficulty of our trek, Bill grumbled something about "f-ing forests" and glowered at the bladesmith, as if this whole uncomfortable journey was his fault. "I'm pretty sure we're safe with him. He's got ties to AE so he has to be on best behavior where we're concerned or good ol' Skeletor will give 'em a rash of shit."

"Okay," I said, sighing deeply, and trying not to relive the feel of the man's sword when it was up close and personal with my neck. I could only hope we were making the right decision in trusting this guy.

"Hopefully Hercules has got some grub," Bill continued, his stomach grumbling as if on cue.

We remained quiet for the next few seconds; the only sound the snow crunching underfoot. The sun had begun its descent in the sky, bathing the forest in an orange hue, the white lights of spirits looking like stars between the trees.

The bladesmith continued to move through the forest, his footfalls barely making a sound against the snow-packed earth, which I found odd, considering how large he was.

Is trusting him a good idea? I asked myself, frustrated when I had no answer. *He came very close to slitting your throat earlier ... what makes you think he's not trying to lure you and Bill into a situation that could be even worse?*

"'He who does not trust enough, will not be trusted,'" I repeated the words of Lao Tzu to myself in an attempt to dissuade my fears.

"What?" Bill asked, glancing over at me with a pinched expression, as if he'd stubbed his toe—which was probably exactly what had just happened.

"Oh, I, uh, like to repeat inspirational quotes to myself whenever I get freaked out about something," I admitted rather embarrassedly. "It seems to always make me feel better."

Bill's frown deepened as he expelled a pent up breath. "Oh, shit, you're one ah them shelf esteemers?"

"I'm one of what?"

He rolled his eyes. "You're one ah them sorry assholes who works on your self-esteem by readin' self-help crap."

"Hey," I started, feeling deeply offended. "Some people just need a little help in their lives."

Bill shook his head, eyeing me pitifully. "You just gotta be careful not to be so busy tryin' to learn how to get a life that you forget to have one."

I felt my jaw drop open as the weight of his words sunk into me. It took me a good few seconds to respond because I couldn't deny the truth in what he'd just said. Maybe I *had* allowed my life to pass me by because I'd been so busy burying my nose in books which were meant to teach me how to live? "That's the most poignant statement you've said thus far, Bill," I said softly.

"I know, right?" he answered, a proud smile peering out behind his lips.

"Right," I responded, shaking my head as I reminded myself of his words again, still taken aback by his insight. The truth of the matter was that I *had* always lived my life and made my choices according to the books I'd read. Maybe in some ways I hadn't allowed myself to make the mistakes in life which would have taught me life lessons I needed to know? I mean, when it came down to it, I was a twenty-two-year-old virgin with a boring job and only my mother and Miranda as friends and confidantes.

As the silence stretched between us, I decided to interrupt it. "So that was some stunt you pulled with those demons." The hike up a small, but nearly vertical hill was in the process of taking its toll on my calves.

Bill shrugged, his huffing and puffing fully back in force. "It was all for show but, hey, it worked."

"For show?"

He glanced over at me and thrust his hands in his pockets before nodding. "Yeah, I can't hurt no one; just like nothin' or no one can hurt me."

"What do you mean?"

He shrugged. "I'm an angel, which means I'm like a spirit. I can't be killed or hurt and, likewise, I can't kill or hurt anyone else, which kinda sucks. There have been plenty of times I woulda really liked to bust out some whup-ass."

"You did a fine job of killing me in that auto accident," I grumbled, frowning as I remembered the particulars.

"I didn't kill you, bubble butt, the truck killed you."

"But ..."

"I was just MIA, that's all."

That seemed like the argument—do guns kill people or do people kill people? But I wasn't exactly in the mood to dispute it. "And just what the he...ll were you doing that prohibited you from seeing to your guardian angel duties?"

He glanced over at me and raised a brow. "You gotta stop nerdjacking the conversation, yo."

"What?" I asked, frowning as I nearly tripped over a tree root, partially concealed in a few inches of snow.

"Who talks like that?" he asked as he reached out and stabilized me. "Nerds, that's who."

"Stop changing the subject," I ground out, pulling my arm from him. "What were you doing at the time of my accident?"

He frowned, glancing down at the ground, and pausing as he carefully avoided another semi-exposed tree root. "I, uh, was gettin' my rocks off with this chick I'd been after for a while."

I shook my head and sighed deeply.

"Hey, don't be mad," he said quickly, offering me a smile of consolation. "I completed my probation and took all my classes and now I'm on the straight and narrow." He held his hand out in front of him, moving it from left to right, as if choreographing "straight and narrow." Then he motioned to his monitor. "I even got this thing, remember? I'm like a new man, honey mounds."

There was no point in beating a dead horse. Instead, I decided to ask about his angel limitations, figuring it was a topic I should be up on. "So how would you have taken me out of harm's way, if you *had* been doing your job?"

He shrugged. "Forced you to hit your brakes harder, or sooner; or created a longer buffer of space between you and the truck. Maybe even jacked your wheel to the side, to make you avoid the truck altogether. Lotsa possibilities."

"So then you aren't really like a spirit, if you can affect tangible things?"

"I can only *affect tangible things*," he said like he was mimicking an English teacher, adopting a pedantic stance and pointing at me, "for you because I'm *your* guardian angel. I couldn't do it for no one else. And I still can't hurt somebody else in order to protect you. Angels are do-gooders, remember?"

"But you had flames coming out of your fingers and it looked like the demons weren't exactly enjoying it?" I continued, not finding it easy to wrap my head around the conversation.

"Yeah, not so much. Think of that whole thing like a light show at the laserium. None of it was real. Them demons are just dumb and don't know any better."

The sun had completely dropped from the sky, and the moon was fully risen. I glanced up at it, admiring the circular orb as it shone its gleaming rays down on us, highlighting the whiteness of the snow. We followed the bladesmith around a bend in the dirt trail and were suddenly standing in front of a small cabin. The trees were so dense, it almost disappeared amongst them, and if not for the lights glowing from the windows, I might have missed it altogether.

"We have arrived," the bladesmith announced, turning to face us expectantly, as if he were surprised we were lagging ten feet behind him.

"Nice digs," Bill chuckled as the bigger man frowned down at him.

"Five hundred ah night for each of ye," he said without losing a beat.

"Come the fuck again?" Bill asked as his mouth gaped open.

The man narrowed his eyes on Bill then he crossed his arms over his incredibly broad chest, and looked really ticked off. He started forward until only a few feet separated us. "If ye want ta test yer luck in the wood, Ah doona care. If ye want mah hospitality, then it will cost ye."

Bill threw his hands on his hips and harrumphed before losing the stare down and facing me. "Fine, pay him."

I felt my stomach drop. "I haven't got any money!" I squealed, recognizing a bad situation when I saw one: camping out in haunted woods wasn't on my bucket list, to say the least.

Bill frowned even deeper and glanced over at the bladesmith apologetically before facing me again, the slack in his jaw disappearing. "Skeletor set you up with an account, didn't he?" he whispered between clenched teeth.

I nodded, remaining just as quiet when I whispered, "Yes, but that doesn't mean I've been to the bank! I don't even know where my account information is!"

The bladesmith held up his hands as if to play the part of peacemaker and faced me. I was surprised he could overhear us. "Give me yer word, an' we'll discoos the particulars later."

I nodded enthusiastically, feeling relief wash over me. "You have my word."

He came closer to me until it felt like there was no air between us, although he was still at least a foot away. "Break mah troost an' ye willna like the outcome."

I swallowed in spite of myself and obediently nodded, feeling his threat down to my toes. I said nothing else, but watched him turn away from us. Then he shooed the demons away, who vanished into the undergrowth. Trudging up to the door of the tiny cabin, he opened it, ducking as he entered so as not to hit his head. He held the door open and faced me. "Well, are ye comin'?"

As soon as I entered the small house, a cloud of warm air enveloped me, thanks to a fire raging in the fireplace. The fire lent a yellow glow to the log walls, reminding me of a cabin in Big Bear where my mother and I used to spend our Christmases. But not wanting to focus on memories which only depressed me, I inspected my surroundings. It smelled like earth—a heady, clean scent that was reminiscent of the forest itself. Above the fire was a large iron pot, bubbling with something that smelled like stew. There was a couch constructed of logs placed in front of the fire. It was covered in animal furs, some of which matched the furs on the dirt floor. A roughly hewn log table with two chairs occupied one corner of the room, and a straw mattress lay in the other, also covered in furs.

"Five hundred clams for this?" Bill asked, shaking his head as he turned to face the bladesmith, disbelief written all over his face. "This doesn't even count as one star ... this is like no star accommodations!" He glanced around himself again, even kicking the fur rug closest to him to show his disappointment. "You should be paying us to stay here!"

"Bill," I started, preferring not to incite the wrath of the Titan known as the bladesmith.

"Ye would do well ta keep yer gob shut, if ye know what's good for ye."

"We're very grateful," I started, offering him a hesitant smile. "And I promise to pay whatever you want, once I can get my account in order. I just ended up in this ... situation very recently and because of that, everything is a bit topsy-turvy. So please excuse our disorganization and thank you again for your hospitality."

The bladesmith simply nodded before facing Bill and frowning again. "Take ah lesson from yer friend."

"Kiss-ass," Bill whispered to me before eyeing the boiling pot on the fire with obvious interest. "What's cookin'?"

***

An hour or so later, the three of us had eaten the entire pot of meat stew (the type of which I wasn't certain). It was surprisingly good, considering the bladesmith didn't strike me as much of a cook. After dinner, Bill sprawled his sated carcass across one of the animal rugs on the dirt floor, basically hogging the heat from the fire. The bladesmith took up one of the wooden chairs beside his makeshift kitchen table and I sat to the left of Bill, my legs pulled up to my chest.

"So what are you doin' with demons anyhow, Conan?" Bill asked as he eyed the man suspiciously.

"Ah doona appreciate pryin' guests," he spat back. He picked up a piece of wood that was lying on the table, then reached behind him and produced a blade. He started whittling the wood into what looked like a spear.

"You know, it's against AE policy to harbor anything from the Underground, right?" Bill continued, but the man didn't look up from his spear-whittling. Bill shook his head and sighed. "You could get yerself into some real trouble, Hulk."

The bladesmith continued to ignore him, honing the end of his spear until it was incredibly pointed and sharp. Bill propped himself on his side, resting his head against his elbow and faced the fire as he apparently gave up on conversation and, instead, turned to me.

"You gettin' tired, sugar lips?"

"A little," I nodded but couldn't say I liked the idea of falling asleep and, consequently, dropping my defenses. I still didn't trust the bladesmith. And judging by the expression on Bill's face, he didn't either.

"An' don't you get any ideas about her, either," Bill piped up. The man simply paused from his whittling, but showed no expression on his face. "You even think about touchin' her and I'll throw a cock-block apocalypse your way faster than you can say eunuch. Capiche?"

"Noted," the man said simply, returning to the spear in his hands.

Bill stood up and yawned, stretching his arms above his head as his shirt rode up and revealed his Buddha-like stomach. Except his was complete with freckles and wiry hair. "I'm sufferin' from major bed gravity, yoze. I'm gonna hit the sack," he said eyeing the straw bedding in the corner of the room with anticipation.

"Ye can sleep on the ground," the bladesmith piped up.

Bill's eyebrows reached for the ceiling as he grumbled something indecipherable. He picked up one of the animal furs from the bed and dragged it to a dark corner close to the fireplace. After spreading it out, he circled it three times, like a dog about to go down for the night. He sat down, twirled himself around so he was facing away from us, and took off his shoes. Using his fleshy arm as a pillow, he laid down. He seemed to stiffen for a second or two, then called over his shoulder: "Egg alert!"

I shook my head, realizing he'd just cut the cheese. Barely two minutes later, he was snoring.

I remained in my seated position with my knees pulled up to my chest, just staring into the fire, very grateful for the silence ... well, silence between Bill's snores anyway. It was the first quiet time I'd experienced since the moment I'd died, and my life was turned upside down.

The flames danced this way and that, burning yellow, then orange as they consumed the remainder of the pine log, rendering it into black cinders. When the bladesmith stood up and lumbered toward the fireplace, I couldn't help noticing the muscles ripple in his arms as he reached for another log. The log was easily the width and length of my thigh, but he handled it like it weighed nothing and tossed it into the fire. The flames devoured it instantly, the log hissing and popping in outrage.

"Did ye get enough ta eat?" he asked in a soft voice as I noticed the black tattoos on the backs of his upper arms. Both arms featured Celtic crosses. Along the upper expanse of his back were the branches of a tree that continued down his middle back, the roots of which sprawled across his lower back.

Remembering his question, I glanced up at him and nodded quickly. "I did, thanks."

He said nothing else as he returned to his chair and resumed his whittling. "Ye said ye are new to this life?"

I nodded again, somewhat surprised that he was interested in making conversation with me. But thinking I could probably learn something from him—well, that is, if he ever decided to open up—I took the bait. "Yes."

"And?"

I shrugged, trying to figure out where to start. "I was in a car accident," I said, instantly wondering if he even knew what a car was. I mean, for all I knew, Bill and I could have traveled back in time. This cabin didn't exactly feature any modern conveniences. "Is this ... place from the same time zone as where I came from?"

"Aye."

"So where, exactly, is here?"

He glanced up at me and the fire reflected in his dark eyes, giving him the look of something not of this earth. Something alien and cold. "The Dark Wood."

There was something familiar about the name. It took me another few seconds before it dawned on me. "Dante!" I said in surprise. "In the beginning of *Inferno*, Dante is lost in the Dark Wood."

The bladesmith didn't seem interested as he simply shrugged, dropping his attention to the spear in his hands, which he continued to whittle. Small pieces of wood littered his lap and the ground around him.

"Is the Dark Wood on the way to the Underground City?" I asked, figuring he wasn't going to offer up any information.

He never looked up from his whittling. "Aye, the first stop."

I nodded, but fear suddenly spiraled through me as I thought about how close we were to the Underground City, that there really was such a place as the Dark Wood, and that this strange man lived here. If it really were true about the forest being unsafe, why would he choose to reside in it? 'Course, he didn't strike me as someone who enjoyed the company of other people. He seemed content in his solitude, happy to only have a handful of demons to call his friends. To each his own, I guessed. "Have you ever been there?" I started, adding quickly, "to the Underground City, I mean."

He nodded. "On numerous occasions."

I wasn't sure why, but that news didn't surprise me. "And is it as bad as I think it is?"

"Worse." Then he glanced up at me. "Is that why ye require ah sword? Because ye have business in the Oondergroond?"

"Yes," I answered, nodding. I swallowed as I shrank beneath his stringent gaze.

He laid his spear on his lap and regarded me curiously. "Are ye ah soldier then?"

"No," I said quickly.

"Ye have trainin' then?"

I shook my head. "No."

He frowned, shaking his head as he tsked at me. "T'will be ah suicide mission, lass."

I gulped hard. "I have no choice."

"Everybody has ah choice."

I sighed, trying not to argue with him, even though I felt forced into this arrangement. "So it would seem."

"Ye were goin' ta tell me yer story?" he picked up his spear and began whittling again. I wasn't sure why I suddenly felt so talkative, but he seemed to have also changed course, and was now being cordial so I figured I should do the same.

"I was in a car accident and, uh, died when I wasn't supposed to," I said quickly. "Then I ended up at AfterLife Enterprises and agreed to become a Retriever in order to live again. I also wanted to skip one hundred years in Shade. Little did I know I was going to be retrieving in the Underground City." Then I exhaled all the pent-up worry that was building within me and dropped my chin to the top of my knees, rocking back and forth.

"Then ye are hardly prepared," he said as he studied me for a few more moments.

"I'm afraid I'm not," I answered as something occurred to me, something I should have asked Jason, but hadn't. "Can I die?"

The bladesmith's eyes widened, as if he weren't expecting the question. Then he simply dropped his attention back to his lap again, but not before nodding. "Aye, ye can die." He faced the sleeping Bill. "Boot ye have yer angel guardian?"

I glanced over at Bill whose leg was twitching as he slept, giving him the look of a sleeping bulldog dreaming of running. I faced the man again and sighed heavily, now aware that Bill couldn't really protect me with anything other than his magical light show. It was disconcerting. "Yes."

Then the bladesmith did something completely out of character, or what I imagined was out of character. He actually smiled, and the smile reached his eyes, brightening his face. At that moment, I could honestly say he was not only a handsome man, but incredibly so.

"He isna much of ah guardian," he said simply, the smile falling from his lips again. He continued to whittle as the silence in the room grew. Then he looked over at me again. "For ah thousand pounds ah day, Ah will provide ye with trainin'. An' Ah will show ye how ta use yer sword."

I swallowed hard, knowing I needed all the help I could get. I wasn't sure what my financial situation was, but remembered when Jason said AE would be in charge of my bills. "Okay," I said quickly, immediately realizing that I needed training and then some. If I had any hopes of navigating the Underground City and returning, I needed the bladesmith and then some.

"Then was the fear a little quieted that in my heart's lake had endured throughout the night, which I had passed so piteously."
— Dante's *Inferno*

SIX

I awoke to find myself lying on my side, facing the log wall of Tallis Black's cabin. The knots in the wood were still ripe with golden sap, which had crystallized into something that resembled amber. I sat up, rubbed my eyes and turned around, wondering if I were alone. I was. And, stranger still, I was sleeping on the mattress in the corner of the room. The same mattress Bill had his sights set on which Tallis had so unmistakably disallowed him. I was fairly certain I'd fallen asleep on the floor, with only the dying fire and a fur to keep me warm. As to how I ended up on the mattress? That was anyone's guess.

I stood up, suddenly feeling my heartbeat in my throat as it dawned on me that Bill was nowhere to be seen. Did my angel guardian pack up and leave? In the depths of my soul, I couldn't imagine he would, but fear of being left to my own defenses with the bladesmith continued to plague me. Not that I got any sort of vibe from Tallis to think he was interested in me in a ... sexual way (or in any way at all, really), but there was undeniably something not quite right about him. It was almost like a natural reflex built into me—that I shouldn't trust Tallis Black.

"Okay, so just what in the hell do you want me to tell him, Conan?"

I heard Bill's voice from outside the door and relief washed over me. Wasting no time, I hurried across the small house, opening the door wide as a gush of frigid air burst in.

At the garish display of sunlight suddenly streaming into my face, I held my hand above my eyes. Once my retinas were able to refocus, I noticed Bill standing right in front of the door, his hands on his hips. He was glaring at Tallis, who was bent over a tree stump, an axe in one hand, the other holding a log in place. The demon herd were behind Tallis, scouting through the bushes like curious dogs. Tallis lifted the axe above his head before bringing it down on the log that rested on the tree stump. He split the log in half, one piece ricocheting through the air and landing beside Bill, who glanced down at it indifferently.

One of the demons lifted its head at the sound of the log splitting, then glared at Bill. Bill growled at it and the ugly thing disappeared back into the undergrowth.

"Tell him she isna ready," Tallis said in a monotone, frowning at Bill before he returned his attention to the task at hand—apparently the chopping of firewood.

"An' you really think he's gonna listen to me?" Bill continued, shaking his head steadfastly. "Shit, I can't even reach the bastard!"

"She needs trainin'," Tallis answered while heaving the axe over his head again. His biceps bulged so much they looked like they were going to pop right off him. Not that I was paying any attention ...

"What are you talking about?" I asked finally, no longer wanting to play the role of detective, piecing the clues together. And besides, I really couldn't say I was exactly comfortable with the fact that I couldn't tear my attention away from Tallis's well-proportioned upper body.

"Mornin', Pollyanna," Bill said, eyeing me with a huge smile. I noticed Tallis didn't even glance up. I just smiled nervously at Bill, still worried about the subject of their conversation.

"Morning," I answered quickly. "What are you arguing about?"

Bill sighed, glancing at Tallis once more, then turned to face me. His eyes were laced with worry. "Skeletor texted me with our first retrievin' mission," he answered, eyeing me sharply as if to judge my reaction.

"Our first retrieving mission?" I repeated, my heart dropping to my feet as sweat started beading along my forehead and the small of my back. "You mean to the Underground?"

Bill bit his lip and nodded, the expression on his face telling me he wasn't happy with the news either.

"But," I started, shaking my head against the idea. I was about to find myself en route to the equivalent of hell. I had a feeling it would end up being a one-way ticket.

"Ye cannae go," Tallis interrupted, still refusing to so much as look at me. Instead, he picked up another log and held it in place. "Unless ye want ta take Streethorn oop on his offer of ah hundred years in Shade."

Roughly translated, that meant Tallis thought I would surely die were I to venture into the Underground City. And even though I didn't know what awaited me in the Underground, I had to agree with him.

"I thought you were going to train me?" I started, my voice sounding strained, panicked.

Tallis finally glanced up at me, his left eyebrow arched in obvious irritation as his navy blue eyes burned with something I had yet to put my finger on. "Trainin' ye will take time ... months. Ye donnae have months."

"So what's the answer then?" Bill demanded, kicking at a demon when it chanced a little too close to his foot.

Heaving the axe over his head again, Tallis cleaved the log in half and tossed both pieces into a pile beside him. Then he lifted the axe one more time and hefted it into the tree stump, standing up straight to face us, all seven feet of him. I guessed his chopping chores were finished for the day.

"Ye take me with ye."

"You would go with us?" I blurted out, surprised down to my toes as a wave of relief rode through me. Tallis, in and of himself, was something fearful, and if anyone could take on the Underground City, I was convinced he could.

Tallis nodded and wiped the sawdust from his hands onto his kilt. I felt my eyes stray to the valleys of broad muscle on his pectorals. My gaze slowly strayed downward, eating up the beauty of his rock-hard stomach to his belly button. I didn't miss the trail of black, wiry hair, which disappeared beneath his kilt either. Catching myself checking him out, and very obviously, I pulled my attention back to his face, suddenly embarrassed when I found his navy eyes studying me intently.

"Aye. For ah price."

"Of course!" Bill railed, throwing his arms up in the air. "Forget philan ... philantrop ..."

"Philanthropy," I finished for him, offering a small, but encouraging smile.

"Thanks, nerdlet," he said with a frown, facing Tallis again. "What's yer price this time? Her firstborn?"

Tallis appeared to ignore Bill and simply faced me. "Fifty thousand pounds."

"Fifty thousand! Fuck, dude!" Bill railed out, covering his heart with his hand as if he were having an apoplectic fit.

"Fifty thousand pounds an' Ah also want the credit for retrievin' the soul Streethorn wants ye to retrieve."

"Okay, done," I piped up instantly, placing more importance on my life than the money and the soul combined.

"What the hell are you gonna do with fifty thousand pounds? You got plans ta buy Sherwood Forest?" Bill continued. "An' for that matter, it's not like you're a Retriever; so what the hell do you want the credit for?"

Tallis finally faced Bill and his expression wasn't a happy one. "Mah reasons are mah own."

"Whatevs," Bill answered, shaking his head before he apparently thought better of it. "Fifty thousand clams is a lot of money, Conan, how do we even know you're worth it?"

"Ah have traversed the Oonderground many times," Tallis started, offering his explanation to me entirely. Apparently, he was well aware of who owned the checkbook. "Ah am extremely strong an' nae one can wield ah sword such as Ah can."

"This ain't an interview, Braggadouche," Bill coughed.

But Tallis ignored Bill and faced me, his jaw tight. "Ye will be safe with me."

They were exactly the words I needed to hear.

"Okay, so what's stopping you from leading us into the Underground and then just leaving our sorry asses there?" Bill continued. "Why should we trust you?"

Tallis never pulled his gaze from mine. "Ye have mah word," he said softly. "Ah willna leave ye."

I swallowed hard as the truth in his words appeared in his eyes. It wasn't like I knew Tallis Black at all, but there was something about him that made me believe that his word was something he never broke. Or maybe that was just my own dumb wishful thinking.

"Ye can pay the debt in installments," Tallis added softly.

"Okay," I said, knowing there was no other alternative. I didn't want to end up in Shade. I didn't want to become another AE Retriever statistic. I wanted to succeed and I was smart enough to realize that I wouldn't succeed without the protection of this man.

"Yer word," Tallis said, his eyes narrowing on me.

"You have my word."

Tallis simply nodded and glanced at Bill, who grumbled something unintelligible, fisting his hands in his pockets as he apparently engaged in a whispered argument with himself. Tallis returned his midnight blue gaze to me again and neither of us said a word, just stared at one another for four seconds ... not that I was counting.

It was Tallis who finally broke the silence. "First things first ... ye will need yer sword."

"What in the hell are we wastin' time with a freakin' sword, yo?" Bill interrupted. "Make her a machine gun!"

Tallis glanced at Bill indifferently. "Ye are an angel an' yet, ye know verra little aboot the Oonderground City."

"Yeah, dude, I've never been there," Bill said sarcastically, rolling his eyes. "We've been through this."

Tallis frowned more intensely, taking a deep breath as if it were all he could do to maintain his personal space without wringing Bill's thick neck. "The only way ta kill ah demon is by way of ah sword forged from iron of this forest."

"Then you will forge me a sword?" I asked softly, the words dying on my tongue as Tallis approached me. I felt myself gulp when he was only a mere foot away, studying me with those intense eyes, eyes that reflected a deep, dark void. Somehow, and I'm not sure why, the scar bisecting his cheek seemed more pronounced.

"Then get on it, yo," Bill interrupted from directly behind Tallis, coming closer to ensure I was safe, I guessed.

"Yer body will dictate how Ah create yer sword," Tallis said quietly, taking another few steps towards me. It seemed with each step he took, my heart rate increased. It was just off-putting and slightly uncanny how he seemed able to stare right through me.

"What do you mean?" I whispered, feeling as if I were succumbing to the seductive tone of his voice.

He said nothing, but held his hands out, so each of his palms were an inch or so away from my face.

"What the hell," Bill started.

"Ah willna hurt her," Tallis snapped at Bill although his eyes were still on mine. Then he simply closed his eyes and dropped his head slightly, as if he were centering all his attention on his palms. I could see his lips moving, as he chanted something only known to him. He pressed his hands even closer to my temples although he never touched me. He brought his hands down my neck to my shoulders, hovering a fraction of an inch above my body. He hesitated only briefly above my breasts before continuing his descent down to my navel where he paused a moment longer. He spread his hands out to encapsulate my hips and stopped, his brows knotting in the middle. Then he opened his eyes and his lips were suddenly tight as he inhaled deeply.

"Ye canna go ta the Oonderground," he said simply, dropping his hands as he took a few steps away from me.

"What?" I ground out, my eyes going wide. "What do you mean I can't go? Why?"

Bill stepped forward and threw his hands on his hips. "What the hell was that, Bubba?" he demanded. "First you're a blacksmith, er a bladesmith, and now a fuckin' mime?"

But Tallis ignored Bill, instead studying me with eyes that were so piercing, I couldn't hold his gaze.

"Ye have never known ah man," he said simply, his eyes narrowing on me with an unreadable expression.

"She never knew what man?" Bill gurgled.

"The lass doesna know what it 'tis ta be with ah man," Tallis said again.

"What the hell are you talkin' 'bout, dude?" Bill continued, grilling Tallis with his beady-eyed expression.

Tallis rolled his eyes. "She is ah virgin, man!" he finally roared out.

Bill was about to continue his word raid, but swallowed whatever was on its way out of his mouth, his shoulders deflating instead as he glanced over at me, and doubt clouded his eyes. "Oh."

"What?!" I started, my cheeks coloring with mortification that this ... stranger knew such an intimate detail about me. I wasn't sure why, but I was suddenly completely embarrassed by my chastity. "How? How do you know ... that? And, really, what difference does it make?"

Tallis shook his head, crossing his arms against his chest. "'Tis mah gift," he said simply, before continuing. "An the difference it makes is that ye are an innocent. Ye willna survive in the Oonderground City."

"Why?" Bill asked before I could.

"The Oonderground is naethin' but strife, sufferin'. All who venture into it have ah past an' it is that past which allows those of us who are able, ta escape." He glanced at me with something like regret in his eyes. He shook his head. "Yer innocence would be ah threat ta yer safety as well as mah own."

I swallowed down the surge of panic suddenly overtaking me as a vision of one hundred years in Shade cast itself before my eyes. "I have no choice," I said in a bereft tone. "I don't want to go to Shade."

"An' if ye venture into the Oonderground, ye will die anyway ... only ta find yerself in Shade ... so what is the point?"

So it was a Catch-22. If I abandoned my post of Retriever, Shade awaited me; but die while on a mission and Shade still awaited me.

But Tallis Black can keep you alive! a voice chimed up inside me. It was that voice, otherwise known as my subconscious, which I trusted.

"This really isn't such a problem," Bill started, eyeing us both, smiling as if he had the answer. "Someone just needs to slip her the sausage."

Although I frowned at him, I couldn't say the idea hadn't crossed my mind. If my virginity was throwing the figurative wrench in my plans, the solution was pretty readily apparent. "If this is just a case of my virginity," I started, flushing from my head to my toes. I couldn't spit out the rest of the statement. Then something occurred to me, something which spared me further embarrassment. "But what if," I started and took a deep breath. "What if my body isn't ... a virgin?" I mean, I couldn't imagine the body I now inhabited once belonged to someone who died a virgin—not looking like I did.

"Ah doona oonderstand," Tallis said as he eyed me speculatively.

I cleared my throat, but Bill beat me to the punch.

"That's just a borrowed body," he said, inclining his head toward me as if I weren't standing there and listening to him. "Skeletor, er Jason, offered it to her 'cause it weren't her time ta go when she, uh, went."

Tallis faced me and narrowed his eyes. "Ah see."

"So maybe my body isn't a virgin?" I continued, not even sure how I should feel about this conversation—it was just so foreign and weird. Furthermore, I didn't know how to feel about Tallis knowing this body wasn't mine. Somehow I felt like an imposter, like I'd done something I shouldn't have. It was a strange feeling and I immediately forced it out of my mind.

Tallis shook his head emphatically. "Ye are ah virgin, an innocent aboot the ways ah men, regardless."

"But if my body has already had sex," I started, getting frustrated and embarrassed all at the same time.

Tallis's lips tightened. "Ah could feel yer innocence in yer spirit."

Okay, so it seemed my virginal status was going to haunt me no matter where I went. Fabulous. Realizing I was now stuck, I quickly weighed the options in my head:

1. Have sex and lose your innocence, thereby allowing yourself a chance in hell, literally, or, 2. Continue being a virgin, die a virgin and spend the next hundred years in Shade ... a virgin ...

Yep, having sex never sounded so good.

I faced Tallis again, forcing myself to hold his gaze. What was about to come out of my mouth wasn't going to be pretty and it definitely wouldn't be easy. I held my chin up high and reminded myself of Robert Schuller's words: *Tough times never last. Tough people do.* And Lily Harper was determined to last. "The only obstacle standing in our way is my ... virginity," I started, spearing Tallis with my determination. "The solution is pretty obvious."

I never expected Tallis Black to be struck dumb, but that's the exact expression he wore as soon as the words left my mouth. He cleared his throat, arched a brow and simply turned to face Bill, as if Bill might be the solution to my problem. He wasn't.

"Somehow, dude, I don't think she's talkin' about me," Bill said and I nodded emphatically, glancing back at Tallis with resolve. When it came down to it, I would rather spend a hundred years in Shade than have Bill for my sexual partner, especially my first.

Tallis cleared his throat and glanced back at me again. I could swear his cheeks were a little redder than before. "Aye, well ..."

"Fifty thousand pounds and you take credit for the retrieved soul," I said simply. "Does your offer still stand?"

He cleared his throat again before taking a deep breath. "Och aye, mah offer was ta act as yer guide in the Oonderground. That doesna include the ..." He dropped his attention to the ground. "The other subject."

"Fuck, dude, you gonna charge her for that too?" Bill demanded, shaking his head, as if he just didn't get it. "Look at her! She's the bomb dot com!"

"Nae!" Tallis thundered at him, anger suddenly infiltrating his expression. "Ah willna deflower her. Ah willna have that on mah conscience."

I felt my stomach drop. "You won't?" I asked softly, not understanding why he wasn't jumping at the opportunity to have sex with me. I mean, Bill was right, I *was* the bomb dot com. Or, at least, I looked that way.

"Why? Are you like ... into men?" Bill asked, taking a few steps closer to me.

"Nae!" Tallis thundered at Bill, who held his hands up in mock submission.

"No need to throw a mantrum, dude," he whispered. "I just wanted to make sure, that's all."

Tallis faced me and sighed, rubbing his head as he realized he owed me some sort of explanation. "Ah have enough ta make amends for. Ah doona need ta add ye ta the list."

"But," I started.

He shook his head and interrupted me. "Besides, Ah dunno for certain if that ... act would remove yer innocence. 'Tis yer spirit that's innocent an' naive."

But somehow I didn't believe him—my spirit being innocent just sounded like a line intended to get him out of having to have sex with me—a subject which still floored me. I'd basically just gotten a smart slap to the face, even with a face that was entirely more beautiful than mine used to be. But none of that mattered anymore. What mattered now was asserting myself. I *would not* spend the next hundred years in Shade. "I'm going," I said resolutely, eyeing Bill and Tallis. "Whether you come with us or we go alone, I'm still going."

"Lass, didna ye hear me?" Tallis asked in an irritated voice, his eyes narrowed and dangerous.

"Yes, I heard you!"

"This mission could cost ye yer life," he repeated, spearing me with his glare as he folded his beefy arms across his beefier chest.

"And if I don't do it, I'll end up in Shade for the next century, which isn't an option," I threw back, holding my lips in a straight line as I gathered whatever strength I could find within me.

Tallis shook his head again and sighed, long and hard, dropping his attention to the ground as he seemed to weigh the argument in his head. Finally, he glanced up at me and there was fury in his eyes. "Ah willna allow ye ta go."

I threw my hands on my hips, anger flaring up within me at the thought that this man, whom I'd only just met, had the gall to tell me he wouldn't permit me to go. "Just who in the hell do you think you are?"

"Nice," Bill said as he smiled at me encouragingly, no doubt pleased over the fact that I hadn't said "heck."

"Ah am the only one of us that will keep ye alive," he said in answer to my question as he returned my scowl. "An' ah am also the only one of us that appears ta have ah speck of intelligence."

So now he was insulting my intelligence? Well, I might not have been beautiful (the old me, anyway) or popular or "cool," but one thing I did know about myself was that if I were anything, I was smart. Damn anyone who tried to convince me otherwise. "You listen here, Tallis Black," I started, not meaning to sound like a ninety-year-old librarian chastising an unruly child, but c'est la vie. "Regardless of what you say, I AM going to the Underground to attempt to do my job. If I die trying, then so be it, but at least I'll know I tried." I took a deep breath. "No one is going to change my mind, not you, not Bill, no one!"

Tallis's eyes narrowed and both of us played the game of stare down for another few seconds before he spoke. "Ye are too stubborn for yer own good."

"Are you in or are you out?" I snapped, no longer interested in his reasons why I shouldn't venture to the Underground.

He stared at me for another few seconds, but I refused to back down. Tallis took a few steps closer to me until we were maybe two inches apart. He was so close, I could feel his breath against my cheeks and smell his earthy scent—a smell I found heady in its raw masculinity. I felt my heartbeat racing as I realized how enormous he was—when it came down to it, he could simply hogtie me to ensure I didn't make it into the Underground. And given the ire in his expression, I wouldn't have put it past him.

"Ah will go with ye," he ground out and then leaned down until his nose was mere millimeters from mine. I felt myself gulp and wanted nothing more than to take a step back, but absolutely disallowed myself. I started to answer, but he cut me off.

"Boot oonderstand that ye will do as Ah tell ye. An' Ah doona want ta hear ah peep out of either of ye," he finished, alternating his glare between Bill and me. Then he grumbled more to himself than to either of us. "Ah'll be damned if Ah let ah lass tell me what ta do."

"You won't hear a peep from either of us," I said, glancing over at Bill for confirmation. He simply nodded.

Tallis continued to stare right through me before he released the breath he was holding. "Ah will do mah best ta ensure yer safety, but Ah cannae guarantee it."

I nodded. "That's good enough for me."

"And if it's good enough for her, Tido, it's good enough for me," Bill weighed in, with a used car salesman's smile.

***

After Tallis's decision to accompany us to the Underground City, he left us to our own defenses, claiming he had to start working on my sword. I didn't see hide nor hair of him for the next few hours and once the sun began its descent, I started to get a little worried. But worrying about Tallis Black was a complete and total waste of my time. It was like worrying about a great white shark or a saltwater crocodile.

"Where the hell is Conan?" Bill asked as he paced the ground just outside Tallis's cabin. It was becoming colder the farther the sun dropped in the sky. Even worse, the less than friendly bladesmith forebade us to enter his home. For the last few hours, we'd basically just hung around a crudely constructed fire pit that Bill put together.

"Ah dinnae know," I answered in a terrible rendition of Tallis, but it made Bill laugh all the same.

The laugh died on his lips as soon as his stomach started growling audibly and he rubbed it as he faced me with a sigh. "I gotta take care of this ragin' food boner."

I just shook my head. "Do you have to be so crude?"

Bill shrugged. "It's the only way I know how to deal with Conan's BMS."

"His what?"

"Bitchy man syndrome," he answered as his stomach started whining again.

I laughed, thinking Tallis did have BMS and then some. I stood up from beneath a large pine tree and sighed. "I'll go look for him and see what the plan is for dinner."

"'Kay," Bill answered as I started forward. "Hey, when he gets back, let's you and me play the penis game with him."

"The what?" I asked, frowning as I turned to face him. One thing I could say for Bill was that I never knew what might come out of his mouth—the only thing I could rely on was that it wouldn't be rated PG.

"We gotta slip in the word 'penis' while we're talking, like it's a normal word in the conversation," he explained, his smile broad. "Like, for example, I would say: 'Yo, Conan, what's for dinner 'cause, penis, I'm starved."

"That sounds like you're calling him a penis."

He shook his head and sighed like it was a damn shame that I didn't see the beauty in his game. "Jesus, you're like the red pen police every second."

"The red pen police?"

"You know, those super annoying people who constantly correct everyone else's lingo," he answered and threw me a frown. "Mucho no bueno."

"Whatever," I said, shaking my head as I started forward again. "I'm not playing the penis game with you anyway."

"Fine, no sweat off my balls," Bill responded, taking the spot I'd previously occupied and leaning his back against the tree. "See you later, masturbator."

> "He seemed as if against me he were coming with head uplifted, and with ravenous hunger."
> — Dante's *Inferno*

SEVEN

I couldn't stop thinking about Tallis Black declining to have sex with me. As I crunched through the snow, intent on finding him, a good part of me was still embarrassed and mortified that he'd basically turned me down flat. Even when sex was the most obvious way out of the dilemma presented by my innocence, he found the idea so odious or loathsome that he opted to endanger both our lives instead. Way to make a girl feel good about herself ...

The more I thought about it, the more it just didn't make sense. Weren't men notoriously horny? Wasn't the big joke that women were always the ones who weren't in the mood? And it wasn't as though I was heinously unattractive and begging him to have his way with me. I was beautiful! My body and my face were every man's dream, yet Tallis wanted nothing to do with me. Was it possible he was gay? I couldn't swallow the idea of Tallis being attracted to men, though. Maybe he was just asexual. Was it even possible for a human to be asexual? Maybe if he were an amoeba ...

But Tallis Black was definitely no amoeba.

I let out a pent-up breath as I shook my head at the anomaly of the bladesmith. The irony of the whole damn situation was that I assumed women as beautiful as I was now had men swooning at their feet. All my life, I wondered what it was like to be gorgeous, alluring and sexy. I always wished men would look at me with blatant awe in their eyes, and view me as something besides Lily Harper, a sweet and smart, but not too pretty girl. Being beautiful now didn't change how I felt about myself at all. How ironic!

Nearly tripping over a partially concealed tree branch, I suddenly became incredibly irritated that Tallis was nowhere to be found. I took a few breaths, feeling the iciness of the air stabbing my lungs. Looking around, I noticed dusky, bluish shadows were falling all around me. Night was on its way and being alone in the forest wasn't a good idea. Actually, it had been silly for me to go after Tallis alone in the first place—especially in these woods. They didn't exactly fill me with feelings of security or safety. I turned around, intent on retracing my steps back to Tallis's cottage. If Tallis wasn't back by the time I returned, Bill would have to figure out his own dinner. I, for once, wasn't hungry.

Looking down at the snow, I searched for my footprints, intending to simply follow them back to the cabin. I can't even begin to explain my shock when I realized there weren't any. Instead of deep shoeprints, only the white snow, pristine and trackless, lay before me. I must have stood there staring for a few a minutes, wondering if my eyes were deceiving me. The snow had to have been three or so inches deep, but there wasn't a track anywhere in sight. It seemed like I'd been airlifted and dropped into the place I now stood. What amazed me even more was that it hadn't snowed during my walk—which would've explained everything.

You didn't walk very far, Lily, I told myself. *Just continue walking straight and you should find Tallis's cabin.*

I started forward, listening to the rustling in the bushes all around me—it was the sounds of creatures, moving through the branches. What said creatures were, I had no idea, but it also wasn't a thought that cheered me up, so I ignored it.

"The whole secret of existence is to have no fear," I whispered out loud, reciting the words of Buddha, hoping they might make me feel better. They didn't.

The bushes continued to crackle and crunch beside me, their leaves shaking with agitation by whatever was moving through them.

Have no fear.

I hurried my steps as an icy wind blasted me. Squinting my eyes, I dropped my face down to shield myself against the relentless battery of wind. As soon as I did, a tree branch lashed across my cheek, the bitterness of the sting almost as sharp as the cold air. Suddenly, it sounded like a large animal was scampering alongside me. I could hear its footfalls in the snow as if it were only a few feet away. With my heart dropping, I nonchalantly glanced to my right, already sensing my fight or flight defenses taking control. But, to my surprise, there was nothing beside me but the pure white snow and endless trees.

No fear.

I didn't know how long I retraced my steps. Maybe two minutes? Ten? It didn't matter, I was lost. There was no sign of Tallis's cabin, not even a spire of smoke to indicate the way to Bill's fire pit. There was nothing but the endless line of trees ahead of me. And something was not quite right about that too. I knew I hadn't walked more than five or ten minutes from the cabin, and now I was walking in the same direction from whence I'd come, with no sign of the cabin anywhere!

My heart continued pounding in my chest as panic began spiraling within my gut.

Thwack!

I stopped dead in my tracks. It sounded like a loud slap. Whatever it was, it definitely sounded like something hard like a book connecting with something soft like skin. I craned my neck, listening for it again. All I could hear was the lonely call of a bird somewhere nearby. As the darkness continued to grow, I had to refocus my concentration on returning to Tallis's cabin. I started forward and that was when I heard it again. This time, it repeated itself within seconds and I realized it was coming from my right. Turning that direction, I noticed a hill, all the scenery beyond which was eclipsed by the hill's crest. I wasn't sure why, but I decided to follow the sound—as if something inside me wanted to prevent me from searching for the cabin, at least until I figured out what was making the sound.

I heard it again—the definite sound of slapping. My feet sunk into the snow as I struggled up the slope, trying to be as quiet as I could, and not alert whatever was making the sound on the other side. When I reached the top, my breath caught in my throat.

There, maybe ten feet in front of me, was Tallis. He was sitting on his haunches, his black kilt covering his legs. His bare back was towards me, the black ink of tattoos in direct contrast to the olive tones of his skin. But it wasn't his tattoos that captured my interest, it was the crimson blood which nearly painted his entire back.

I felt like I was suddenly frozen, and couldn't move my legs even if I wanted to. Instead, I just stood there, rooted to the spot, unable to pull my attention from the pumping of Tallis's blood as it gushed down his back, seemingly following the lines of the branches and roots of the tattoo of the tree on his back. His blood stained the snow beneath him.

A small creek flowed in front of him, and his broad sword lay still beside him on the white snow. On his other side a narrow rivulet of blood, fed by the multiple lesions on his back. It looked as if it flowed into one channel, inexplicably drawn together by an invisible force. It continued down his back, looking like a crimson braid, before leaking into the snow. What struck me as completely odd, and even impossible, was that the snow didn't absorb his blood at all, but appeared to reject it. It looked like the snow was sealed or something because his blood simply ran down the face of it like water in a funnel, before being carried away by the creek.

I didn't move. I don't even think I breathed as I watched Tallis pick up what looked like a cat o' nine tails.

He held the black leather handle above his head and pulled his hand back toward me before coming down, flogging the multiple braided leather ropes against the skin of his back. As soon as they made contact, fresh blood from the lacerations poured freely. Looking closer at the weapon he held above him, I noticed that there were small, silver blades attached to the ends of each individual braid.

When the cat made contact with Tallis's back again, he didn't so much as flinch, but continued sitting there, as if it was no physical discomfort at all. I had no idea what to do. Should I stop him from further harming himself? Should I walk away and pretend I hadn't seen him ... what? Punishing himself, for lack of a better word?

Before I could decide, I heard his voice. It took me a few seconds to realize he was speaking in a tongue I didn't recognize. The sounds that came from him were like chanting of some sort—delivered in a low-pitched monotone. Hoisting the cat above his head again, he brought it down harder this time. Blood splattered off the ends of it, staining the white snow behind him. The snow again rejected the beads of blood, while the creek eagerly swallowed them. Meanwhile, the lacerations he'd gouged into his back continued to bleed. Watching the rivulets of blood running down his back, into the snow and eventually the creek made me snap. When he brought the cat up over his head again, I couldn't take it anymore.

"Stop!" I yelled, emerging from the top of the small hill and nearly tripping down the other side. I stopped short when I found the tip of a blade aimed at my nose with Tallis at the other end of it. It happened so suddenly, I didn't even get a chance to blink. We stared at one another for a few agonizing seconds while I wondered if he intended to run me through.

"Lass!" he finally stammered, his voice on the verge of outrage. "Dinnae ever sneak up behin' me again!" he railed against me, dropping the blade in the snow. His eyebrows knotted in the middle as he glared at me. "Ah could have killed ye!"

"I'm sorry," I said quickly, looking from the blade, to the wrath in his eyes. "I, just ... just wanted to stop you from ..." I glanced at the cat o' nine tails lying against the bank of the creek, deceptively innocent from disuse. I glanced up at Tallis again, frowning as I tried to make sense of what I'd just seen. "I wanted to stop you from hurting yourself."

He narrowed his eyes, but kept staring at me. His expression was unreadable. I expected some shock or embarrassment at being discovered doing something so hideous to himself, but he showed neither. He wore the same stoic expression he always did.

"Ye should mind yer own business."

"I'm sorry," I repeated, not knowing what more to say. Looking at the snow, I saw the last of his blood running into the creek, which eagerly embraced it. Looking up at Tallis again, I found his eyes still fastened on mine.

"What were ye doin' out here anyway?" he demanded.

I took a deep breath and tried to remember the answer to his question. I was still so shocked by seeing him abusing himself that every other thought completely vanished from my mind.

"Answer me, lass!" he insisted.

"Um, I, uh," I started, but grew suddenly nervous, and felt clumsy and awkward with words. *What in the heck ... no, what in the hell was I doing out here?* Then I remembered. "Bill was hungry and we didn't know what your plan was for, uh, dinner, so I offered to look for you."

Perhaps it was my imagination, but I could have sworn Tallis's dark blue eyes suddenly turned black. "Ye should know better. How many times must Ah tell ye how dangerous this forest is?"

I didn't say anything but simply nodded, suddenly consumed by an irrational fear of the man standing before me. His eyes seemed like bottomless pits of nothing and his jaw was clenched so tightly, it illustrated perfectly what he thought about me traipsing around the forest and spying on him. I suddenly hated the silence between us, and my mouth dropped open of its own accord. "I tried to find my way back to your cabin, but I couldn't find my footprints to follow. The snow swallowed them up."

Tallis nodded. "Aye. The woods were tryin' ta make ye lose yer way."

"You make it sound like the forest can think, or that it has a brain," I said softly.

"Och aye, it does."

I didn't say anything as I swallowed down the fear that was climbing up my throat. I wasn't sure who scared me more: the haunted forest or the man standing in front of me. Actually it wasn't much of a contest: Tallis did.

He suddenly made a sound in his throat and started forward, grabbing me by my upper arm to let me know in no uncertain terms that I was to follow him. Shrugging out of his almost painful grip, it made me angry that I couldn't do anything right as far as this man was concerned. After basically saving him from self-inflicted torture, all I got was a lecture. But even worse, I didn't like being afraid of him.

"What were you doing back there?" I demanded then I stopped walking. Tallis didn't pause for one second, and after realizing he probably wouldn't hesitate to leave me out here, I hurried forward to catch up with him.

"Ye need nae concern yerself."

I gritted my teeth and ached to even out the playing field. I didn't want Tallis Black to think I was just a vapid, shy, intimidated woman that he could order around. Because I wasn't. I was Lily Harper, Director of Marketing. Plus, I was incredibly educated with a master's degree and there was no way that I would let some … woodland lumberjack intimidate me.

"Excuse me for caring."

Instantly, Tallis turned on me with a fire in his eyes that scared the hell out of me. His irises grew darker, taking on the inky blackness I'd witnessed earlier. "Ah donnae want yer carin' nor yer questions. Once this mission ta the Oonderground is over, Ah dinnae want ta see ye or that damned angel again."

My jaw dropped open at his complete lack of humanity. I could honestly say I'd never come across anyone as cold and distant as this man. Tallis Black was the biggest jerk I'd ever met!

We continued walking forward, neither of us saying anything. I was so angry, embarrassed and shocked, I couldn't decide if I wanted to scream at him or cry. One thing I was certain of though, especially based on my reaction to him, was that I genuinely cared about Tallis. And I hated the fact that I cared—that he got under my skin so much. Really, I shouldn't have given two hoots about him. I shouldn't have cared that he was such a jerk—it shouldn't have bothered me because it wasn't as though Tallis meant anything beyond a guide to the Underground City to me. After that, I would happily be free of him, just like he said. If we never crossed paths again, that would be just swell in my books.

Then why were you so upset when he refused to have sex with you? a voice suddenly piped up from inside me. I felt my stomach flip-flop on itself. "About that sex thing," I started, blazing forward on my steed, bedecked in armor and defending the flag known as "Lily Harper's Pride."

"Nae, that conversation is over," Tallis growled without looking at me as he maintained his breakneck walking speed.

"No, it isn't," I demanded, crossing my arms against my chest, determined to salvage some of my dignity. "The only reason I even mentioned ... sex ...was purely because I saw it as a means to an end," I said with authority. "It absolutely had nothing to do with me ... wanting to uh, do it with ... you," I finished with less authority.

Tallis gave me a side glance and a raised brow, which I interpreted to mean that he wasn't exactly buying my explanation. And that fueled me all the more. I stopped walking and this time, so did he. I threw my hands on my hips and faced him with all the fury I could muster. He just had this way about him where he could strip me to my core with only a word or glance my way. "Listen," I told him loudly, "if we are going to travel together through the Underground, you need make yourself a little easier to be around."

Tallis didn't say anything right away. Instead, he closed the distance between us until he was maybe only an inch from me. I refused to budge though, and crossed my arms over my chest, forcing my chin up just to glare at him. He mirrored my expression, but his was a lot scarier.

"Listen here, Besom. Ah dinnae give ah damn aboot what the hell ye want. Ah would never have agreed ta be yer guide if Ah'd known ye were an innocent. Oonderstan' me now that if ye give me even an ounce ah grief, Ah'll leave ye an' that stookie angel ta find yer own way in this forest alone."

I was so angry and dumbfounded, I just said the first thing that occurred to me. "My name isn't Besom, Conan!"

"Aye, boot it describes ye well," Tallis responded, a slight smile turning up his lips.

"What does it mean?" I demanded.

Tallis started forward again but I kept up with him, especially after hearing he would leave my stookie angel and me out in the forest to find our own way out.

"It means ye are ah difficult woman."

I thrust my lower jaw out and glared at him. "Well, you are the most difficult, irritating, rudest man I've ever met!"

"Then we are even in our mutual dislike of one another." He gave me a frown. "All the more reason ta finish this silly mission apace."

"Agreed," I answered, my lips tight.

"Dude, where the hell have you assholes been?!" Bill's voice interrupted the previously tranquil air and caught me by surprise, since I didn't even realize we'd returned to

Tallis's cabin. Bill jumped up from the exact same position I left him, and threw his hands on his fleshy hips as he shouted at us. "You left me Macaulay Culking it for so long, I thought you dumbasses forgot about me!"

Neither Tallis nor I said anything. Bill continued to berate us, although his anger gave way to curiosity as he looked us up and down. "What did you bring back for dinner?"

Tallis threw the sword against the base of the tree where Bill was sitting. The blade stuck into the snow, swinging the rest of the sword to and fro. I remembered Tallis leaving the cat o' nine tails back in the snow, beside the creek. Looking at Tallis's wide back, I noticed all the blood was gone, and the lacerations had completely healed. I shook my head in wonder over how Tallis had healed so fast.

Bill turned his beady-eyed, hungry expression from Tallis to me, reminding me that he'd asked where dinner was. I simply shrugged, as if to say we hadn't brought anything back. The whole of my thoughts, though, were still centered on how Tallis Black managed to heal so quickly.

"You mean to tell me that while I've been sittin' here so damn long that I taught myself how to be ambisextrous, neither of you caught anythin' to eat?" Bill demanded.

Tallis faced me and shook his head. "What is he goin' on aboot?"

Bill held both of his hands up and turned to Tallis. "Ambisextrous, man! I can masturbate with both hands!"

Tallis shook his head just as the mob of demons suddenly appeared from the rear of his cabin. The one in the front carried a carcass of something. The other demons brought up the rear and the one carrying the bloodied rabbit (I think that's what it was) carefully made its way to Tallis's feet. It dropped the carcass, which turned out to be two rabbits, before Tallis.

"Well done," Tallis said with a slight nod at the creature. He leaned down and picked up the two blood-soaked rabbits.

I glanced at Bill and saw the horror on his face. "Please tell me that isn't our dinner, Conan?"

"It isnae yer dinner," Tallis answered quickly, facing the wooden door of his cabin. He turned the knob and walked inside, while the demons surrounded the doorway, looking like super-ugly dogs begging.

"Amen to that, nerdlet," Bill said with a smile as he walked over to me and we both took a seat in front of the fire. "You okay, sugar mounds?" he asked, draping his pudgy arm around me.

Looking back at the cabin, I watched Tallis shut the door. I turned back to the fire and shook my head. "You do realize that he meant the rabbits are solely for him, and we have to fend for ourselves?"

The smile on Bill's face vanished as he eyed the closed door of the cabin and frowned before asking, "You sure?"

I just nodded with a smile that said I was very sure, in no uncertain terms.

"What the fuck?!" Bill railed. "What the hell are we supposed to eat?" As he stood up, the demons caught his attention. "Hey, you," he called, and all the demons turned to face him as one. "Yeah, you ugly, little shits, go bring me something to eat!"

But the demons simply turned back to the door of the cabin again, clearly unimpressed with Bill. Tallis opened the door, throwing out a large bowl of what looked like leftovers—old vegetables and even older meat. The demons dove for the scraps, growling and biting one another as they wolfed down whatever they could get into their mouths.

"Garbivores," Bill said in disgust as he watched the demons licking the dirt and snow for any leftovers they might have missed. "The lowliest of animals in the food chain because they only eat garbage."

I couldn't help laughing, but stopped as soon as Bill sighed. We both stared at the fire as his stomach continued to growl. "Bill?"

When he looked up at me, I almost felt sorry for him because he seemed so dejected. "Yeah, nips?"

"Do you think we could make our way back to the car ourselves?" I asked. I kept one eye on the doorway to make sure Tallis wouldn't show up anytime soon.

Bill frowned. "No way," he said with a "duh" undertone. "You heard Conan. He said this forest ain't safe."

I nodded quickly. "I know but I'm also not so sure we can trust him."

"You weren't singing that song earlier," Bill responded. His eyebrows reached for the sky before he returned his attention to me. "You were, like, in love with the dude."

"I was not!" I said with utter irritation.

"Oh, we can't even think about goin' into the Underground without the bladesmith," he said in a sing-song voice. He held his hand up to his cheek like he was in distress. It was the worst impersonation of a woman I'd ever seen. "And once he finishes our tour of the Underground, I hope he'll take a tour of my panties!" He finished in his girlie voice before erupting into a fit of chuckles.

"Are you done?" I demanded vehemently.

"Yeah, geez," Bill said, holding his hands up in mock submission. "What's up your bug?"

"Nothing," I said as I shook my head. I took a deep breath. "I just don't trust him and I don't know if it's smart for us to consign ourselves to traveling in the Underground City with him."

"Well, he sure as hell isn't any friend of mine," Bill started, staring down at his feet as he shook his head. "But he's the only one who knows the Underground and without him, we'll be shit outta luck."

I nodded. "That's what I thought you were going to say."

"Then why did ya ask, babydoll?" He didn't give me the chance to respond. He looked over at the demons, who were cleaning themselves off using their tongues just like cats do. They'd already made themselves comfortable around the fire pit. Bill studied the one closest to us for a few seconds before turning to face me. "You think we could eat one of them things?"

"Oh my God," I said, curling my lips up in disgust. "No!"

Just then, the door to Tallis's cabin opened. Tallis strode out, carrying a wooden bowl with him. He walked up to me, and to prevent him from towering over me any more than usual, I stood up. He thrust the bowl into my hands. I saw it was one half of a rabbit in a stew of what looked like boiled potatoes and something else I couldn't quite put my finger on.

"Rabbit, neeps an' taddies," he said, which I figured meant potatoes and turnips. "Ye must eat as ye'll need yer strength in the Oonderground."

I didn't say anything as I took the plate and stepped away from him before he started walking back to the cabin.

"Hey, what about me?" Bill called after him.

Tallis turned to face him and frowned. "Ah dinnae approve of men that cannae provide for themselves." Then he closed the door behind him.

"Dick!" Bill yelled as he faced me, shaking his head.

I took a seat next to him and offered my bowl. "We can share."

Apparently "sharing" never entered Bill's mind because by the time the plate was clean, I only got to eat turnips for dinner, the only things on the plate that Bill hadn't liked. I stood up and took the empty plate back to Tallis's door, knocking on it cautiously. When he didn't respond, I knocked louder. He opened the door and looked down at me, saying nothing as he took the bowl from my hands. His eyes settled on mine for another few seconds. I was actually uncomfortable because I couldn't understand why he was staring at me. Then he cleared his throat and lifted his eyes to the sky.

"Ye will come in. Night is upon us an' 'tis nae longer safe in the woods."

Bill was beside me in a split second. Tallis held the door wider for him, but frowned at the much smaller man as he made his way into Tallis's house. Just as I was about to follow Bill, Tallis stopped me with his hand on my upper shoulder. I wasn't sure why, but his touch sent shivers down my spine. Looking up at him in question, I found him studying me.

"Retrieve the sword afore ye enter," he said in a low tone. He tilted his chin and motioned to the sword he'd carried back with him, which still lay against the tree. I nodded and turned around, heading for the sword. It felt like slow motion as I reached for it. Once my fingers made contact with the hilt, an incredibly bright light flashed out from it. I drew back and closed my eyes, shielding them with my arm. When I tried to release the sword, however, it wouldn't allow me.

"Accept it!" Tallis roared at me.

Not knowing what he meant, I tightened my hold around the hilt and lifted the sword. As I did, I felt heat radiating within me and a gust of wind blew my hair right off my face. I closed my eyes to an onslaught of images that flickered behind my eyelids. There were so many, I found it difficult to focus on any one. After the images faded before me, I was left with the memory of a beautiful landscape, complete with craggy, verdant hillsides. The lush foliage on the mountain's face touched the dark blue of the ocean, somehow reminding me of Tallis's navy blue eyes. The sky was covered with grey storm clouds, their color emphasized in the ancient stones of a castle that occupied an island as wide as the castle's base. It was maybe two hundred yards from the mountainside, and connected by a stone bridge that looked straight from Roman antiquity.

I opened my eyes and looked at the sword, realizing I was panting. I turned to face Tallis and shook my head, still trying to catch my breath. "What was that?" I demanded finally.

"What did ye see?"

"What does it matter what I saw?" I lashed out. "What I want to know is what the hell just happened?"

"What did ye see, lass?" he repeated.

I swallowed, taking another breath, and trying to calm my heart. "I saw a lot of ... things, but the only one I remember is a castle."

Tallis's eyes widened for a split second before the surprise disappeared from his face. "Describe it to me."

"You said it was dangerous for us to be out here at night," I said with a quick scan around myself. "Do you mind if I describe it inside?"

He simply nodded and stepped aside, allowing me to enter. As soon as I walked through the door, the warm fire in the hearth hit me immediately. I gently brought my sword to the table near the door, half wondering if I set it down, would it separate from my hand? Luckily, it did.

"What the hell?" Bill started, but Tallis silenced him with a "shush" as he raised his hand in the air. Then he faced me again.

"Explain what ye saw."

"The castle sat on an island at the base of a green mountain. I think the island was in a lake maybe. There was a bridge that connected the castle to the mainland." Tallis nodded as if he knew exactly what I was talking about, as if he recognized my description of the castle. He didn't say anything, though, so I continued. "Do you know the castle I'm describing?"

He immediately shook his head, and I knew he wasn't telling the truth. There was real recognition in his eyes when I described it ... "Now it's your turn to answer me," I said with steely resolve. "What happened when I touched that sword?"

Tallis shrugged. "The sword became one with ye. 'Twas ah test ta ensure that Ah created it correctly, that it was truly meant ta be yer sword."

"That's the sword you made for me?" I asked, surprised.

"Aye," Tallis said with a nod. "A claidheamh mhor."

"A what?" Bill called from the corner of the house where he'd made himself comfortable in front of the fireplace. "Sounds like a venereal disease."

"In English, ye call it ah Claymore sword. In Gaelic, 'tis known as the claidheamh mhor, the great sword."

I eyed the sword on the table and approached it, watching Tallis. "If I pick it up, will it freak out on me again?"

He shook his head. "It already knows ye are its mistress."

I reached for the hilt and lifted the sword, as though it was the first time. The blade was long, maybe four feet, and it had two handles. Each handle terminated in a honeycomb pattern. The hilt was carved of wood that appeared to be twisted, but fit my small grip perfectly. Taking my eyes from the sword to focus on Tallis's face, I asked: "Did you create it correctly? Is the sword really meant for me?"

A strange thing happened then. Tallis actually smiled. I was so shocked to see the semblance of happiness on his face that it completely threw me. Luckily, the smile didn't last long and his regular sourpuss demeanor quickly returned. I was then able to regard him once again as the arrogant jerk I'd come to expect.

"Aye, 'tis yer sword."

Without another word, Tallis opened the door and stepped outside, before quickly closing it behind him. I looked at Bill, who simply shrugged as if he could care less about Tallis. "Shocker," he said. "Conan can actually smile."

> "Thee it behooves to take another road."
> — Dante's *Inferno*

EIGHT

I wasn't sure how many hours passed before Tallis returned. I spent the time sitting in front of the fire and thinking, Bill's sonorous snoring playing the part of soundtrack to my overwrought mind. My thoughts were pretty much wholly centered on the enigma called the bladesmith. There was something supernatural about him; of that I was convinced. Otherwise, how could he have healed himself? How was he able to bewitch my sword to make it ignite into a light show as soon as I touched it? And how could he survive in a forest that he, himself, described as treacherous? Furthermore, he'd somehow managed to domesticate the herd of Grevels, something which seemed counterintuitive, seeing that they were demons! And that whole thing with his eyes ... More than once I'd watched their midnight blue eclipsed by a colorless, dark void, of pure, inky blackness. Yes, I was convinced that Tallis Black was otherworldly. But the question still remained: what, exactly, was he? Definitely not an angel, so I crossed that off my list. Perhaps a demon? Hmm, that would explain a lot of things.

"Why are ye still awake?

I jumped when his voice interrupted the stillness of the air, and cranked my neck toward him so quickly, a shooting pain stabbed through it. I didn't answer him as I brought my hand to the back of my neck and rubbed it, trying to end the jabbing agony. I hadn't heard him when he opened the door and entered the cabin and I also didn't hear him when he closed the distance between us, and came up behind me. The only reason I knew he was there was because I suddenly felt his hands on my shoulders.

My instinctive response was to shrink away from him as the fleeting thought that he could very easily break my neck crossed my mind. "What?" I started in a voice laced with anxiety, but he interrupted me.

"Relax. Ah wilna hurt ye." His tone of voice was soft and reassuring. He didn't say anything more, but I felt his large, callused hands massaging the back of my neck, and moving down toward my right ear. "Is this where ye feel pain?"

I just nodded, my heart in my throat as I resisted the urge to close my eyes. His hands just felt so incredibly good, warm, big and ... strong. He continued to manipulate the muscles of my neck, and the tensile strength of his fingers soon melted the pain away. I again reminded myself that he could snap me in two effortlessly, yet he could also be so incredibly gentle.

"Are you a demon?" I asked, focusing on the mottled brown fur on the floor that Bill was noisily sleeping on.

Tallis chuckled a deep, luxurious and infectious sound. "Nae, Ah am nae demon."

"Then what are you?" I persisted, figuring if he were in a good mood, I might as well drill him for more information. Who knew when he'd be in another good mood again? "I know you're not an angel, or an ordinary human like me."

"Why do ye think Ah am anythin'?"

I found it strange that he continued to massage my neck even though the pain was gone. Then I realized I hadn't told him the pain had ceased. The truth was that I loved feeling his warm skin touching mine and I didn't want him to stop his ministrations. "You can heal yourself and ... others; you live in this forest even though you told us it's a perilous place; you're the leader of a pack of demons; and you did something to that sword when I touched it."

He chuckled again, this time softer and I could feel his breath on the naked skin of my neck. My entire body responded with goose bumps.

"How is the ache in yer neck now, Besom?"

"It's gone, thanks," I answered, deciding to ignore my nickname for the time being. Frankly, I was embarrassed that he'd had to ask me about the pain at all. It had to be pretty obvious that I didn't want him to stop touching me.

He pulled his hands from my neck and I couldn't staunch the disappointment that rose up inside me. Instead, I turned around to face him and offered him a small, hurried smile of gratitude, as a creeping blush heated my cheeks. He didn't make any motion to stand up from where he'd been kneeling over me. Instead, he just leaned back on his haunches and stared at me. He was wearing a kilt, but a different one to what he'd worn earlier, or maybe I just hadn't been paying attention. In the low light of the fire, I could make out the deep blue and green shades of his tartan. He crossed his arms over his bare chest and I wondered how he maintained his incredible physique. His muscles were the type that men would kill for, dedicating hours upon hours at the gym. One thing I knew for sure, though, was that Tallis Black definitely didn't go to the gym.

"If you aren't a demon, then what are you?" I repeated, trying to wipe the awe from my expression. I was just so obvious sometimes.

Well, it's not like you've had much experience with the opposite sex, I reprimanded myself. *Give yourself a break!*

"Ah Celt," Tallis answered in a steely tone.

"A Celt?" I reiterated, baffled by his response. I even felt my eyebrows drawing into the middle of my face. "As in a Druid?"

"Aye," he said, as if it was nothing to raise one's eyebrows at. He narrowed his gaze as he studied me and a slight smile played with the corners of his lips. Perhaps his smile was because he found it amusing when my mouth dropped open and my forehead furrowed into a unibrow.

"You mean you're a direct descendent of the Celts?" I corrected him, more than aware that the Celts were long extinct. "As in—your ancestors were Celts?"

He shook his head. "Nae. Ah, mahself, am ah Celt."

"But the Celts don't exist anymore?" I argued, shaking my head as I tried to understand what in the hell he was getting at. Despite speaking the same language, his ship had passed mine a while back where this conversation was concerned. Yep, his crazy Scottish brogue was definitely a hindrance.

"Aye, for the most part 'tis true that the Celts nae longer exist. An' 'tis ah damn shame," he continued. "Ah am the last of mah line."

I closed my eyes and brought my hand to my forehead as I tried to decipher if his words could possibly mean anything else. I opened my eyes when I realized exactly what he was trying to tell me. "If I remember correctly, the Celts existed around the time of the Romans," I started, shaking my head with disbelief. "And that was, what? Two thousand years ago?"

"Aye, yer memory serves ye well, lass."

My mouth was still agape. "So you're saying you are two thousand years old?"

Cocking his head to the side, he appeared to ponder the question before facing me again. There was no sign of jocularity in his features; nope, none at all. He was back to that stoic, poker face that I was beginning to know so well. "Thereabouts, aye."

I shook my head. "If you aren't a demon and you aren't an angel, how is it possible that you could be two thousand years old? I guess next you'll tell me you're a god?"

He shook his head and that smile of amusement returned to his lips. "Ah am nae god, Besom."

"Then what are you?" I demanded, irritated that he seemed to be talking in riddles.

"The Romans called us *Galli*."

"Galli?"

He nodded again, his eyes suddenly appearing harder than they were a moment ago. The smirk on his lips vanished just as quickly as it had materialized. His expression was now harsh, as if he'd just recalled an unhappy memory. Then I remembered that the Celts and the Romans had pretty much been at war with one another throughout history. So if Tallis really were an ancient Celt, he must have despised the Romans and, apparently, still did.

"Aye, *Galli* ... Barbarian," he answered in a low, heated voice. "Ah prefer the term warrior."

Suddenly the scar bisecting the left side of his face made sense. A warrior ... It fit. Tallis Black was the epitome of a warrior—not only visibly, but also in his speech and his disposition. He was intimidating by any and all accounts. And yet, there were moments, such as this one, where I sensed a softer side to him. It was a side I'd only seen a few times. He definitely appeared to be more comfortable playing the role of the daunting, controlling brute.

Looking back at his scar, I traced it with my eyes. It started at his outer eyebrow, now reduced to just a faint, pink line. It grazed his eye, moving down his angular cheek and widening to maybe an inch in width at the base of his cheek. Then it narrowed again before disappearing into his lower jaw. The scar was about a half an inch from his full lips making me instantly thankful that it didn't traverse the perfect arc of his cupid's bow. Without realizing it, I brought my index finger up to his face, to touch the tissue of his scar.

He nearly doubled over on himself to escape my reach. When he seemed a safe distance away, he speared me with eyes that were suddenly ignited with anger. "What the bloody hell do ye think yer doin'?"

I shook my head, flushing with indignation as well as mortification, demanding the same question of myself. What in the hell *was* I doing? It was as if I'd fallen into some sort of trance while looking at him. I couldn't remember a moment, (well, in recent history anyway,) when I'd been more embarrassed. "I, I'm sorry," I said, dropping my eyes to the dirt floor beneath me.

"Ah dinnae like ta be touched," he explained. The fire in his eyes no longer burned and his tone of voice became slightly softer. Perhaps it was his way of apologizing.

I just nodded, still angry with myself that I'd tried to touch him. It was a totally weird thing to do, especially since Tallis and I weren't exactly friends. Shoot! We weren't even acquaintances. With the weight of silence closing in on me, I glanced up at him again. I suddenly wanted to break the quiet between us, so I asked the only question that still baffled me. "How did you get that scar?"

"Ask me nae questions, Ah'll tell ye nae lies."

So, back to being evasive. I couldn't understand this man at all. Sometimes, he was almost forthcoming with information about himself, and other times, seemed to want nothing to do with me. Well, call me nosy, but I wasn't about to let him get away with it. "Why were you nice to me just now?" I demanded, shaking my head for emphasis.

Tallis didn't respond but offered me a bemused grin as if to say my question was a silly one. His response made me feel like I had to explain myself. "I just don't know what to make of you. Sometimes you're a horrible bully, whom I can't stand; and other times, you actually seem ... nice."

Tallis eyed me from where he leaned against the wall of the cabin, his arms crossed over his chest. His short, black hair nearly reached the ceiling. In the low light of the fire glow, I could just see myriad tiny scars, like tattoos, over his chest and upper arms. There were hundreds of them, like tiny, pink ants marching this way and that. Why I hadn't noticed them before? No clue.

"Ye are the daftest lass Ah have ever met," he said, shaking his head as if he didn't get me. "Ye just say whatever comes ta yer mind."

I frowned at him, cocking a brow to show I didn't appreciate being called "daft." Then I put on as haughty an expression as I could muster and answered: "As Confucius says, 'Speak the truth.'"

A slight smile curved Tallis's lips and I was left with the sudden observation that when he was borderline happy, he was incredibly handsome. The smile managed to imbue him with an innocence he otherwise lacked. It gave him a certain boyishness. After thinking about it, I realized when Tallis wasn't glowering, frowning, yelling or lecturing me, he was easily one of the handsomest men I'd ever seen.

"Och aye, an' it was yer sixteenth president who said, 'Better ta remain silent an' be thought ah fool than ta speak out, an' remove all doubt.'" He chuckled and appeared pleased with himself.

For myself, I hadn't realized Lincoln was the author of the quote but I filed it away in my memory all the same. It *was* a good one.

"Ye saw Alba, mah homeland," Tallis suddenly said, like he was responding to a question I'd just asked.

"Excuse me? I thought we were talking about fools and presidents?"

"Alba ... Scootland."

I furrowed my brows, still lost. "Yes, I get it—Alba means Scotland. And yes, I have seen it. I live in Edinburgh now, so it naturally follows that I have seen Scotland." I couldn't keep the irritation from seeping into my tone. Truth be told, he had me at my wit's end.

Tallis shook his head, a smile still playing on his lips. "Nae. Ye asked me why Ah was suddenly bein' nice ta ye. Mah answer was that ye saw mah homeland of Scotland when ye touched yer sword."

"I saw a castle," I said simply.

"Aye," Tallis nodded. "It is known as *Fearghus Castle*, in Gaelic."

"Oh." Although we were finally on the same page, I was only precariously hanging onto a letter or two.

"Fearghus castle has been in mah family for generations."

I wasn't sure if I should congratulate him or what. "So what did it mean when I saw Fergus Castle after I touched the sword?"

He shook his head again. "Ye need nae concern yerself, lass, ye need nae concern yerself."

I threw my hands up in the air and glared at him. "Forget I ever asked anything! You are so frustrating sometimes! Why don't you just stay the jerk bladesmith that I've come to know so well, because then at least, I'll know what to expect!"

He shook his head as if my outburst were completely unwarranted. Then he brought his beautiful blue eyes to mine, but they seemed heavier somehow, as if a weight had descended on the otherwise lovely navy. "It takes ah long spoon to sup with the devil."

All I could do was shake my head. "I give up." Then I stood and went over to Bill's corner of the small room. He was still snoring blissfully, completely unaware of the frustration consuming me. He twitched a few times before a serene smile plastered itself across his pasty face. I sat down next to him, unhappy to discover there wasn't another fur on the floor. When I looked back at Tallis, his eyes were narrowed on mine.

"Keep yer distance when dealin' with the devil," he said in a soft, but arctic tone. There was no expression on his face so it took me a second or two to understand he was translating his last bizarre statement. Before I could tell him to put a sock in it, he turned on his heel and approached the door. When he opened it, a wintry breeze invaded the house and I heard the sounds of the Grevels' paws hurrying over to him. Saying nothing, our eyes met before he shut the door.

***

I awoke in tears with a sob trapped in my throat. Sitting up immediately, I found night was still upon me. The room was dark except for the fire's embers dying in the fireplace. They created a muted, yellow glow and sent strange shadows all around the room.

Orienting myself, I discovered I was lying in the middle of Tallis's bed. I shook my head, wondering how I'd ended up here when I remembered going to sleep on the ground, beside Bill. Speaking of whom, Bill remained in the same position I'd left him, still snoring away, his thick body twitching spasmodically. Tallis was nowhere to be seen.

I couldn't stop wondering why Tallis had put me in his bed. It was the second time he'd done it and I was as shocked this time as I had been the first.

I wonder if that's all he did to you? my inner voice interjected from inside my head. I looked down at myself, noticing I was still dressed in the clothes I'd gone to sleep in. It didn't look as though I was in any way disheveled. Additionally, I was all buttoned up. And, really, if Tallis wanted to take advantage of me, wouldn't I have woken up?

Not necessarily, that voice barked back at me. *You heard him, he's a two-thousand-year-old Druid so he must possess some type of magic. For all you know, he could have been sexually molesting you all along.*

Somehow, I couldn't believe that. Not after Tallis appeared to want absolutely nothing to do with me from a physical standpoint. Shaking my head, I banished the thoughts right out of my brain. Instead, I exhaled a deep, pent-up breath and felt a tear slide from my left eye. I caught it with the back of my hand as I tried to ignore the dreams that had plagued me all night.

They were dreams of my mother, dreams of her realizing her only child was dead. There was a huge hole within me, a hole that had been growing since the death of the old me. It seemed to grow larger every time I thought about my mother and the sheer grief she'd been enduring all this time. All I wanted to do was call her and tell her that I wasn't dead, that I was all right, but I knew I couldn't make that phone call. Yes, I was well aware that Jason Streethorn had also insisted as much, but it wasn't Jason's dictum that concerned me. It was because I couldn't show up on my mother's doorstep and announce I was her daughter. Not when I looked nothing like the old Lily Harper. Besides, even if she bought the whole reincarnation thing, how would she take the news that I was a Soul Retriever, now living in the equivalent of hell? She wouldn't be able to handle it.

Sadly, I had to continue allowing my mother to believe I was dead, and it was that thought which ate at me. I clenched my eyes shut tightly and gritted my teeth, trying to ignore all thoughts of Josephine Harper. They would do me no good. Since I couldn't do anything to improve the situation, there was no point in hurting myself even more by dwelling on it.

"Either you run the day or the day runs you," I whispered. The words belonged to the self-help guru Jim Rohn, and they made me feel a little bit better.

I had to focus on my own survival, and whatever it took to ensure my first mission to the Underground was successful. As much as I loved my mother, and would always love her, and despite missing her with my entire being, I had to close that chapter of my life. I had to move on or risk the chance of failing.

Failing wasn't an option.

Lying back down, I stared at the log ceiling of Tallis's home. I tried to close my eyes and go back to sleep, but my mind was racing, my heartbeat just a few paces behind. I sighed and sat up again, stretching my hands over my head. Then I stood up and approached the nearest window. I pulled the dark muslin curtain to the side and noticed the moon still lighting the sky, although some nimbus storm clouds obscured its milky glow. The branches of the trees seemed more skeletal and the overall vibe outside the window was menacing. If the woods didn't look haunted before, they definitely did now.

As I continued to watch the branches of the trees scraping against one another in the ruthless wind, I caught something moving just beyond the tree line. I brought my face closer to the window pane and saw the glint of steel reflecting in the dull moonlight.

Tallis.

I didn't know why, but I immediately started for the door, throwing it open as I shivered in the cold wind. I knew it was only my imagination, but the sudden gust of wind seemed like it was trying to keep me inside the sanctuary of Tallis's home, to keep me from taking a step outside into the haunted woods.

Treading onto the dark earth, I took a few more steps toward the trees, still watching the blade's silver flashing in the moonlight. I continued forward until I was shrouded by the darkness of a tree. I leaned against it and watched Tallis slice the air with an incredibly long blade. It had to have been five or six feet long, and was balanced by two handles of solid steel, with the grip of the sword bound in black leather.

As always, Tallis wore only a kilt. This time, however, his sandals were missing. As he turned his back to me, I could see red blood staining the tattooed image of the tree on his back. My stomach dropped as I realized what the crimson stain meant—he'd whipped himself again. Images of Tallis brandishing the cat o' nine tails in the snow flashed through my mind and I swallowed down a sour taste.

Tallis whirled around, wielding the sword high above his head, and the lacerations and blood on his back simply disappeared. Just as before, Tallis's body managed to heal itself. I watched, transfixed, as Tallis sliced the air with his sword repeatedly, above his head, in front of him, and to his right and left. He moved with incredible fluidity, as though gliding along the earth, his feet never touching it. He kept his feet shoulder-width the entire time. When he moved, he appeared to slide over the dirt. His posture rigidly straight, he kept his chest and torso forward to aid his equilibrium. With every thrust and parry, Tallis's elbows were bent and close to his sides.

Watching his grace and skill with the sword, I realized his was an art form equal to any ballet. The effortless way in which he wielded the blade was stunning and, more so, awe inspiring.

He suddenly stiffened and dropped his sword into the earth while wheeling around on the ball of his foot, his eyes focused directly on mine. With my breath in my throat, I thought of hiding behind the tree, but it was too late. He'd already seen me.

"Ah dinnae appreciate ye skulkin' behind the trees an' watchin' me."

"Oh, I, uh," I stammered, feeling embarrassment hot on my cheeks. "I, uh, I'm sorry. I just couldn't sleep and, uh, saw you out here and I, uh, didn't want to interrupt you so …"

"Aye, Ah get it," he said, silencing me with a wave of his hand. "Perhaps yer inability ta sleep is fortuitous."

"How so?" I asked, approaching him from behind the tree.

"Ye need trainin' on how ta wield yer sword." He inclined his head toward the base of the tree nearest him, where I saw my sword leaning against it.

"Why is my sword out here?" I cautiously approached the beautiful sword he'd forged and reached for it, half wondering if the visuals of exotic castles would blind me again. When I wrapped by fingers around it, however, I didn't see or feel anything.

"Ah was teachin' it."

"What?" I asked rather indignantly. When I got within a few feet of him, he took my sword from me, and held it before him with admiration.

"Aye, Ah was teachin' it ta recognize mah hold, an' the feel of mah fingers." He stretched his fingers out before tightening them around the grip of the sword again. "Ah was teachin' it ta recognize me."

I swallowed hard, feeling slightly uncomfortable with the way he touched the sword, running his fingers down the blade as if it were the skin of a woman's leg. "You almost sound like you think the sword is alive."

"Och aye," he snapped, turning his attention from the shiny steel and narrowing his eyes on me. "Everything from the haunted woods is alive, lass."

I had no clue what to make of that so I remained silent. Tallis apparently took my silence as a tacit sign that I was ready to learn how to wield my sword, and handed the sword to me. After crossing his arms over his bare chest, he stood directly in front of me, wearing his poker face.

"What?" I demanded with annoyance. I guessed I was grumpy because I never felt exactly comfortable around this man. It seemed like I was always walking on eggshells.

"Which is yer dominant hand?"

I figured by that he meant which hand did I use most often. "This one," I answered, waving my right one at him. He arched a brow, apparently finding my little wave slightly amusing. In the blink of an eye, though, any hint of humor was bleached right out of his expression.

"Grip yer sword with yer dominant hand," he barked. "Take control of it. Show the sword that ye are the master, not it."

Wrapping my fingers around the sword's grip, I held it out before me, and tried to imagine how a master would hold a sword. Unfortunately, I'd never met any sword masters, so I didn't have a very good feeling about the success of this task.

"Nae, nae nae, woman!" he guffawed as he ripped the sword from me. "Show yer dominance, damn ye!" His reprimanding roar made me wince in response, and he threw the sword into the dirt while closing the distance between us. I felt my heart climbing up my throat and averted my eyes from the blade of my sword, which was now sticking out of the ground. I felt Tallis's fingertips on the bottom of my jaw as he lifted my chin, and forced me to look at him. "Ye wilna survive the Oonderground unless ye assert yerself. Ye cannae show ah semblance of weakness. An' given yer innocence, ye will have ta prove yerself all the more."

"Okay, I understand," I said between gritted teeth.

"Again," he ordered, motioning to my sword, which was still planted in the ground. "Take yer sword."

With every ounce of willpower and courage, I reached for the sword and pulled as hard as I could. I nearly toppled over when the earth released it. With my eyes narrowed on Tallis, I gripped the sword tightly and held it out directly in front of me, aiming the tip right between Tallis's eyes. I didn't even know what I was doing until after I did it. But now, after seeing the utter surprise in Tallis's midnight blue gaze, I was pleased with myself.

With his eyes riveted on mine, he simply rested his fingers on the tip of my blade before pushing it down. He stared at me for another few seconds, both of us engaged in a war of wills, me striving to prove that I was much stronger than he gave me credit for, while he had to decide whether or not I was telling the truth.

"Grip yer sword with yer dominant hand," he repeated again, this time in a raspy-throated voice that set butterflies fluttering in the pit of my stomach and kindled a burning that radiated from the depth of my core. His husky, low voice exuded something decidedly sexual. The more I thought about it, the more I began to see Tallis Black as the epitome of everything sexually attractive in a man. From his obvious masculinity and incredible strength, to his eyes, which could tear my clothes off with just a glance, Tallis Black equaled unparalleled lust. What made it so bizarre though, was that he was also celibate, well, as far as I could tell anyway.

"Grip below the guard an' take hold of the pommel."

"What's the pommel?" I asked with no ounce of apology. Instead, I held his gaze and narrowed my eyes, while holding my chin higher.

"The bottom of the sword," he whispered.

I did as he instructed before facing him with tight, dry lips. "Now what?"

"Usin' yer left hand, grip the sword tightly with yer ring, middle an' yer wee finger."

I figured he meant my pinky. As he examined my grip, he nodded before approaching me again. This time, he yanked on the bottom of my shirt before lifting it. "What the hell do you think you're doing?!" I demanded, moving away from him.

He grabbed my shoulder and pulled me toward him again. "As Ah am yer tutor, ye will pay me the decency of trustin' me." Glaring at me until I nodded, he reached for my shirt again and lifted it up to expose my midriff. He swiped his index finger across my waist and settled it right on top of my belly button. I didn't know if the goose bumps were from the chill in the air or his touch.

"Hold yer sword so that the pommel is just above yer belly button," he said while placing his index finger on my belly button, apparently in case I forgot where it was. With his stern gaze on me again, he continued. "Never rest the sword on yer stomach an' always point the tip between yer sternum an' throat." He took a breath. "When strikin', stab at the sky, bringin' yer left hand up past yer eye," he said as he backed up a few paces. Hefting his enormous sword, he enacted what he'd just told me. I was grateful he used body language to show me what he meant, considering half the time I didn't understand a word he was saying. "Then come down, usin' yer right hand ta guide the blade an' usin' yer left hand ta set the force into the blade." He brought his sword down, slicing the air. Then he set it on the ground again and faced me. "The right hand should be yer axis point."

I didn't budge in my stance and my fingers were still wrapped around the sword's grip with the blade awfully close to my throat.

"Now ye try, Besom," he said, crossing his arms over his chest, ready to judge my every move.

I nodded and tried to remember his instructions. Lifting the sword up past my eye, I came back down, and hoped my right hand did most of the work. Thinking I was rather adept with my move, I eyed Tallis with a large grin. "How was that?"

He shook his head. "Ah've seen wee bairns do better." The smile dropped right off my face but I wasn't given any option to respond. "Never mind that now though. Now we focus on the footwork. Put yer left foot behind yer right foot an' stand on the ball of yer left foot." I tried the fancy footwork and nearly toppled over. "Keep yer balance, lass!" Hitler ordered.

"I'm trying to!" I snapped back at him.

"When ye strike, ye push with yer left foot, slidin' yer right foot on the ground an' raise yer sword like this." Pushing back with his left foot, he slid his right foot along the ground while raising his sword. With no other options, I tried to follow suit, but the incredible weight of the sword, combined with my own wobbly balance didn't manage to impress Stalin.

He quickly barked the next set of orders, acting them out in perfect harmony. "Now bring yer left foot back inta position an' strike!" He stressed the last word and then glared at me when I made no motion to imitate him. "Dinnae stand there like ah stookie!" he railed. I hastily moved my left foot back and lurched out with my sword, managing to demonstrate the perfect face plant. Luckily, the sword fell first and I only ended up with a face full of dirt instead of steel blade.

Tallis offered his hand and I accepted it. Pulling me onto my feet, he wore the expression of disappointment. After fully regaining my balance, he simply shook his head. "Thank goodness for yer bonnie face, lass."

I figured he meant without it, I wouldn't be worth my weight in feathers. I frowned and dusted myself off before standing up to my full five foot eight inches. "Let me remind you, Mussolini, that this was my first time handling a sword!"

Tallis continued to glare at me, but seconds later, he burst into raucous laughter. He shook his head, hoisting his sword over his shoulder then did the same with mine. He turned and started for his ramshackle home as the nascent sun began to ascend.

"Mussolini!" he repeated with another loud chuckle and another shake of his head.

> "I entered on the deep and savage way."
> — Dante's *Inferno*

NINE

I had no idea where Tallis disappeared for the rest of the day. After seeing him early in the morning, when we returned from our unsuccessful sword lesson, he more or less vanished. I imagined the Grevels had gone with him as they were also nowhere to be found. Tallis had taken both my sword and his, but I spotted four discarded swords behind the cabin so I stayed busy by practicing his instructions on how to grip a sword while wielding it. Although I preferred having privacy while I practiced, Bill insisted on watching me. And, yes, he more than adequately filled the role of the peanut gallery, as expected.

The sun dropped from the sky and night stretched her cloak of darkness, I finished my practicing for the day and headed inside with Bill at my heels. Tallis had left his cabin unlocked so we made ourselves comfortable. After Bill made a roaring fire, I heated up a potful of water. When it was hot enough, I took the pot off the fire and demanded Bill go outside so I could give myself a full body wipe down. I couldn't remember the last time I'd bathed, but I wasn't about to go traipsing through the haunted woods in search of a stream or lake to wash in. Nope, it was better to be dirty than dead.

"Dude, I'm tired of being a soap dodger," Bill said after I opened the door and allowed him back inside again. With a frown, he reached for the pot of hot water I'd heated up for him. Without saying anything, I offered him an understanding smile, handing him a two-foot wad of muslin I'd found wedged in the corner of the house. I'd used the other half to wash and dry myself. Bill reluctantly accepted the piece of material with a frown, but opened the front door of the cabin, and closed it behind him.

A few minutes later, the door opened again and I was about to reprimand Bill for not washing himself thoroughly enough when I recognized Tallis. Glancing at me as I sat on the floor in front of the fire, he merely nodded quickly in greeting. I knew better than to ask him where he'd been all day. Instead, I watched him deposit a large sack he was carrying onto the ground.

"Where is the angel?" he asked.

I inclined my head to the door. "He's in the back, washing up."

Tallis nodded. "We leave tonight."

My eyes widened involuntarily. "We leave for where tonight?"

"To the river," he answered, walking to the far corner of the small room, where he shifted the table to the side, along with the makeshift chair. He leaned down and opened the top of a roughly hewn pine box that resided just below the table. He fished inside it until he procured a small sack. Shaking the sack, the sound of coins jingled through the velvety material. Then he looked over his shoulder at me. "Dinnae think ta steal from me."

"Really?" I asked angrily, shaking my head as I wondered if it was even possible for Tallis Black to be any more disagreeable. "As if I would steal from you!"

Without another word, he turned back to sorting through the box as I stood up and started for the door. I was already fed up with him even though we'd only been in one another's company for a matter of minutes.

"Lass, Ah didnae mean ta offend ye."

I paused, but kept my hand on the doorknob. "Well, whether you meant to or not, you're really getting good at it."

"Ah donnae believe ye would steal from me."

I figured that was as close to an apology as I would get. And the truth was that I was more than curious about the river we were bound for. It was better to focus on Tallis's plan moving forward. Yep, getting offended wouldn't help anybody. "What river are you talking about?"

I couldn't help my eyes as they fell from his head to... his forearms. As soon as I focused on them, I felt my jaw drop open accordingly. He had two serious gashes on both of his arms. The wounds started at his wrists and extended all the way to his elbows. It looked like he'd slit his entire forearms open. There wasn't any blood, but the flesh was filleted, the gashes maybe a quarter of an inch wide. They were an angry red, and beyond swollen. After witnessing his rapid healing abilities, I didn't know why these wounds hadn't already mended themselves.

He noticed me noticing him and frowned at me. I lifted my eyes from his shredded forearms to his face, and watched him narrow his gaze. His expression said in no uncertain terms that he didn't appreciate prying guests. So I didn't pry. If he wanted to flog and cut himself, then so be it. That was his business.

"The river Styx," he offered, in response to my question.

"What?" I asked in shock. "You mean, we're going to the Underground City... now?"

He nodded as he reached inside the pine box and produced three small daggers. Each one was faded with weathered wooden handles and uneven steel blades that looked hand-chiseled. He put them on the floor beside the sack of what I assumed were coins. "We have waited long enough an' now we will make our move."

"But, but I'm not ready!" I almost screamed as my heart plummeted to my feet. If we went to the Underground now, I was as good as dead. There was no way I could defend myself. "You saw how poorly I used my sword! There's no way I'm ready yet!"

"Ah received ah sign that said we must leave now," Tallis said, ignoring my outburst.

"Maybe you didn't hear me," I started stiffly. "If I go to the Underground City now, I will die!"

But Tallis didn't seem overly concerned or concerned at all. Instead, he continued to search through the pine box for God only knew what. "Ah have taken care of it."

"Taken care of what?" I railed back at him, my heart hammering so hard, I wondered if I was having a heart attack.

"Everything," he answered succinctly, placing a handful of what appeared to be fishing hooks beside the daggers.

I was so angry and scared, my hands were shaking. "Look, I know you don't give a damn about me," I started, but as soon as the words left my mouth, the anger fueling them dissolved. Instead, I became consumed by an inordinate sense of despondency and terror.

My words finally sparked some interest in him because he stopped rifling through the box and turned to face me, flattering me with his full attention. "I know you don't care if I live or die," I continued. "I know I mean nothing to you, and am more of a hindrance than anything else." My voice wavered as tears flooded my eyes. "But you also don't understand what I've been through and how hard I want to succeed." I closed my eyes and fisted my hands, digging my nails into my palms to stop myself from crying in front of him. "I have to succeed." After regaining my composure, I opened my eyes and took a deep breath. "I don't want to go to Shade." The mere thought of one hundred years in limbo had my whole stomach turning on itself. "If there is any humanity left in you at all, please don't make me do this, not yet … not until I'm fully prepared."

He stared at me for a few seconds with those hollow eyes as I continued resisting the urge to cry. Whatever happened, I didn't want to show any more weakness than I already had.

There was no expression on his face at all. "As Ah said, Ah have taken care of it."

I wasn't prepared for what I did next. My body must have been on autopilot because I didn't even think about my actions before executing them. I launched myself at him and grabbed his upper arm. He shot to his feet, but I didn't release him. Instead, I stared up into his face as tears began bleeding down my cheeks. They were not tears of sadness, however, they were tears of outrage. "You cold bastard!" I screamed at him. "I'm not ready to go! I won't go!"

"Ye will be safe," he growled, between clenched teeth.

"Safe?!" I yelled at him, shaking my head at the absurdity of it. "How can I be safe if I can't protect myself?!"

His eyes were angrier than I'd ever seen them. Shoving me away from him, he pushed me so hard, I nearly fell over. I had to support myself on the wall. Before I could respond, he held his forearms out to me, yelling, "Ah ensured yer safety with mah own blood!"

I was speechless for a few seconds as my eyes returned to the gashes down his forearms. Completely bewildered, I stared into the void of his eyes. "I don't understand," I admitted softly, hot tears still rolling down my cheeks.

He dropped his arms and returned to the pine box, kneeling down again, and refusing to look at me. "Ah bathed yer sword in mah blood."

"Why?" I whispered. I suddenly had the urge to reach out to him and apologize, but I knew better. He was like a feral animal.

"'Twas the only way ta ensure yer safety."

"How would that," I started.

"Druid magic," he interrupted. Before I could further interrogate him, the door opened to reveal Bill in the entryway. His mouth was open as if he wanted to say something, but when his eyes settled on me, his eyebrows knitted in the middle and an angry grimace captured his entire face.

"Why is she cryin', you son of a bitch?" he yelled at Tallis. Tallis immediately stood up and glared at the much smaller man. "What did you do to her, dammit?" demanded the angel.

"Naethin'."

"Nothing, Bill," I said, holding my hands up in submission. "It's okay. He didn't do anything to me."

"Then why are you crying?" Bill asked, his anger still evident as he continued spearing Tallis with his glare.

"It's a long story," I answered as another round of tears fell from my eyes. I must have been experiencing an emotional breakdown after enduring so much in the last ... I didn't even know how long. When Bill threw his arms around me, I realized how much I needed the consolation, and dropped my head on his shoulder.

"Listen to me good, Black," Bill started, anger tainting each word. "You ever make her cry again an' you'll have me ta deal with! Capiche?"

"Aye," Tallis said in a monotone.

It wasn't much of a threat, especially since Tallis could grind Bill into mincemeat in two seconds flat, but I appreciated his intentions all the same. "Thank you," I whispered as he nodded and held me tighter, even leaving a kiss on the top of my head.

"No one messes with my nerdlet."

***

We trudged through the snow in complete silence. Tallis led the way, with Bill and me two paces behind him. As I'd expected, the forest floor swallowed our tracks as soon as we lifted our feet.

I found my attention settling on Tallis's broad back as I watched him carve the way through the forest. He wove this way and that, back and forth through the endless trees. The reflection of moonlight on his black hair made it look so glossy, it almost seemed liquid. For once, he wore more than just a kilt—a black T-shirt and boots. The boots looked like he'd turned an animal pelt inside out and stitched it into the shape of two socks.

The large sack he'd brought with him into the cabin was now securely fastened to his back, looking like the ancient relative of the backpack, and it was full to the brim. Above that, he'd fastened a silver, oval shield that was really quite beautiful. The moonlight made the raised circles and diamond patterns stand out until they almost looked like jewels. Both my sword and his were in their scabbards, strapped across his chest. The gashes in his forearms were still visible although the cuts seemed a little less crimson than before, and his flesh didn't look quite as swollen. I still didn't know why he'd made himself bleed, or what his blood on my sword meant. How could bathing my sword in his blood protect me in the Underground? I chalked it up as one of those mysteries which might never be solved. I only hoped that whatever lengths he'd gone to wouldn't be for naught.

As our footsteps brought us ever closer to the Underground City, my nerves were more than present and accounted for. My heart beat frantically and a solid lump of angst was rapidly forming in the pit of my stomach. I assumed Bill felt the same thing because he was strangely quiet for once. The only sounds were our footfalls crunching on the snow.

"Wait!" I blurted, my heart lurching into my throat as I came to an abrupt halt. Bill faced me curiously, but Tallis never broke pace. I looked at Bill, my eyes wide. "I forgot the book!" I admitted, aghast. "I forgot Dante's *Inferno* in the car!"

Shaking his head, Bill began to smile while patting his back pocket. "Figured we might need it."

"Thank God for you!" I chirped happily, relief pouring through me, even to the farthest of my extremities.

"Amen ta that, sistah!" he replied with a large grin.

Seeing Tallis much farther in front of us, I inhaled deeply and jogged to catch up to him, Bill right beside me. I pulled the fur Tallis had given me tighter around my shoulders to ward off the frosty evening air. Despite my efforts, I was still freezing. Clad in only the black leather pants and long-sleeved, red T-shirt Jason Streethorn packed for me, I would have frozen, were it not for the fur. As for Bill, because he was an angel, he couldn't feel the cold. Lucky him.

"Be cannie," Tallis announced when we reached what looked like a cliff.

I figured that meant to be careful. I watched him remove the swords, and place them on the ground. Leaning forward, he gripped the side of the cliff and jumped down to what must've been a ledge of some sort below him. He landed in a crouched position, with both his hands on the ground. Then he glanced up at me, motioning for the swords, which I handed to him. He leaned them along the ledge before scaling down the face of the rock wall again.

"I'll bring up the rear," Bill said, winking at my butt. He dropped behind me as I unwrapped the fur shawl from my shoulders and handed it to him. Then I looked over the edge of the cliff. Tallis was already on another ledge of rock, waiting for me to reach the first ledge so I could hand him both swords again. Only a few shelves of flattened rock led down the cliff to a sandy beach alongside a river. It was mostly just a sheer precipice with a long drop. If I had to guess, I'd say it was maybe five stories tall. Figuring there was no time like the present, I got down on my stomach, and using the toes on my boots, I searched for a toehold on the rock face. I felt Bill's hands on mine and found him smiling down at me.

"I got ya, honey nips! Just find a place to put your toes and descend slowly. The first ledge is maybe another ten feet down."

I nodded as my toe found a footing, and I carefully lowered myself. Once my entire body was flush to the rock face, I felt for the next toehold. Pulling my hands from Bill's, I took my time as I scaled the cliff. Glancing down, the ledge was now maybe only eight feet down. Finding two more toeholds, I descended still further. After several more repetitions, I reached the ledge. When I felt the ground, unimaginable relief washed over me. Reaching for both swords, I had to kneel over the edge just to hand them to Tallis since he was so much further below me.

"Nicely done, Pippi Long Legs," Bill said as he materialized directly beside me. I frowned at him, irritated that he just Mary Poppins'd right down with little or no effort while I'd had to struggle for the last ten minutes, at least. There were definite drawbacks to being merely human.

"I didn't know you could do that," I grumbled.

Bill shrugged. "Neither did I. Usually only works in the Kingdom. Go figure."

"Nae time for dilly-dallyin'," Tallis yelled at us. Placing the swords on the ledge, he started down the cliff face again.

The moonlight was suddenly eclipsed by a large grey cloud, leaving us in near pitch darkness. "I can't see anything!" I yelled to Tallis.

"Aye, just bide 'til the cloud passes."

"I'll wait with ya," Bill said with an encouraging smile.

"Thanks," I muttered. "Can't angels fly while holding someone else?"

"Sorry, Skipper, but no can do. I ride solo, hot cheeks."

"It figures," I murmured. The cloud eventually passed and allowed the iridescent moon rays to light our way again. I glanced down the cliff side to find Tallis already on the beach, waiting for me. I had two more rock ledges to conquer. The next one seemed relatively close, but the last one was a fair distance away. Heaving a sigh, I dropped down onto my stomach before pushing my legs off the end of the ledge, to search, yet again, for another foothold.

After a few minutes, I felt flat ground, so I hopped down and took a deep breath just as Bill materialized next to me again. Gripping both swords, I dangled them over the edge, unsure how Tallis could reach them when he was still at least thirty feet away.

"Just drop 'em, lass," he called out. "Try ta throw them so the blade sticks in the sand!"

Feeling more concerned with my own safety than either of the swords, I didn't argue. I hastily flung my sword over the edge, flipping my wrist as I launched it in the hopes that it might help to make the blade sink into the sand. The sword responded by crashing onto the face of the mountain before bouncing into the rocks at the base of the cliff.

I heard Tallis expelling an exasperated breath. Then he addressed me. "Bloody hell, Besom! Dinnae go throwin' mah sword willy-nilly."

Irritated to even be in this position to begin with, I gripped his heavy sword and sort of just dropped it over the ledge. And what do you know? The blade sunk straight into the sand as Tallis looked on with a smile.

Two ledges down, and one really far one still to go. Getting down on my belly again, I threw my legs over the edge and tried to ignore the jagged rocks scraping against my stomach. I assumed my shirt had to be ripped to shreds, but I didn't care. Getting down from this cliff in one piece was the only issue on my mind.

I found another toehold and settled my foot into it as I clung to a rock that jutted out. After I made the mistake of glancing down, I felt fear radiating through me. It was probably a good twenty feet to the next ledge. And from there, at least another ten feet to the ground.

Joy is of the will which labors, which overcomes obstacles, which knows triumph. I repeated the famous quote by Yeats in my mind. Yep, Yeats was so right. If and when I made it off this cliff, joy couldn't even begin to describe the bliss I would feel. Maybe more relief than joy ...

"You're almost there, Lily," I encouraged myself.

"Just take it slow," Bill advised from where he stood on the ledge above me. I half-wondered if he, as my guardian angel, could save me if I happened to fall? I could only hope the answer was yes, although I didn't dare test my theory.

Locating another toehold, I continued down the cliff, although my fingers were beginning to ache from grasping the rocks so tightly. It probably also didn't help that the air was so cold, I could see each cloud of my breath.

Something shifted underneath my foot and I gasped. Scrambling to find another toehold, I thought I had one until the rocks crumbled away beneath my foot. Now panicked, I tapped for another crevice, grateful the foot currently supporting my weight was still snugly wedged into the rocks. Suddenly, the rock beneath my right hand began to loosen, and before I could find another grip, the rock pulled free from the mountain's face.

Then I felt nothing but weightlessness and cold air rushing past me.

Everything that happened next occurred within mere seconds. I faintly heard Tallis yelling something in Gaelic before a huge gust of wind blasted my face and I had to close my eyes. No sooner did I blink when I felt myself hitting something, or was I landing on something? Bracing myself for a painful collision, I was surprised to find there was no pain at all—no bone shattering agony like I expected. My eyes snapped open to see Tallis's face barely five inches from mine. He was panting. Shock overtook me, and after a second or so, I managed to catch my breath. Miraculously, Tallis had caught me.

"How," I started, but was unable to form the rest of the words. It felt like my lungs had collapsed because I found it near impossible to take a breath.

One of Tallis's arms supported my back and the other my legs, so that he was holding me bride style. Neither of us said another word, but just stared at each other while struggling to catch our breaths. I didn't know why he didn't put me down.

"What did it mean?" I asked at last. My lungs still ached as I tried to regulate my breathing. "What did you say?" I continued, referring to the Gaelic I'd heard him yell as soon as I fell. My voice sounded raspy.

Tallis still didn't set me on my feet. "Ah ordered ye to slow an' to fall away from the mountain," he answered in an equally breathy voice. "Had ye fallen strait down, the rocks would have scraped yer face to ah bloody mess an' yer ... breasts."

"Oh," I said, unable to tear my eyes from his. At the mention of the word "breasts," something blossomed deep inside me, a feeling of yearning, a stinging that I wasn't familiar with.

Tallis didn't say anything more as he continued to study me. Our eyes were locked, riveted by an invisible force. No matter how hard I tried to look away, I couldn't.

Suddenly, Tallis cleared his throat before quickly setting me down on my feet. It seemed as if he was uncomfortable with what had been and was transpiring between us. As to just what "it" was, I had no clue. I certainly had never experienced anything like it before. Except in a contest, I'd never stared so long at someone, and I'd never lost myself in someone else's eyes before, not like that. I suddenly felt cold and shivered.

Tallis took a few steps away from me and I saw fresh blood on his arms. At first, I thought it was my blood, that the rocks had scraped and cut me, until I remembered his forearms. "Your wounds," I said softly, reaching for his arms.

He jerked away immediately and his lips went tight. "Ah am fine."

I didn't respond. The weight of Tallis's fur fell onto my shoulders, and when I turned around, I found Bill smiling at me.

"Cirque Du Soleil hasn't got shit on you two!"

"Well, I guess that answers my question of whether or not you could protect me in the haunted wood," I grumbled.

Bill shrugged. "Hey, I tried. I guess my mad skills aren't so mad in this fucked up place that Conan calls home."

Speaking of the bladesmith, I turned to face him, and found his attention on the river ahead of us. The moonlight emphasized the water's darkness, which only appeared in patches beneath a fog so thick, it looked like a dense layer of whipped cream. I doubted Tallis found the fog so intriguing, so I continued to look at the river, while trying to understand what he was so focused on. Taking a few steps forward, I had to take a few more before I was shoulder to shoulder with the enormous man.

"Ah must summon him," Tallis said quietly.

"Summon who?" I asked just as the answer dawned on me. "Wait, is this the river Styx?"

"Aye."

"Then you have to summon Charon, the ferryman?"

"Aye."

"Well, get on it with it, Conan," Bill interjected from behind us. Stepping up beside me, he stood on my left side, with Tallis on my right.

Tallis frowned at Bill before bending down on one knee and closing his eyes. He said something in a foreign tongue, which I figured was Gaelic.

"What? The ferryman doesn't speak English?" Bill asked as he elbowed me in the ribs and laughed at his own joke.

Tallis didn't hear him, or maybe just ignored him because he continued to chant something with his eyes closed. When he opened his eyes, he reached beneath his kilt and produced a dagger. Before Bill or I could say another word, he brought his arm straight out in front of him and slit the top of his wrist. Rotating his hand, he allowed some of the drops to sink into the sand.

"Jesus, what the hell happened to Conan's arms?" Bill asked in shock, having just noticed the gashes. From my vantage point, they looked quite a bit more healed.

No one answered Bill's question and it was just as well because no sooner did the sand absorb Tallis's blood before something appeared in the distance, hovering over the river. At first it looked like a tree or something that fell into the river and was now making its way toward us. The harder I looked at it, though, the more I saw it was no tree, but Charon, the ferryman. He stood up in the center of a small wooden boat, his figure and head shrouded by a dark cloak and hood.

"Shit just got real," Bill whispered and then elbowed me in the ribs again. I was about to snap at him to quit it when he motioned to something just behind me. I turned around quickly and couldn't help but gasp. I glanced over my other shoulder, awed to find that we were completely surrounded by what appeared to be ghosts. They looked like whitish puffs of steam that trembled this way and that as the wind rode through them. There had to have been hundreds of them, maybe thousands. All were nearing the river although none of them ventured beyond the icy tide.

"They must be waiting for the ferryman to take them across," I said in a mere whisper, my gaze still fixed on the specters, none of which seemed to notice us. For that matter, they didn't even notice one another. From what I could see of their faces (which wasn't much considering the background of trees showed right through them), they stared straight ahead, not speaking. There was no emotion on their faces.

Tallis eyed both of us with tight lips before focusing his attention on me. "Ye will sit in the rear of the vessel."

"What about them?" I asked, glancing at the myriad souls who obviously wanted a place on the boat.

"Dinnae bother aboot them," he answered, shaking his head as if to reiterate the sentiment. "When ye enter the boat, dinnae speak, an' dinnae look the ferryman in the face."

I didn't even imagine I could have spoken if I'd wanted to. Instead, my heart had taken up residence in my throat. I couldn't remember being more frightened in all my life. Tallis turned back toward the river and I noticed the top of his wrist was now healed. As to why his forearms hadn't healed more quickly, I still had no clue.

I watched the boat approach us and then stop about four or five feet from the shore. The ferryman moved slowly, turning toward us as he nodded to Tallis. None of the spirits made any attempt to approach the boat.

As to looking the ferryman in the face, I didn't have to because he didn't have one. There was nothing but darkness under the hood, air. I glanced at Tallis, who simply nodded back at the ferryman before facing me.

"Lass, ye will enter the vessel first."

With a nod, I took his outstretched hand when he offered it. He led me into the water which was so cold, it felt like a thousand tiny mouths biting my ankles. Bill was behind me and I silently thanked my lucky stars that for once, he was obeying Tallis's command and not making a sound.

The boat was still a good two feet away. I inched forward, the water now up to my knees, and smarting just as much as when I'd first stepped into the river. When we finally reached the boat, Tallis tugged on my hand to tell me I wasn't supposed to get into it yet. Fishing inside the sporran he wore on the front of his kilt, he produced the small sack of coins he'd taken from the pine box earlier. He opened the satchel and dropped three gold coins, each the width of a small apple, into the palm of his other hand. The ferryman extended his cloaked arm, but there was nothing visible where his hand or arm should have been. Unfazed, Tallis simply dropped the coins into the open air of the ferryman's cloak. I expected the coins to drop straight into the arctic water, but they simply vanished upon making contact (or not, in this case) with the ferryman's invisible hand.

The ferryman withdrew his cloaked arm and nodded at Tallis again. Tallis looked at me and nodded in turn, apparently to let me know all was good now. With his eyes on mine, he propped his hands on either side of my waist and lifted me into the boat, only releasing his hold when the boat started to wobble. Gripping the side to keep it from tipping, he pointed to one of two wooden planks that were more or less benches in the back of the boat. The planks ran from starboard to port.

I ignored the first bench and took a seat in the middle of the second one, turning to watch Bill and Tallis. With a big smile, Bill hefted his fleshy arms into the air, showing he was ready for Tallis to lift him up onto the boat as he'd just done for me. Tallis muttered something unintelligible beneath his breath and Bill's grin broadened even wider. When Bill simply materialized into the boat, it rocked so violently, I worried it might capsize. Tallis again stabilized it as I scooted over and Bill plopped down next to me.

The ferryman dropped his oar into the water adjacent to Tallis. I figured it was his way of saying he wanted to get a move on. Tallis took off his shield and backpack, before removing both his sword and mine from their scabbards across his chest. He handed them both to me. Then, gripping the sides of the boat with both hands, in a move that would inspire Mary Lou Retton, he crouched down into the water, leapt up and over, and managed to land right into the boat. He took a seat on the wooden plank ahead of us, and reached for the swords which I'd put in my lap.

For some unknown reason, my attention immediately dropped to my feet. Maybe I was just nervous about locking eyes with Tallis again. Whatever the reason, I was momentarily distracted when I saw that neither my boots nor my pants were soaking wet as they should've been. I reached down and touched my lower pant leg, only to find it completely dry. Eyeing Bill's discolored, stained, and ripped pants, I saw that they, too, were dry. With visible surprise, I looked up at Tallis. His slight smile suggested that things were different here and about to get even more strange.

The ferryman started rowing and my heartbeat sped up again. I was well on my way to the Underground City, a place that housed only the vilest of souls. And that thought frightened me much more than the ferryman had.

"Through me the way is to the city dolent;
Through me the way is to eternal dole;
Through me the way among the people lost."
— Dante's *Inferno*

TEN

Sitting next to me, Bill began to struggle with something and when I glanced over at him, I realized he was wrestling with his back pocket, trying to extricate Dante's *Inferno*. He huffed and puffed before managing to free the tattered book (which wasn't quite so tattered before it was in Bill's possession), and gave me a dramatic sigh. Tallis looked over at us while firmly shaking his head as if to say we, er, Bill, was making too much noise. Bill immediately held up his hand and nodded to assure Tallis he had everything under control.

Bill opened the book and started leafing through the pages, clicking his tongue against the roof of his mouth as he scanned the words. For my part, I couldn't tear my eyes from the scenery around us. The farther we sailed down the river Styx, the darker the night sky became until only the starlight offered any illumination. Strangely enough, I could still see just as clearly as when the moonlight dominated the sky. Odder still, the scenery appeared to be changing. We were no longer surrounded by immense pine trees, verdant mountainsides and sandy beaches. Instead, it looked as if we were floating through some sort of bog or swamp. The trees gave way to the stick-like outline of leafless branches and trunks, long dead.

The only sound in the stillness of the night air was the ferryman's oar lapping through the water as it propelled us forward. I found my attention riveted on it every time it came up and out of the water. From what I could see, the droplets rolling off the oar were pitch black and thick. It seemed more like inky sludge than river water.

"Oh, hell no!" Bill suddenly yelled out. Both Tallis and I faced him, my eyes wide, while Tallis's narrowed in irritation. Bill, however, took no notice of either of us. Instead, he stopped reading the book in his hands, and looked at me with disbelief written all over his face, before turning his stricken expression on Tallis. "We're on the wrong fuckin' river, yo!" he railed out, shaking his head. "Unfreakingbelievable!"

The wrong river?

I looked at Tallis, my heart hammering as I wondered what Bill was talking about. Could there be more than one river to the Underground City? And if so, why would Tallis have led us to the wrong one? He said he'd traveled to the Underground many times! "Bill, what are you talking about?" I whispered. My eyes fell on the form of the ferryman, as I wondered what his reaction would be to Bill's outburst. Tallis had been pretty emphatic about telling us not to make any noise … Luckily for us, the ferryman paid Bill no attention at all. He just dipped his oar into the water, first over one shoulder, then the next.

Looking back at Bill, I found him gaping like a fish out of water, with an expression that said he'd been duped. "Right here!" he bellowed, pointing to the open book in his lap. "Fuckin' Dante says we're s'posed ta cross the Acheron, not the Styx!" Then he eyed the ferryman. "So I don't know who the hell this goon thinks he is, or where he gets off pretendin' ta be Sharon!" He took a deep breath before nodding furiously. "I call that getting swindled and pimped!" he sang out in a terrible rendition of Macklemore's "Thrift Shop."

"Nae," Tallis began to intervene, but Bill's diatribe wasn't over because he silenced Tallis with a wave of his pudgy hand. "Turn this shit around, yo!" he called out to the ferryman while frowning at Tallis. "Do ya think someone needs ta go back and read his *Inferno?* I don't know, Slick, but somebody sure got his rivers wrong." Taking another breath, he sang: "This is NOT fucking awesome."

"'Tis the same bloody river!" Tallis growled, his voice growing increasingly louder. "The Acheron flows into the Styx, ye bleedin' dunderheid!"

Bill was silent for a second or two as he bit his lower lip. "Oh," he finally said with a frown. "Well, run and tell that to Dante, yo!" He closed the book and flicked his fingers at the cover. "Flippin' useless thing."

Tallis looked more than frustrated, but I was more nervous about the ferryman's reaction. Strangely enough, the ferryman just continued to silently row the boat and I could only wonder if he could talk, since he didn't have any vocal cords, or a face, or even a body, well, one that I could see anyway. Could he even hear us?

"Sorry, yo," Bill said to the ferryman's back. "Honest mix-up, that's all. Didn't really mean ta call you a goon. I actually think you're pretty cool, ya know, diggin' the cloak thing."

"Bill, shush!" I whispered to him, elbowing him in the arm while shaking my head in utter annoyance.

"Okay, okay," he whispered back. "I just wanted to make sure everything was cool so the dude didn't drop me off in some ..." his voice trailed off as he glanced around, "... scary ass tree."

After Bill's outburst, everyone remained quiet for the remainder of the ride, which was maybe another fifteen minutes. The scenery didn't change much, the eerie, skeletal outline of dead trees still dominating the landscape. The darkness was just as murky and engulfing as before.

The ferryman steered the boat to a long, wooden bridge that led from the river to the shore. Tallis stood up and reached out to grasp the wooden railing. Taking my hand, he supported and stabilized me as I stood.

"Dinnae let the river touch ye," he said in a throaty voice, his eyes piercing.

I watched the waves slosh against the rocks that lined up like a natural staircase, leading up to the bridge. The only step that wasn't wet was four steps up and required that I do the splits at a forty-five degree angle. "Um ..." I started dubiously.

"Ah shall assist ye."

Bracing his feet shoulder-width apart, Tallis tried to compensate for the shifting of the boat. Once he had his balance, he secured both of his hands around my waist. Then he lifted me up and over the side of the boat as I gripped both sides of the railing and hoisted myself over the top step. Bill simply materialized beside me while Tallis reached for our swords in the bottom of the boat to hand them up to me. I accepted them and watched him hold the shield and backpack up to Bill before he gripped the railing and started up the stairs, the inky water seeming to swallow up his boots.

It took me a second to realize he was standing in the same water he'd just warned me to avoid. I didn't say anything, but continued to watch him as he nodded at the ferryman. The ferryman took off, no doubt on his way to retrieve the souls I'd seen earlier, waiting on the banks of the river.

"Your feet touched the water," I pointed out.

"Aye."

"But you said ..."

"Ah am not ye," he answered evasively.

Not knowing what else to say, I refrained from further conversation, and turned to take in my new surroundings. They looked very much like the surroundings we'd just left. Aside from the bony outline of trees, there was nothing more to speak of. It looked like we'd just entered a charred forest. But unlike any woodlands I'd experienced, this one was eerily silent, absolutely noiseless. Not even the sound of a lonely bird or a rodent scuffling through the dead branches littering the ground broke the silence of what reminded me of the macabre hush of a graveyard.

"Is this the Underground City?" I asked, my doubt unconcealed. I figured the Underground City would be at least that, a city.

"Nae, 'tis ah long way off. 'Twill take us the better of three days ta reach it."

"Your next sentence better include something about your garage where you have a Range Rover waitin' for us," Bill said testily.

"Three days on foot!" Tallis clarified, giving Bill a raised brow expression.

"Shit! Exercise," Bill griped as he kicked something that rattled before it clunked against a lifeless tree trunk. "I liked my stealth abs." I frowned at him, and he patted his gut. "I gotta ripped six pack … it's just covered by a layer of insulation." Then he smiled and shrugged. "Stealth abs."

I rolled my eyes and refocused my attention on the three-day journey that lay ahead of us. Tallis was busily sheathing our swords into the scabbard against his chest, before donning the backpack and pulling each of his arms through the handles of the shield.

Bill, looking at Tallis, immediately started laughing. "Dude looks like a turtle." He took a breath. "Tallis Mutant Ninja Turtle!"

"So if the Underground is a three-day journey from here, where are we now?" I asked, ignoring Bill.

"We are nowhere. The land between here an' there."

Sometimes I wondered if I'd get clearer answers from the Riddler, but call me a glutton for punishment because I wasn't ready to give up. Not yet anyway. "So if Dante's directions said to get to the Underground City by way of the Acheron, why did we come up the Styx?"

"That's what I've been sayin'," Bill interrupted, shaking his head.

"Short cut," Tallis responded, without turning around to make sure we were still behind him. Instead, he continued his breakneck speed, although I had to admit I was getting used to it now. Good thing my long legs could sort of keep up with him.

"A short cut?" I repeated.

"Aye. Had we gone the other way, it would have been ah five-day trek to the city," Tallis replied with unmasked annoyance.

Yep, three days were better than five. Good thing Tallis knew his shortcuts. "So we're going to have to camp out in this forest tonight?" I asked, hoping and praying Marriott had real estate in pseudo hell.

"Aye."

Well, so much for that thought. "Is this forest safe?" I asked hesitantly, glancing sideways, as well as over my right shoulder and then my left. There was nothing except the looming figures of blackened trees as far as I could see.

"Ye are near to the Oonderground City. Nothing is safe."

I wasn't in the mood to further interrogate the bladesmith. His negativity drained me. Instead, I eyed my stubby neighbor, who looked back at me with a smile.

"Never fear, Bill is here!" he said with a hearty chuckle.

"Except for the fact that you can't protect me here," I replied in a worried and dejected tone.

He nodded. "There is that."

The three of us walked in silence for the next ten minutes or so, each absorbed in our own thoughts. Mine traveled from studying Tallis's large physique, which I couldn't help admiring, to his less than affable personality. Although I found his company exasperating (and sometimes downright hostile), I couldn't help my inordinate sense of relief knowing he was on this trip with us. I couldn't even begin to imagine how I would have flagged down Charon and, more so, how Bill and I would have made our way through this forest without Tallis. I might have given up before our journey ever really started.

But, don't forget, you won't have Tallis beside you much longer. After this trip, you might be on your own, I reminded myself.

But he said he would train me! I argued back in somewhat of a panic.

Maybe he was just referring to this outing, which came along a lot faster than anyone expected ...

Unable to fathom the idea of doing this same thing without Tallis, I had to banish the thoughts right out of my head.

"Focus on where you want to go, not on what you fear," Anthony Robbins's words reminded me.

"There you go again with that self-help shit," Bill grumbled.

"It makes me feel better," I snapped back at him. "And at this point, I need all the help I can get."

After studying me, he nodded, sighing to convey his acquiescence. "Yeah, I guess you gotta point. What else you got in that head of yours?"

"Um ..." I tried to remember the various quotes I'd committed to memory, never imagining in a million years that I'd need them in this situation. "Ah, here's one. 'All that we are is the result of what we have thought,' Buddha."

"That one's dumb. Say another one."

I frowned at him but lacked the urge to argue. "How about this one: 'You are essentially who you create yourself to be, and all that occurs in your life is the result of your own making.'"

Bill considered it as he chewed on his lip in silence. "I like it. Who said it?"

"Stephen Richards," I answered before another quote popped into my head. "I always liked this one: 'Life's managed, not cured,' Phillip McGraw."

"Life's managed, not cured," Bill repeated before nodding. "I like that one too."

"Bill?" I asked, as something occurred to me. "Do you know other guardian angels?"

"Sure I do, why?" Then a glower came over his features. "If you think you can exchange me for another one ..."

"No, I have no intention of doing that," I interrupted him. I'd never even considered exchanging him for another angel. Well, at least not in the last few days, anyway. However, if given the opportunity, I wasn't sure if I would exchange him. Miraculously, over the last few days, I'd actually begun to like Bill. His jocular presence provided some comic relief, which I appreciated. As much as I couldn't imagine attempting this trek without Tallis, I also couldn't think about doing it without Bill. He helped soothe my relentless anxieties, which were mostly caused by this mission and heightened by Tallis.

"Good, 'cause there ain't no refunds, sistah," he said and then studied me, as if he weren't sure if I was telling the truth.

"I like you, Bill," I said with a smile. "I wouldn't think of exchanging you."

"Well, thanks, sugar lips, I like you too." He threw his arms around me then, hugging me tightly. When he released me, I wobbled a bit before regaining my balance.

"The reason I asked," I continued, before clearing my throat, "was because I wanted to find out if you might know the guardian angels of people that I know?"

"Well, seems like the only people you know are me and Tallis, and he ain't got no angel," he said, lifting his chin in Tallis's direction. "An' I guess you could say I'm my own angel."

I looked at the bladesmith who was doing a good job of managing to maintain at least a ten-foot lead on us. "Why doesn't he have an angel?"

Bill shook his head. "Dunno. Prolly because he's in a different category than you or me." As he exhaled, he finished, "I'd call it the 'Asshole' category."

I laughed, having already reached the same conclusion about Tallis, myself. But I still had reasons for asking the question about guardian angels in the first place. I needed to steer the conversation away from the Tallis tangent. "I meant in my old life, people I knew in my previous life."

Bill cocked his head to the side. "Yeah, I might have. Who'd ya have in mind?"

"Um, my mom," I answered in a soft voice. "Do you know her angel?"

Bill shook his head. "I know of her angel, but don't know her personally. I can tell you she's a woman, though. She ain't hot or nothin', which is prolly why I don't know her." With a laugh, he added. "I make it my bidness ta get in the know when they're hotties."

I shook my head and rolled my eyes before focusing on a subject that was more than important to me. "Is my mother's angel a good one?"

"Yeah, I guess so. Never heard of her havin' any problems, if that's what you mean?" Then he eyed me more pointedly. "Why are you askin'?"

I exhaled a long sigh. "I'm worried about my mom. She's all alone now," I tried unsuccessfully to keep my tears at bay and wiped them away with my shirtsleeve. Glancing up at Bill, I attempted to smile. "I was all she had."

Bill nodded and was politely silent for a few seconds. "You know you can't contact her, right? That sort of thing is strictly prohibited … it only leads to problems."

"Yes, I know," I answered in a hushed tone, wiping my eyes again. "That's what Jason told me." I exhaled. "I was hoping you could put in a good word to her angel, just let her know that my mom needs extra help right now."

"Sure, I'll do that as soon as we get back," Bill said with a comforting smile.

"You mean *if* we get back?"

"We'll get back, don't you worry none," he said with enthusiasm. "An' when we do, I'll be sure to talk to your mom's angel."

"Thanks, Bill."

"Keep in mind, that part of our work as angels isn't just protecting you guys but it's also about helping you through shit times like this, so your mom's angel prolly is already helpin' her through it."

"What do you mean?" I asked hopefully.

"Think back to when you were going through a tough time in your life. Did you ever feel like someone was there with you to help you through it?" I nodded. "Yep, that's us," he finished and then paused for a second. "Your mom's angel is right there with her, baby doll. Don't you worry."

"Do you think my mom knows that?"

Bill shrugged. "It's hard to say." Then he grew quietly pensive. "You remember that time when you were maybe ten or so, and your mom took you to the pet store in town?" I gave him a puzzled look, wondering where this story was going, to which he just nodded and continued. "I know you're gonna say your mom took you to the pet store lotsa times, but this time was different. You were looking at the rabbits and she went ta pick out some dog food, and while you were oohing and aahing over the bunnies, a strange man walked up and stood next to you. He was maybe thirty-five. You remember?"

I looked at Bill, and my mouth dropped open as I recalled everything he'd just said as though it were only yesterday. "He asked me what I liked to do in my free time, and I told him I liked going to the movies."

Bill nodded. "And then he asked you who you go to the movies with, and you said your mom."

"Yep, and he said he'd like to take me to the movies sometime," I finished for him. "He asked me to meet him in the pet store the following Saturday so he could take me to the movies." I never had forgotten the incident, and looking back on it now, as an adult, I realized the man's motives for what they truly were.

Bill nodded, his face hard and angry. "You remember hearing a voice inside your head that told you to get away from him and go find your mom?"

I nodded just as something dawned on me. "That was you?"

He smiled widely. "That was me." We just stared at one another as the weight of his words sunk in. When he spoke again, his voice was softer. "Whenever you find yourself in a bad situation, or feel overcome with grief, we can and do reach out, but we do it in ways that aren't obvious. We have to be subtle."

"Is that why your voice in my head sounded like my own?"

Bill just nodded and we were both silent for another few seconds. Then he added, "Your mom is gonna be fine eventually, baby doll. It will take a while because the pain is so fresh and new, but she'll get through it. I promise you."

Looking down at my feet, I wiped a few more tears from my eyes, but I could honestly say that his words did make me feel better.

***

"We will stop here for the night," Tallis announced, dropping his shield and backpack beside the charred trunk of a tree. We'd arrived at a clearing of sorts, maybe a ten-by-twelve-foot open space in the skeleton-tree forest.

"Don't you mean we'll stop here for the day?" I corrected him. Since we'd just spent many hours walking through the forest, daytime had to be arriving soon.

"Nae," he said as he studied me pointedly. "There is nae daytime here. Only dark. An' ye must accustom yerself to the neverendin' darkness or ye wilnae know when ta sleep an' when ta wake."

I swallowed hard, looking up at the black sky and realizing that was all we would see for who knew how long? Bill dropped down onto the dirt beside me, resting his back against a tree, as he stretched his short legs out in front of him. Then he crossed his ankles, wrapped his arms around himself and closed his eyes. "I'll be takin' a snooze if anyone needs me."

"Each one of us will take turns keepin' watch while the others sleep," Tallis started.

"Good, I'll volunteer to sleep first," Bill interrupted without bothering to open his eyes.

Tallis frowned at me, but neither of us said anything. Instead, he removed my sword from the scabbard around his shoulder and handed it to me. "Keep this close ta ye at all times."

Standing up, he opened the backpack and pulled out what looked like an ancient relic. It was a bow with three even more primeval arrows. After retying the backpack, he slung it behind the closest tree.

"Where are you going?" I asked, afraid to be left alone.

"We have ta eat," he answered simply. Before I could argue, he stomped off, disappearing into the line of burnt trees.

My stomach flopped at the thought of being basically alone. I could already hear the sonorous hums of Bill snoring and had to shake my head at the fact that he was comfortable enough in this … place, that he could fall asleep so easily. But then I remembered he was an angel and couldn't be harmed. Such was most definitely not the case for me. I sat down against the tree where Tallis left his things and pulled my knees up to my chest, fingering the blade of my sword, which lay on the ground beside me.

All I could think about was the deathly stillness of the woods. Aside from Bill's rhythmic snoring, there wasn't another sound. The uncanny quiet started to undo my nerves. Was everything dead here? If so, what did Tallis plan to hunt? 'Course, Tallis knew these woods since he'd traversed them many times on his way to the Underground City, so I imagined something managed to survive in them. And it was that something that was starting to give me heart palpitations.

I had no idea how long I sat there, frozen. My own fear crippled me and even though I could feel pins and needles starting up my legs, I couldn't move. Hearing the sounds of footfalls on the dead tree branches covering the forest floor, I grasped my sword and hopped onto my feet. In response, the stinging pins and needles ran all the way up to my knees but I ignored the pain. Instead, I planted my feet shoulder-width apart and held the blade in striking position, ready for whatever was out there to make its presence known.

"At ease, Lass," Tallis's rich baritone interrupted the thudding of my heart. I couldn't help the inordinate sense of release that washed over me.

I didn't say anything but leaned my sword against the base of the tree and watched him fling something bloody and heavy beside it. I couldn't see all of it, but what I did see looked decapitated. Tallis kneeled down and started rummaging through his backpack. I took a few steps closer to him without knowing what I was doing. It was just as if my body knew Tallis meant safety as much as my mind did, and consequently, it wanted to be close to him. With a raised brow expression, Tallis let me know he didn't like me hovering over him.

"Um, what can I do to help?" I asked quickly, trying to cover for basically crowding his personal space.

"Can ye build ah fire?"

I nodded emphatically, pleased there was something I could do to help. Acting the role of a peasant in "Middle Ages," my medieval reenactment group, I'd managed to learn how to make a fire using nothing but wood and my bare hands.

"Ye can build ah fire?" Tallis asked again, disbelief in his tone.

"Yep, I can," I answered with steely resolve, already having decided that the hand drill would be my best bet. Determined to prove myself, I searched the nearby surroundings for small sticks and something to use as tinder. The sticks were easy to find, the tinder not quite as easy.

After gathering an armful of branches and twigs for kindling, I dropped them into a pile at the base of the large opening Tallis designated as our camp. Then I started scouting the area for something flammable—something very dry that would ignite quickly and start my fire.

"At the base of the trees ye will find dead lichen," Tallis offered.

"Thanks," I muttered, irritated that he felt the need to advise me when I intended to prove myself useful in at least something. The base of the closest tree had no dead lichen or moss, so I moved to the tree where Bill lay snoring away. There was a mass of brown and fibrous-looking stuff that I assumed was the lichen. After scraping off a few handfuls of the stuff, I added it to my twigs and branches. Placing my tinder to the side, I separated my kindling from the rest of the branches and piled it into a pyramid shape. I reached for half of the dried moss, which I placed inside the kindling at various spots.

Then came the task of finding a suitable fireboard. I scouted through the branches I'd assembled, trying to find something for my board and spindle. For the fireboard, I needed wood that was relatively soft. In "Middle Ages," I'd passed the fire-starting test by using a juniper fireboard. With no idea what sort of trees were in this forest, I could only hope some were soft wood. I found a branch that had a relatively flat surface, then realized I needed Tallis's help.

"You didn't happen to bring an axe by any chance, did you?" I asked hopefully.

"Aye," he answered from where he was leaning against a tree, watching me.

"Great! Could you cleave this in half so I can use it as my fireboard?"

"With pleasure, lass," he answered. He took the branch from me before rummaging through his backpack until he found his axe.

Using a nearby stump, he placed the broad branch down and cleaved it in half. Then he knocked off the rough side of one half, creating a nice looking plank. He handed it to me as I thanked him with a smile, and prayed the wood was soft. Pushing my fingernail into the board, I watched my nail indent it, which was exactly what I was hoping for. I glanced up at Tallis again. "Could you cut a V-shaped notch into it, please?"

He simply nodded and did as I asked, handing it back to me with the glimmer of amusement in his eyes. I noticed he also put a small depression on the edge of the notch for my spindle. Concerning which, I still needed to find one.

I searched through the kindling I'd collected and spotted a thin stick that was maybe two feet long. The top of it was a bit gnarled, but I could use the bottom half. My tinder close by, I pinched off a bit of it and dropped it in the groove Tallis carved for me. Placing my spindle on top of the tinder, I started spinning the stick rapidly between my palms.

Making fire from cold sticks would be no easy feat. In "Middle Ages," it had taken me the better part of two days and countless blisters before I even got the knack of it. And during my fire-making test, it had taken me twenty minutes before I saw the telltale wisps of smoke.

My hands were getting raw and were beyond tired, but I continued rolling the stick between my palms. My new body included hands that were a callous-free study of beautiful skin. Well, that beautiful skin was about to get a crude lesson in survival.

After ten or fifteen minutes, I felt like my arms were about to detach from my shoulders, they were so tired. And my palms were a lost cause. But I didn't stop; I didn't even pause. I just kept the momentum up, thinking about what a fire might mean for my safety. It would, undoubtedly, ward away whatever creatures lurked in this horrible place. At least, I hoped it would.

At last, the welcome beginnings of an orangey-red glow and white smoke began to spiral up from my spindle. I knew better than to stop rolling the spindle, though, and continued until there was an actual spark, which ignited the tinder at the base of my spindle. Once that happened, I grabbed the fistful of moss I'd put to the side and added that to the flames. Gently blowing on them, I urged them to consume the lichen. The flames inhaled the tinder greedily, and pretty soon, I had a fairly large blaze going. Lightly blowing on the flames, I couldn't stifle my elation as the tinder caught fire and the kindling began to crackle. Reaching for some smaller branches, I loaded them on top of the fire and watched in silent anticipation as the flames grew larger.

Turning to face Tallis with a broad grin on my face, I asked, "How d'you like them apples?" I slapped my hands against my thighs victoriously before wincing at the pain.

Tallis chuckled and moved away from the tree, approaching me. "Ah must confess, Ah am impressed," he answered with a hearty laugh. When he reached for my hands, I felt my heart climb up into my throat as soon as he touched me. I didn't know what it was about him but my body definitely seemed to answer to his. 'Course, maybe that was just because he was a handsome man and I had little to no experience with handsome men or men at all, really.

Tallis rolled my hands so my palms faced him and studied them for a moment or two. I couldn't help looking at his forearms and noticed the gashes were completely healed. I didn't say anything though. I knew better. Instead, I stared at my sore palms. "It's just a few blisters. They'll be fine in a couple of days."

Tallis shook his head. "Ye willnae be able to hold yer sword." Taking a deep breath and releasing one of my hands, he reached into his sporran, and retrieved a blade. Thinking he meant to use it on me, I started to pull my hands away, but he held me steady. "Dinnae be afraid. Ah willna hurt ye," he said softly, as I realized this was probably the third time he'd repeated the same words to me.

"Then what …?" I started, but lost my voice when he sliced the blade across his palm. Blood gushed from the cut immediately. He clamped his palm down on mine, smearing his blood over my blisters. He did the same to my other hand and then closed his eyes as he muttered something in Gaelic. When he reopened them, he didn't say anything but reached for his backpack. He pulled out a steel canister of what I assumed was water. Unscrewing the cap, he poured the water across my palms, washing away his blood along with my blisters. "They're … they're gone!" I exclaimed in astonishment.

"Aye," he answered casually.

"Your blood … can heal?"

He simply nodded as I reached for his hand, knowing full well that he wouldn't like me touching him. In general, he seemed okay with contact as long as he was the initiator. I had a feeling he was a control freak and couldn't tolerate that control being shaken. Gripping his wrist, I turned his hand around so his palm was facing me. The gash was healed. I shook my head in amazement as I dropped his hand. "What are you?" I asked in awe.

"As ah told ye, Ah am a Druid."

"All cowardice must needs be here extinct."
— Dante's *Inferno*

ELEVEN

"How did ye know how ta make ah fire?" Tallis asked quickly, apparently wanting to change the course of our previous conversation, when I'd asked him what, exactly, he was. Yes, yes, yes, he'd insisted more than once that he was simply a Celtic Druid, but I wasn't convinced. 'Course, for all I knew, maybe the Celtic Druids possessed incredible powers and he wasn't covering up the truth ... but maybe he was.

I shrugged as my thoughts drifted back to his question about how I learned to make fire by rubbing two sticks together. "I was part of a medieval reenactment group, and in order to be accepted into the peasant league, I had to learn how to make fire."

Tallis studied me for a moment or two, his bushy eyebrows centered in the middle of his forehead as he frowned, obviously not comprehending me. Then he stood up and reached for the carcass he'd dumped beside the blackened stump of a tree and brought it closer. He sat down, leaning against the tree, and retrieved a blade from his sporran, wasting no time removing the dark, blood-soaked pelt of whatever was unfortunate enough to cross his path. Whatever "it" was, appeared to be the size of a basset hound, now looking like a fleshy, bloody mess.

"Ah what?" he asked, eyeing me with interest, his hands covered in blood.

"A medieval reenactment group. We called ourselves 'Middle Ages.'" I directed my attention first on my fingernails, then on the sleeping Bill, and finally, the charred woods. Anything to avoid watching Tallis skin the animal. After feeling famished a half an hour ago, my hunger had long since tucked its tail between its legs and hit the road.

Tallis cleared his throat and I brought my attention back to his face as he studied me pointedly. In his expression, I could see he still didn't get my gist and worse, seemed to suspect I was trying to pull his leg. "Ah doona oonderstand," he admitted finally.

I sighed. I wasn't really in the mood to talk about my time in Middle Ages, especially since I was practically living the real thing now. "There were a group of us, maybe sixty or so, and we acted out periods of history."

His frown deepened. "Ye put on ah play, ye mean?"

I shook my head. "No. We actually pretended like we were living history." Before he could interrupt me with another confused expression, I continued. "All of our costumes were hand-stitched and created from fabrics that would only have been available during the high middle ages. And each costume was tailored to whatever class we happened to be members of. Since I played the part of a merchant's withe, I wore fabrics of higher quality wools and linens. When I played the role of a peasant, I only wore the cheapest wool available, which was scratchy, hard to clean, and usually the color of mud."

"Why elect ta enter the class of the peasants or the merchants?" he asked with knitted brows. "Why nae the kings?"

"Well, obviously everyone wanted to enter the class of the royalty, but it wasn't that simple. You had to work your way up, and everyone started as a lowly peasant. Then, as you mastered each rank, you would eventually enter the class of kings and queens. However, that took quite a while, as I'm sure you can imagine."

"Ah oonderstand," he nodded, briefly glancing at the bloody thing in his hands before offering me his full attention again. "Prithee, continue."

I shrugged, not really sure what more I could say about it. "So, basically, we just acted out the average daily life in our village, each of us interacting with one another as befitted our station, trading and the like."

"An' did ye live in this town?"

"No. Our group met a couple of weeknights and weekends." Then I shrugged. "I mean, we *did* have day jobs."

Tallis nodded like he finally understood but then started worrying his lower lip as if he wasn't completely satisfied with my answers to all his questions. Overall, a definite expression of interest and slight bafflement remained on his face. He glanced over at me, his eyebrows furrowed. "An' were ye paid ah good wage to do this?"

I shook my head and rolled my eyes, now getting frustrated. And, no, it didn't surprise me in the least that his line of thinking tended toward the "What's in it for me?" Tallis Black definitely struck me as an opportunist. But returning to the subject, this conversation really was a total waste of my time. Since Tallis had basically lived through the middle ages, he probably couldn't fathom why anyone would want to relive them. "No, I received no wage. I did it because I thought it was ... well, fun."

"Fun, lass?" he barked at me while shaking his head, all of which was followed by a mocking laugh. "Ah didnae consider those days fun, not with the constant worry of invasion, the black death an' starvation."

"So if you are an immortal Druid, like you claim to be," I started, intending to change the subject while spotting an opportunity to drill him for information.

"Ah am."

"Then why are you the only one? Or are there other immortal Druids out there like yourself?"

He shook his head and dropped his gaze to the now skinless creature in his hands. Its fur lay folded on the ground beside him, looking like bloodied linens. After rotating it a few times, he began cutting it in half. That done, he cut each half into halves. Then, eyeing my pile of sticks, he motioned for me to hand him a branch. I sorted through them until I found a fairly straight and sturdy one. Handing the stick to him, I watched him run it through a hunk of the meat. He motioned for a few more sticks, which I gave him. Then he skewered the last three pieces of meat, all of which were about the width and length of my foot. He handed two of the skewers to me, which I held over the fire. The other two he rested on a tattered piece of muslin. Then he stood up and retrieved his canister of water, washing off the blood on his hands.

"Ah am the only one, the only Druid left of mah kind."

"Why?" I demanded, carefully keeping both pieces of meat away from the flames so as not to scorch them.

Tallis cleared his throat and looked decidedly uncomfortable. He didn't sit back down, but stood over me, which was incredibly intimidating, owing to his immense stature. "It is mah cross ta bear," he answered forlornly.

"What did you do in the past?" I threw the words at him, afraid they wouldn't come out otherwise. When he didn't respond, the weight of the silence descended on me, and I nervously continued. "Obviously, you're doing ... penance for something and anyone can see you're haunted by it."

"Ah doona care ta discuss it."

But I wasn't listening to him. Instead, I was still too absorbed in solving the riddle of what had turned him into the broken person he now was. "I'm sure something happened in your past which is why you flog yourself?" Even as I uttered the words, my brashness in asking surprised me.

As I imagined he would, Tallis shook his head and crossed his arms over his chest while regarding me with a glower. "Nae, that has naethin' ta do with mah past."

"Then why do you lash yourself?" I continued, my tone of voice curiously conversational. With nothing to lose, I figured I might as well push as far as he would let me.

"That is mah business."

I took a deep breath, wondering how Tallis would take the self-help advice of Steve Maraboli that I was about to offer him. "Unless you let go, unless you forgive yourself, unless you forgive the situation, unless you realize that the situation is over, you cannot move forward." Once the words left my mouth, neither of us said anything for a few seconds. Something twitched in Tallis's jaw, a jaw which seemed incredibly tight. I was suddenly worried I might have said too much, and gone too far. "I was just trying to help."

"Keep yer help ta yerself," he answered tersely.

I shook my head, feeling annoyed. "When you asked me about my life, I willingly told you."

"Aye boot this isnae about tit for tat. Ye made the choice ta tell me aboot yerself just as Ah make the choice nae ta tell ye."

"Fine, I'll remember that." Hunching over, I paid full attention to the fire, suddenly realizing I'd held the meat on the same side for too long, and now both pieces were charred. I rotated them while exhaling a deep breath, averting my eyes from my unfriendly companion. But my anger ended up getting the best of me, and I glared at him. "Don't for one second think that I'm some stupid idiot." Tallis's eyebrows reached for the sky as if thinking I was an idiot was the last thought that would occur to him. I further narrowed my eyes. "I'm onto you. I know there's a reason why you decided to escort Bill and me on this mission to hell, and it wasn't out of empathy."

His eyes were just as hard as mine. "Empathy?" he scoffed, his lips curling up into a mockery of a smile. Seconds later, the smile vanished and his lips became painfully straight. "Nae, empathy plays nae role in mah plans."

"Then what does?"

"Ye do recall Ah named mah price ta escort ye?"

I nodded, but that didn't mean I bought his explanation. "Yes, I remember. But there's more to it than the money for you; and if you think I'm going to buy that lousy explanation, you don't give me enough credit."

"Och aye! Ah give ye plenty of credit. It's yer bloody intelligence that makes ye dangerous."

I continued to study him, taking his words as a compliment even though I knew they weren't intended to be. I felt my jaw tighten as I further considered him. "Why do you want credit for the soul we're going to retrieve?" He was completely silent, but I didn't miss the rigidity of his posture. His chest rose and fell quickly, with his increased respiration. The question made him uncomfortable at the very least, although "nervous" was probably more fitting. "Do you want to know what I think?" I continued, seeing that he wasn't going for my bait.

"Even if Ah didnae, ye would tell me anyway, Besom." I ignored the jibe, raising one brow to let him know I wasn't impressed. He just shook his head like I was infuriating. Well, if that wasn't the pot calling the kettle black! Tallis Black was the most infuriating man I'd ever had the misfortune of encountering!

"I think you're really a Retriever, just like me; but for some reason, you won't admit it." He just stood there with his arms crossed and his expression just as safeguarded, as I continued. "What? Are you too ashamed to admit that AfterLife Enterprises is your employer?"

He finally shook his head and his acidic laugh cut through the air. "Ah am nae Retriever an' Ah am nae employed by anyone save mahself."

I glared up at him. "Then why are you here with me now? And why do you insist on taking credit for this mission? What do you need the credit for if you aren't a Retriever?"

Scowling at me for another few seconds, his eyes became so consumed by ire, they almost appeared closed. He finally exhaled a long breath, staring at the ground in front of my feet. Releasing a disgruntled "harrumph," he sat down, resting against the stump he'd occupied earlier. "Ye are stubborn as ah bloody mule!"

"Hee-haw!" I brayed at him with a smile, recognizing that he'd just caved.

He shook his head, but couldn't keep the amused smile off his lips. "Afore Scotland was as ye an' Ah now know it, 'twas called Alba, ah land of numerous tribes," he started in a faraway voice that sounded both deeply resonant and soft. "Ah was of the Votadini clan on the Lothians coastline."

"What are the Lothians?"

"Ah region, lass. It lies atween the Firth ah Forth an' the Lammermuir Hills. Ye live in the Lothians as ye reside in Auld Reekie."

"Auld Reekie?" I asked, shaking my head.

"Edinburgh," he finished with a slight chuckle, as if entertained that I wasn't in the know. But just as quickly as his laugh appeared, he extinguished it and the familiar, brooding glower which characterized him returned. "In the Votadini, Ah was of the chief's kin, the elite. Given mah physique an' mah size, 'twas natural that Ah should be leader of the chieftain's warband."

"Yes, that only makes sense."

He glanced at me as though he'd forgotten I was even there. He seemed so captured by his own thoughts that he'd been taken somewhere far away, somewhere that only lived in the deep cavity of his memories. Judging by the expression on his face, the land of his memories was a dark and foreboding destination.

"Ah was especially accomplished as the leader of the other warriors. Ah drunk mah ale an' mead, wrestlin' with mah brothers of the warband an' gettin' numerous dalliances with the lasses. Ah wanted for nothing."

I started to blush as he recalled his sexual escapades. Well, at least this conversation put to bed (no pun intended) one of the mysteries regarding the Scotsman—that being that he hadn't always practiced celibacy. 'Course, on second thought, maybe he wasn't even practicing it now—maybe I just wasn't his type. I couldn't help but think, were I his type or not, that given the subject of my virginity and its associated perils in the Underground City, that he would have just sucked it up and "given me the sausage," as Bill so aptly put it.

"Boot then the Roomans came," Tallis continued with a tight jaw, both fists clenched at his sides. "Aye, they came an' they conquered, as they say." He took a deep breath and swallowed hard. When he lifted his eyes to mine, they seemed hollow and shadowy, in a word, pained. "'Twas Samhain, the festival of the new year, the only time when the gate between this world an' the world beyond this one is open. The only time when spirits of the dead wander among us."

I eyed the meat, having again forgotten it, and noticed both of my shish kabobs were black on both sides. Taking them off the fire, I handed them to Tallis, unsure how he preferred to dish them up. He accepted both, holding them at eye level, and inspecting each one, but making no motion to get up from where he leaned against the tree.

"Sorry, please continue. I just didn't want to char them anymore than I already have," I offered by way of explanation.

Tallis nodded, but remained oblivious to the overcooked meat. "Although 'twas dangerous, Ah convinced the old priestess to brew me ah tea made from the spores of the rye fungus."

"What is the rye fungus?"

"When brewed into tea, the spores allow yer soul ta separate from yer body so ye can see beyond this world an' into the next."

"Why would anyone want to do that?" Keeping your soul within your body seemed like the best place for it to be.

"Ah didnae want to," he answered in a snippy tone, apparently annoyed at my interruption. "As 'twas Samhain, by drinkin' the tea, Ah was openin' mah body to the spirits, an' to one certain spirit in particular." Then he took a breath.

"Donnchadh, the most powerful of warriors. The bards would sing of his ability with ah sword an' his brutality when it came ta destroyin' his enemies."

"So you possessed yourself?" I asked askance. My mouth dropped open just as an image of Linda Blair in *The Exorcist* flashed through my head. "Willingly?"

Tallis shook his head and speared me with another expression of utter annoyance. "Ye dinnae oonderstand the risk of the Roomans. They were conquerin' our clans, township by township. As Ah saw it, Ah had nae other choice."

"So the spirit of Donchad took over your body?" He glanced at me with a raised brow over my mispronunciation of the spirit's name. "Potato, *potato*, whatever," I grumbled.

He didn't drop the smile but continued. "Aye. Ah allowed him into mahself. After three nights of infernal pain, the rye spores passed from mah body."

"So did the possession work?" I demanded. "Did the spirit of this warrior help you defeat the Romans?"

Tallis was quiet for a few long moments before he shook his head and sighed despondently. The look in his eyes became one of utter despair. "The Roomans wouldnae be defeated so easily. Instead, mah bravery an' mah ability in battle only attracted their attention." He looked down at his hands, each of which held the skewers of meat. He handed one to me. "Ye should eat."

"What happened with the Romans?" I asked, accepting the skewer he offered me without taking a bite.

"What happened? Ah was captured in combat an' given the option ta help them or ta die."

"To help them?" I shook my head, not understanding.

"They wanted the Votadini land an' as they saw it, they had only the chieftain an' the warbands standin' in their way. If Ah, as leader of the Votadini warriors, sided with the Roomans an' betrayed mah own folk, they could triumph."

"But you didn't do that," I started, shocked, as I shook my head against the mere idea of Tallis selling out his tribesmen. "You ... you hated the Romans," I stammered. "You hate them now!"

He inhaled deeply and released his breath a few seconds after as his eyes settled on his fingers. Cracking his knuckles, he raised his stricken gaze to mine. "The Roomans promised me riches, fame an' the kingdom of the Votadini lands."

"The kingdom?"

"Aye."

"But what about the old chief, er, chieftain?" I asked, feeling a lump forming in my throat. I just didn't want to believe, couldn't believe, that Tallis would have even considered taking the Romans up on their offer. I hated to think he was capable of such utter and complete treachery.

He shook his head, his eyes boring into mine and his were empty pits, never ending voids of nothing. "The chieftain was ah lost cause, regardless. The Roomans planned ta kill him anyway."

"But ... but wasn't the chieftain your family? You said you were the chief's kin?"

He gritted his teeth. "Aye, he was mah uncle."

I didn't say anything for a few seconds, but listened to my heartbeat while it pounded through my head. I didn't realize I was holding my breath until I released it. "Please tell me you didn't backstab your own people."

He didn't say anything, but simply stared at me. But he also didn't need to say anything because the answer was there in his eyes. "Then you agreed?" I asked, my mouth agape. A stabbing sense of disappointment began penetrating every fiber of my being. I shook my head against the inanity of my own disappointment. I didn't know Tallis Black from anyone, so why I should be disappointed in him, I didn't know. Furthermore, once this mission was over, he'd go his way and I'd go mine; that would be the end of it. Yep, his sordid past had absolutely no effect on me whatsoever.

So why was disillusionment still cresting inside me? I didn't have an answer to my question and, instead, focused on this side of Tallis that I never imagined existed. Despite being anything but friendly, he appeared to live his life according to some moral code. 'Course, ratting out your family and fellow clansmen wasn't exactly upholding the code.

"Aye, Ah agreed," he spat the words out, as if they disgusted him.

"But what of the other warriors in your warband? You called them your brothers?"

"Massacred."

His answer hit me just as keenly as a palm across my face. "The Romans slaughtered them?"

"Aye," he answered, exhaling deeply and dropping his eyes down to the dirt on the ground. He drew circular patterns in the dirt, using the end of the skewer. It was pretty apparent that neither of us was interested in our dinner.

"Then what happened?" I asked, almost dreading his answer. I was still reeling with the realization that he wasn't the person I thought he was. It was as if someone ripped away the façade that I first believed was Tallis Black and I was now looking at his changeling.

"Ah was ah fool to trust the word of ah Rooman," he said with a bitter laugh.

"Then they didn't keep their word to you either?" I asked, thinking he probably deserved any ill treatment he received at their hands. Whatever the options, or lack thereof, backstabbing your own family was beyond wrong.

"Nae, they didnae, not when they realized they couldna control me such as they hoped."

"So what did they do to you?"

He laughed out. "They murdered me."

"They killed you!" I almost choked on the words while shaking my head in a cloud of confusion. Could Tallis Black simply be a spirit, a ghost? "You must mean they *tried* to murder you?"

He laughed again, a deep sound totally devoid of humor. "Aye, they tried. Boot the spirit of the warrior within me, imbued me with immortality." His eyes bored into mine. "Ah couldna be killed … just as Ah cannae be killed now."

I nearly swallowed my own tongue. There was something horrible but familiar stirring in my gut that felt very much like fear. "Then the spirit of the warrior is the reason you're immortal now?"

He simply nodded, the expression on his face unreadable.

"You're still possessed by him?"

"Aye."

I just stared at him without knowing what to think or say. Was it customary to offer your condolences to someone possessed? I wasn't sure. For that matter, what did possession really mean? Was I talking to Tallis or to the ghost? There was only one way to find out. "So, uh, are you like Dr. Jekyll and Mr. Hyde?"

Tallis chuckled and shook his head. "Nae, 'tis nothing like that. Ah've learned ta suppress Donnchadh's spirit. Sometimes, Ah even forget he's with me. The only reminder Ah have of his presence comes every morn Ah wake up."

"If the spirit left you, you'd die?"

He nodded. "Ah believe so."

I still didn't know what to make of Tallis claiming to be possessed by some ancient spirit, but one thing was becoming quite clear: why he flogged himself. "You flog yourself as penance for backstabbing your clan?"

"Aye," he answered in a smaller voice, his eyes suddenly appearing as dark blue pools of ancient pain. "Boot nae matter how much pain I bear at mah own hands, it cannae wipe away the pain of mah betrayal."

Feeling like my mind would collapse on itself, I tried to organize my myriad thoughts. "So do you have some sort of agreement with AfterLife Enterprises whereby if you retrieve enough souls, you will have paid penance?" That was the only reason I could see for why he wanted credit for saving the soul of our first mission.

He was quiet for a second or two as he appeared to contemplate my question. Then he simply nodded.

"How many souls do you have to retrieve?" I continued.

He shook his head and sighed. "Ah doona know."

"You don't know?" I tripped on the words. "Then how will you know when you've been forgiven?"

He chuckled, but it was a hollow, weak sound. "Yer guess is as good as mine, lass." Then he took a deep breath and brought his eyes to mine from where he'd been focusing on the crop circles he was drawing in the dirt. "Mah hope is to someday nae wake up. For then Ah will know that the spirit has been washed from me an' Ah have been forgiven." He stood up and stretched his arms above his head, sighing as he did so. Then he turned his haunted expression on me. "For mah part, Ah will never forgive mahself."

I just exhaled, suddenly feeling very sorry for him. Two thousand years was a long time to suffer immense self-loathing and guilt. Whereas before, I envied his immortality, knowing it meant his safety in the Underground City, now I recognized it as the true curse it really was.

"Abandon hope, all ye who enter here."
— Dante's *Inferno*

TWELVE

I didn't know what time it was, or whether it was day or night, as everything in this horrible place amounted to nothing but endless dark. And even though it was my turn to sleep, after Tallis took it upon himself to play the role of watchman, I did nothing but toss and turn. My thoughts were a jumbled mess, all centering on the story Tallis told me about being possessed by the ghost of some Celtic warrior and how he'd sold out to the Romans. It almost sounded like the setup to a bad joke …

But, unfortunately, there would be no punch line.

Coming to the realization that my mind was too busy to sleep, I rolled onto my back, opened my eyes and focused on the stars as they blinked in the black sky. The sound of Bill's loud snoring further pushed me toward the decision that I was definitely awake. I rolled onto my side and looked over at Tallis, who was leaning against a tree, his attention centered on me.

He held a small piece of wood in one hand, a blade in the other. Wood shavings on the ground around him as well as in his lap told me he was whittling a spear or something of that nature.

"I can't sleep," I grumbled as I cleared my throat and sat up. I could feel the effect of sleep deprivation on my body—lethargy, a feeling of being drained, and almost sick. But, there was no way I could rest in this dreadful place, having already tried and failed.

"Ye need yer sleep. 'Tis important." Tallis's voice was a monotone, his attention riveted on the spear he whittled.

"Yeah, well, unless some of your Druid magic can make me sleep, there's no hope."

"Ah cannae force ye ta sleep," he answered, frowning at me before refocusing his attention on the spear.

I nodded and took a deep breath, my stomach grumbling loudly as I felt the heat of embarrassment flooding my cheeks. Despite eating the shish kabob earlier, it obviously hadn't been enough.

"Are ye still hungry, Besom?" Tallis asked. He motioned to the two uncooked skewers that lay on a strip of muslin beside him, one of them reserved for Bill. Laying my eyes on the one unaccounted for, I immediately felt my stomach growling even more loudly. But moments later, I shook my head. Tallis was more than twice my size, so if anyone deserved seconds, he did.

"You should eat it," I answered with an encouraging smile. "I'm fine, really."

"Ah have learned ta survive on minimal edibles. If ye are hungry, ye should have it."

Unwilling to argue, I accepted the kabob when he handed it to me and faced the warmth of the fire while holding it over the flames. "You should sleep now; I can take over watch duty," I said, although the thought did leave me slightly concerned. I couldn't help wondering what lurked out there that required me to be on watch duty in the first place.

Tallis said nothing, but simply nodded. He dusted the wood splinters from his kilt as he laid the spear on the dirt, with the blade beside it. Then he made sure his sword was propped next to him, against the tree. Convinced everything was present and accounted for, he wrapped his arms against his broad chest and closed his eyes. I forcibly moved my gaze to the fire and watched it flickering as it spat flames and roiled this way and that. At the sound of sputtering, I looked at Bill. His mouth was half-open, with a clear stream of drool traveling down his cheek and dripping into a small puddle in the dirt. Catching his breath, he began to snore more evenly, and looked as comfortable as if he were lying on a bed of down.

Unable to suppress a smile, I shook my head and returned my attention to the hard planes of Tallis's face. I couldn't help staring as I studied him in his repose, grateful to be able to gaze at him without worrying about him realizing what I was doing. 'Course, all he had to do was open his eyes and I'd be caught. I figured it was a chance I was willing to take since I couldn't unfasten my eyes from his face. It was strong, masculine and handsome, despite the long scar that bisected his cheek. Actually, the more I thought about it, the more convinced I became that the scar wasn't so much a flaw, but rather an embellishment to Tallis's face. The scar emphasized his masculinity with more rawness, and more edginess. His long, black eyelashes settled against his high cheekbones, and his eyebrows and mouth free of their usual glower, gave him a peaceful, even happy appearance.

But I knew better. Happiness was not in Tallis's repertoire. I sighed, remembering the details of our conversation and, more pointedly, the details of his past. Tallis was damaged, that much was clear. And I wasn't sure why, but somehow knowing he was broken drew me closer to him, almost as if I wanted to fix him. Knowing his story, I no longer dismissed him as the hostile, intimidating and argumentative bladesmith. Nope, the situation wasn't black and white anymore, or cut and dried. Now, I knew why he was the way he was. He needed to bury his past, and let it go. And a part of me wanted to help him cease his self-loathing, and prove to him that he could overcome his past and be proud of himself, not ashamed.

Another part of me wanted to avoid any involvement and protect myself. I sensed the more I got to know Tallis, the more invested in him I would become. And that thought scared me because getting close to Tallis was like befriending a wild lion. Not to mention, I didn't think Tallis wanted much to do with me.

Just stop thinking about him, will you? I yelled at myself. *Tallis isn't your problem to fix! I mean, hello! You've already got more than your fair share of issues facing you!*

But, try as I might, I couldn't forget the angst in Tallis's eyes as he recalled his past. Furthermore, I was shocked to hear him admit as much as he had to me. Sometimes, he seemed so guarded and withdrawn, while at others, it seemed as if he wanted or needed someone to talk to. There were moments when it almost seemed like he trusted me, or maybe even considered me his friend.

He was a dichotomy, for sure. Not only that, but he was in obvious pain. It was pretty clear that he couldn't forgive himself. One piece of the Tallis puzzle that I couldn't quite put my finger on was why he had ever agreed to side with the Romans in the first place. I mean, yes, he said it was either that or death, but Tallis didn't strike me as someone who feared death, or anything else, for that matter. But, who knew? Maybe in his long lifetime, he'd changed. Maybe the Tallis of two thousand years ago was very different to the Tallis I only recently met.

"Hey, nerdlet, please tell me you're cookin' that shiznit for me?" Bill grumbled in a sleep-heavy voice as he sat up and stretched, with a gaping yawn. Cupping his palm in front of his lips, he blew and cringed when his breath wafted back at him. "Shit, I got nap mouth," he muttered. He crinkled his nose and swallowed three times, trying to rid his mouth of the offensive smell. Then he looked around himself, belched, and tipped his chin in Tallis's direction. "He dead or just sleepin'?"

I shook my head and offered Bill a smile, pleased to have his company because it meant the end of my mental debate about Tallis. "He's asleep and, yes, you can have this," I said, indicating the skewer. "It's almost done now."

Bill nodded in thanks before yawning again. He rubbed his eyes, which made them look even puffier. With his cowlick causing his hair to stick up in the middle, he reminded me of Alfalfa from *The Little Rascals*.

"Damn it!" he blurted as he rubbed his stomach and curled his lip into a pout.

"What?" I asked, worried. It looked like he was in some kind of pain.

With a quick glance over both of his shoulders, he made sure we were really alone, then frowned at me, still grasping his stomach like he thought it would drop. "I gotta go number two, but this place is givin' me pooformance anxiety."

I laughed out loud. For all Bill's off-color and idiotic jokes, some of them were actually pretty funny. "Well, just make sure you don't venture too far."

"Easy for you to say when you don't gotta go."

"When you don't have to go," I corrected him, shaking my head. "If you want me to learn your bizarre lingo, then you have to speak mine correctly!"

"Blah," he spat back at me and stood up. He hopped from toe to toe as he looked right and then left. Finally, with a shrug, he walked behind the tree he'd been sleeping beside. A tree that was maybe five feet from me.

"Oh my God, Bill, go farther away than that!" I yelled at him, absolutely not wanting our friendship to degrade into watching him defecate. Hopping over to a burnt-out trunk, beside the other tree, he began to squat. "Not there, Bill! I can still see you!"

He grumbled something unintelligible as he gripped his waistline with one hand and his bottom with the other. Then he waddled over to a tree maybe three feet away from the other one. Hiding behind it, he poked his face around the charred trunk and scowled at me, shaking his head. "I gotta go now, yo. I got major poo pains!"

Still able to sort of see him, I immediately turned my attention to the skewer in my hand. I rotated it carefully to make sure I didn't burn this one. Then realizing that Bill and I weren't exactly quiet in our last exchange, I chanced a glance at Tallis, and was relieved to find his eyes still closed. It looked like he was sleeping, or at least trying to. I scolded myself for being so loud—as much as I needed my sleep, Tallis needed his more.

Before I could think another thought, Bill bellowed from behind the tree and rent the still of the air. I felt my stomach knot and I instantly released my hand, dropping the skewer into the fire. I jumped up and turned to face Tallis, who was already on his feet, his sword ready. Hearing unsteady but hurried footsteps, I watched in shock as Bill ran at us full bore, while holding up his pants. His eyes were as big as two saucers and his mouth was even larger and screaming.

"What is it?" I shrieked at him.

"Uglyasfuckasaur spider!" he wailed in terror. He caught up to me and stood still, trying to catch his breath.

"Really, Bill?" I glared at him, throwing my hands on my hips to show my annoyance and disbelief. "All of that over a spider?"

"This ain't no ordinary spider!" he squealed, shaking his head just as he remembered he hadn't zipped or buttoned his pants. "This thing is the size of a fucking hippo!" he roared out as his fleshy, fin-like fingers wrestled with his zipper and button.

"Yer sword!" Tallis railed at me, motioning to the sword that lay beside me. I lurched for it, my heart in my throat as I wondered what was out there, and what Bill had seen. I had to admit I'd been skeptical about the danger of the spider, that is, until Tallis ordered me to pick up my sword. Now I was just scared. I held the blade up in front of me, completely forgetting all of Tallis's lessons.

Bill, now beside and slightly behind me, addressed Tallis. "Go kill it, Conan!"

My breath caught in my throat as the spider in question suddenly appeared from behind a tree. Although not quite the size of a hippo, it was abnormally large—standing as tall as my knees. Its tubular body was maybe two feet in diameter, and its legs had to be four feet long when extended. Its body was covered in a pelt of white hairs that looked like fur. Its legs, also covered in the strange hair-fur, were mottled white and grey. Long, black hairs extended from the top of its legs, matching the glassy black of its six eyes. But it was the two large eyes on top of the other four that were repugnantly terrifying. All eyes watched Tallis as he approached it. The thing reared back and held its four front legs out, obviously adopting an attack pose. In this new vantage point, I could see what looked like two large, yellow, furry fangs that were just below its numerous eyes.

"Be cannie," Tallis called out. "It jumps!"

No sooner were the words out of his mouth than the creature launched itself at Tallis, flying over his head as he swung his sword and missed. Bill and I both screamed, in exactly the same pitch, and ducked in the same direction and at the same time, squarely ramming our heads together as the thing sailed past us. It caught its foot on the trunk of the tree where Tallis had been sleeping and thrust itself forward again. This time, Tallis came up behind it and speared it right through the abdomen.

"We must move on," Tallis said as he pulled his sword free of the spider. He glanced down at it briefly, just to make sure it was dead. "They hunt in packs an' it wilna be alone."

After cleaning the blade of his sword with a piece of muslin from his backpack, he sheathed it. Then he motioned for my sword, which he stashed beside his own, in the scabbard across his chest. Pushing his arms into his backpack, he did the same with his shield.

"What about the fire?" I asked, as I watched Bill's attempts to avoid the flames as he tried to save the skewer I accidentally dropped.

"'Twill burn itself out. We leave now," Tallis finished. He started forward without waiting for either of us to ask any more questions.

Bill inspected the completely charred shish kabob, now with small sticks and other debris stuck to it. After studying it for another moment, he took a hesitant bite, before finally shrugging and starting in on the rest of it. Figuring he might be hungry later (I'd since lost my appetite after being attacked by the enormous spider), I wrapped the other skewer in the muslin and decided to bring it with us.

We walked at a breakneck pace for maybe thirty minutes before Tallis finally slowed down and I could actually take a deep breath. My legs were aching, as were the soles of my feet. I was sweaty, headachy and under the circumstances, pretty grumpy. "So what was that thing?" I asked, waiting to discuss the spider until we were far enough away from it to be able to. Obviously, I knew it was a spider but I wasn't sure if maybe it was more than that.

Tallis looked over at me and arched a brow, a slight smile tugging at one corner of his mouth. "It was yer supper."

I felt my stomach drop at the thought of the disgusting creature which now lay in my stomach. Then I caught Tallis's grin and a wave of relief washed over me. As soon as the wave crested, though, I wondered what we'd *really* eaten for dinner. "It's comforting to know you're joking about the spider being our mystery meat, but that begs the question of what our dinner really was?"

Tallis cocked his head to the side and offered me another quick grin. "'Tis better nae ta ask, lass."

***

We traveled through the charcoal forest for another night and two days, although the days and nights mingled together into one dark blur. The landscape was unchanging, and the burnt out hulls looked just the same as they did the day or night before. How Tallis could navigate was beyond me. I guessed he used the stars though, because he constantly checked the sky every hour or so. Or maybe he was just looking out for flying monsters.

I wasn't sure how, but Bill never lost his cool. He didn't seem the least bit put out that we were living an absolute nightmare. I felt like I could lose my mind at any given moment, but Bill continued to rattle off politically incorrect, and often graphic and disgusting, jokes, although he was the only one who laughed at them. At least he kept himself amused. Tallis, too, seemed unruffled by his surroundings, and remained recalcitrant and mostly withdrawn. Apparently, I was the only one who didn't take everything in stride …

When I finally hit my breaking point, and felt like the never ending dark sky combined with the skeletal forest would certainly be the undoing of my sanity, the landscape changed. Bill and I stopped dead in our tracks at the new scenery before us. We faced an uneven, muddy dirt road with weeds and overgrown grass on either side of it. There were no trees at all, skeletal or otherwise. The road started where the tree line ended. Ominous black clouds eclipsed what appeared to be the moon. The pale, yellow-grey glow of the moon's reflection against the clouds lit up the center of the road, and became so bright, I had to shield my eyes against it.

"We have reached our destination," Tallis announced.

I was surprised and returned my attention to the dirt road, which disappeared into the cloud cover. "This is it?" I asked, expecting to see a city, not a dirt road to nowhere.

"Aye," he answered robotically before continuing forward, as though to discourage any more questions. Bill and I watched him walk onto the dirt road and proceed toward the shadows of the clouds. Then he simply disappeared on the horizon, at the same spot where the road vanished into the clouds.

"Well, it was nice knowin' him," Bill said with a shrug as he spun around on his heel and started back for the forest.

"Come on, Bill, you know we have to follow him," I called out. I had to run the few steps that separated us, so I could grab the back of his collar and yank him to a stop. I wasn't sure what was worse, following the unknown dirt road or traveling back through the skeleton forest with the monster spiders.

Bill sighed, shaking his head. "All right, nips, ladies first," he said, holding his arm out in front of him theatrically.

I started toward the dirt road, looking back to make sure he was right behind me. He was. I took a deep breath, gave Bill an encouraging smile, and stepped onto the path. My heart was in my throat as Bill and I walked side by side, neither of us knowing what to expect. Strangely enough, both of us were completely silent, as if our own thoughts were distraction enough. My own mind was completely racing, plaguing me with questions I didn't have the answers to ...

What happened when Tallis disappeared? Did he just materialize somewhere else? And if so, where? My thoughts collided in my brain until I wanted to scream with frustration. Instead, I strained to see the end of the road, where it simply disappeared into the nether. My heart climbed into my throat.

"This is it," Bill said in a low tone, frowning as he faced me. "Ready, Betty?"

"I guess so," I answered, looking toward the end of the road, which simply T-boned into a black wall of nothing.

"Aye, we'll be back!" Bill said in a crummy imitation of Tallis combined with Arnold Schwarzenegger.

"You do realize that line isn't from *Conan*, right?"

"What you talkin' 'bout, yo?" Bill asked, shaking his head, like I was the one with my movies crossed.

"That line was from *The Terminator*."

Bill waved me away with an unconcerned hand. "Whatevs, *Terminator*, *Conan*, they both fit Tallis to a T. Maybe I'll just start calling him the bitchmaster instead. Get it? Beastmaster ... bitchmaster?" Then he erupted into a roar of chuckles.

"I'm sure he'll love that," I grumbled as I reached for his hand, and together we stepped forward. Seconds later, I blinked and found a completely different landscape around me. Luckily, Tallis was present, off to our right side. His hands were propped on his hips as he glared at us, no doubt unimpressed by our cowardice. But I couldn't say my attention was wholly centered on Tallis, beyond the relief at knowing he was still with us. Nope, I was much more interested in the Underground City.

It was comprised of large high-rise buildings, maybe twenty-five or so, all of which stood huddled together amid a backdrop of parched desert. In fact, the earth was so dehydrated, deep valleys pitted the ground, imbuing the landscape with the look of very old skin. The sky was an ugly, muted burnt shade of dark orange, with a lighter area of yellow centered over the city. It looked like the sky was on fire.

"Come," Tallis said as he started forward.

I dropped Bill's hand and inhaling the dry air deeply, followed Tallis. I had to be careful as I walked so as to avoid catching my toes in the deep fissures of the earth. Sprain my ankle or break my leg and I'd be SOL for sure. I sincerely doubted there were any doctors in hell.

The closer we walked to the Underground City, the colder the air became. It seemed the temperature dropped by five degrees with every step we took. "It's freezing!" I announced as I tightened my grip on the fur around my shoulders. I could see my breath on the air.

"Aye," Tallis answered. "Warmth doesna exist in the Oonderground. Only the cold of despair."

"And on that happy note, let's get this party started!" Bill said in a chipper voice as I tried to calm my frantic heart.

Tallis faced Bill and me with a dour expression. "An' how do ye propose ta find this soul we must retrieve?"

"Ah, shit!" Bill called out with a laugh as he slapped his thigh like the joke was on him. "I almost forgot, yo!" He reached inside his pants pocket and pulled out the pack of pills we first took when we entered Tallis's forest, and I thought Bill was taking illegal narcotics. He flipped open the tin and handed a green pill to me and one to Tallis, before taking one himself.

"What is this?" Tallis demanded, eyeing the pill with suspicion.

Bill shrugged. "Skeletor said to take it before each of our missions."

With that, Tallis threw his on the ground. It rolled off the edge of the parched earth, only to vanish into a deep ravine. I had yet to swallow mine and faced Tallis with the question of whether or not I should written on my face.

"I doona trust Streethorn," he said simply, before facing Bill. "Furthermore, ye, as an angel, have nae need ta take pills that are intended for human consumption."

"How do you know?" Bill eyed him warily.

"Aye know," Tallis answered, his jaw tight and his expression warning he wasn't in the mood to argue.

Bill simply shrugged as he faced me. "I just thought they might taste good. So hurry the hell up an' take yours, sugar loaves! You heard Frankenstein—they're for human consumption."

Before I could so much as open my mouth to speak, Tallis slapped the pill out of my hand. "Ye doona need it."

And that took care of that. Bill and I just looked at Tallis in surprise. "Okay," I said as I turned to face Bill, putting to rest the subject of taking pills. "So where are we going and how will we know when we get there?"

Bill chewed on his lip while he reached into his back pocket and retrieved his phone. With all the grey duct tape holding the thing together, I was amazed it even worked. He powered it on and clicked a few buttons. I glanced over his shoulder and noticed he was reading through text messages. "What are you doing?" I demanded.

"Checking my messages. Amazing, but I got service here." Then he focused on his phone again before shrugging at me. "All from my common-law girlfriend."

"What does …?" I started.

He shrugged. "We been hookin' up for a long time, but neither of us wants to call it a relationship, ya know? We just can't seem to shake each other though," he finished with a sigh.

"Bill!" I yelled at him, feeling frustration up to my ears. "I don't care! Back to the subject! How are we going to find the soul to retrieve?"

"Cool your panties, sweetie," he said, holding out the palm of his hand as if he were stopping an enraged bull. "Skeletor told me he programmed my phone with a sensor or something. I'm trying to make sure the damn thing downloaded. Now just busy yourself with Mr. Party over there"—he pointed to Tallis—"while I figure this shit out, namsay?"

"What?" I snapped.

"Ugh," Bill scowled at me and drooped his shoulders. "Know. What. I. Am. Saying?" Then he arched his eyebrows to see if I followed him. "Namsay?"

"Yes, I get it!" I grumbled back at him. "Just download the freaking sensor already."

"Workin' on it, sweetcheeks." Then he continued to click buttons and appeared, for all intents and purposes, like he had no idea what he was doing.

Annoyed, tired, scared to death, and in no mood to end my life in the Underground City, I huffed out a breath of impatience and eyed Tallis. He was standing a few feet away from me, his arms crossed against his chest, observing Bill and me with the whisper of a smile on his lips. "What are you so amused about?" I asked gruffly.

"Atween the two of ye, Ah doubt ye could navigate to yer own feet!" He chuckled loudly as he shook his head, as though pitying Bill and me.

"Shut it, Conan," Bill said and shot Tallis a discouraging glare. Moments later, he started to hop around while twirling his hips. "That's right! Big daddy Billy just got the sensor to work!" After thrusting his pelvis forward repeatedly, and looking like he was having sex with the air, he broke into the running man.

"He looks as if he's havin' ah seizure," Tallis said as he observed Bill.

Bill mistakenly took the comment as an invitation to dance in Tallis's personal space. He continued thrusting his abdomen forward, only in much closer proximity to Tallis, who recoiled with repulsion. "That's right! Bill found the spirit to retrieve! That's right!" he sang as he squatted down and got onto his hands and toes. He appeared to be mounting the dirt.

Tallis stepped backward while I wrenched the phone from Bill's grip. Peering down at it, I noticed what looked like a map. Directly east, there was a glowing white dot that seemed to move back and forth, as if it were a person walking on screen. I looked at Tallis who was busy trying to swat Bill away. The much smaller man was bent over, gripping his thighs while pumping his bottom up and down, and singing the wrong words to "I'm Sexy and I Know It."

"Bill, will you quit that?" I yelled at him as I handed the phone to Tallis. "I think the white dot is our spirit, but do you know where he or she is?"

Tallis inspected the screen for a few moments and then nodded. "Freak Show," he answered as if either Bill or I had a clue what he was talking about.

"Um, come again?" Bill asked between pants, apparently winded from his terrible dance moves.

"The amusement park," Tallis continued.

"There's an amusement park called Freak Show in the Underground City?" I asked, sounding completely baffled.

"Aye, the Oonderground City is just that, ah city. Everything you'd expect ta find in ah normal city, ye will find here."

"But Dante's *Inferno* says there are levels of hell!" I continued, perplexed at how this could be.

"Each level is ah destination within the city," Tallis explained.

I shook my head. "But Dante never described an amusement park!" Then I saw the skyscrapers in the distance. "And he definitely didn't describe modern buildings!"

Tallis looked like it was taking every last ounce of his self-control to remain patient with me. "Just as the world evolves, so does the Oonderground City."

"So can we, like, go on some rides, yo?" Bill chimed in.

"And after he had laid his hand on mine with joyful mien, whence I was comforted, he led me in among the secret things."
— Dante's *Inferno*

THIRTEEN

"So, dude," Bill started, glancing down at the copy of Dante's *Inferno*, which he held in his hands open to Canto Three, "it looks like we, uh, missed a few stops along the way."

"What are you talking about, Bill?" I asked, even though I couldn't say my attention was wholly focused on him. Instead, I stood gaping at the entryway to the Underground City, gulping despondently. The entry was comprised of an iron and brick gate that towered over us, maybe twenty feet high. The iron, a bluish-grey color, looked incredibly aged and worn, while inside the ironwork were layers of bricks. The bricks also looked ancient, as if they'd vanish into dust if you so much as swiped your finger across their rough surfaces. The remains of long dead and sticky vines clung to the gate and bricks, making the macabre reliefs of animal and human faces appear even more gruesome.

The black clouds overhead were moving on fast-forward, and the light of the moon refracted in rays of jaundiced illumination. Try as I might, I could not tear my repelled fascination from the sculptures that flanked the entry. Crowning the gate was an urn, guarded on either side by two enormous snails. Just beneath the urn was a woman's expressionless face, positioned so the rays of the moon arced out behind her. Below her was an antique-looking oval window, the color of algae. The ornate iron pattern on the glass resembled a spider's web, even though a few of the glass panes were broken. On either side of the window were two lion heads, with their mouths wide open in a roar. The largest of the reliefs was that of a man, perhaps in his late fifties. He sported a close-cropped beard, had a furrowed brow and wore a hood that looked like a lion's mouth mid-roar. I couldn't tell whether it was meant to appear as if the lion was eating his head, or if the man was simply modeling a lion's carcass. As I gawked at the morose sculptures, I had the uncanny feeling that the relief of the man was staring right back at me.

"I'm talking about Dante's directions, yo," Bill said, snapping my attention back to him. He even stepped in front of me and waved, obviously intent on grabbing my attention. "I'm thinkin' we mighta taken a wrong turn somewhere."

"Why?" I asked, now fully focused because his information was alarming.

"'Cause Dante was talking about some place called Limbo and then some other place, which was 'sposed ta come before the Acheron River but …"

"Aye, both are just products of Dante's imagination," Tallis interrupted with a frown, shaking his head. He wore an uptight expression and raised one brow, looking completely irritated with Bill. "Ye dinnae need ta consult the book as Ah know this city as well as Ah know the back of mah own hand."

"Well, if it's just the same to you, Conan," Bill spat out, puffing up his chest like a powder pigeon and imitating Tallis in a highfalutin way, "I'd like to see what *Dante* has to say about this place," he added before facing Tallis with a mirrored expression of annoyance.

"Then doona bother me with one more of yer bloody questions!" Tallis railed back at him, shaking his head in exasperation.

"Enough!" I shouted, giving both of them warning glances before settling my attention on Bill. "We made it to the Underground, right?"

"Yeah," Bill admitted, albeit reluctantly.

"Right!" I continued, unable to hide my exasperation. "At this point, we have more important things to worry about than that book!" I caught my breath and exhaled deeply before facing Tallis. "Are we going into the city now or what?"

"Aye," he answered with a stiff jaw as he pushed past me, and approached the immense gate. He paused in front of it and then turned to me. "Afore we enter, ye take yer sword," he said, unsheathing my sword from the scabbard across his chest and handing it to me.

"Okay," I started but he interrupted me with just a look. The intensity of his gaze was so riveting, I felt my heartbeat increase and my breath caught in my throat. Any other words I was about to say simply died on my tongue. His eyes were so focused on me, it almost seemed as if he could see right through me.

"Dinnae, for even one second, release yer sword," he said in a steely voice. "Keep it attached to ye." He paused for a few seconds, just staring at me in his soul-searching way. "Do ye oonderstand?"

I nodded as the meaning of his words sank in. If I lost my sword, I was as good as dead against whatever awaited us in the Underground City. I could read as much in Tallis's eyes and that realization, the possibility of losing my life as soon as we stepped behind the double gates, left me completely breathless.

Gripping the sword as tightly as I could, I began to think of it as my only lifeline, the one protection from impending doom, aside from Tallis, himself. How the sword could protect me when I still had no idea how to use it, I didn't know. But I figured Tallis had more surprises up his sleeve, so his word was good enough for me.

I suddenly felt light-headed, even dizzy, as the gravity of my predicament rained down on me. But fear would do me no good. I had no choice—I had to proceed, and enter the Underground in order to retrieve my first soul. Otherwise, Shade awaited me ...

Death is not the biggest fear we have; our biggest fear is taking the risk to be alive. I spoke Don Miguel Ruiz's words in my head, closing my eyes tightly in order to concentrate. Whether or not I was unsuccessful in this first mission, I would do my damndest to rescue the soul and to survive. If I failed, it was completely up to fate; but there was no way I would go down without a hard fight.

I opened my eyes and took a deep breath, centering myself. Then I focused on Tallis, who took off his shield, followed by his backpack. Rummaging through his pack, he found what he was looking for, and using both hands, reached into the large sack and pulled out what looked like a human skull, except there were two horns protruding from the top of its head. The horns were incredibly long, maybe two feet and very shiny. Ridges circled the horns from the base, where they blended into the bone of the skull, all the way up to their glossy black tips. The thing was so hideous that my heart began pounding as soon as I saw it.

"What the fucking fuck!!!!" Bill screamed in a high pitch, nearly doubling over on himself to get away from it. He took a breath, his eyes wide as he addressed Tallis, shaking his head. "You just carry around random ..." he inspected the skull again, trying to figure out what it was, "goat heads?"

"That is no goat," I announced, pointing at it with obvious repulsion on my face.

"Aye," Tallis answered with a slight smile curving his lips.

"So what is it?" I managed, trying my best not to look at it. With the almost obscene way its lower jaw met the upper, it looked like it was smiling at me, and I wanted nothing to do with it.

"Conan is one crazy ass bitch," Bill muttered beneath his breath, as he shook his head and stepped away from us. He acted like the horned skull was going to come after him or something.

"'Tis protection," Tallis answered simply, completely ignoring our outbursts. Instead, he took out a long piece of rope from his backpack. He wound the rope around the skull's horns, knotting it to ensure a tight fit around each horn. Then he slid his arms through his backpack, and followed with his shield. Looping the rope over his head, he turned and faced me. "Ah need ye to hold it against mah back, lass."

I looked at the dreadful thing again which, even in death, seemed to be amused. That was when I noticed the two long fangs where its canines should have been. The fangs were incredibly sharp at the tips and so long, they reached its lower jaw. "Protection against what?" I asked as I leaned down and, resigning myself to my task, placed both of my hands on either side of the skull and lifted it. The thing had to weigh twenty pounds! Holding it above my head, which was no easy feat, I placed it against the middle of Tallis's back, doing my best to avert my eyes.

"Lift higher," Tallis ordered.

"This is as high as I can reach," I snapped as I continued to wrestle with the burdensome weight of the relic. Tallis didn't respond as he pulled the rope tauter, which helped me secure the skull in place. With one more tug on the rope, he managed to move it up another four or five inches. Not wanting to look at it any longer, I turned around and walked in front of Tallis, watching him tie the rope into a tight knot around his waist.

"You didn't answer my question. What is that thing?" I demanded.

"Ah Grenelly demon's skull," he answered. At my confused expression, he continued. "They are notoriously foul-tempered an' difficult ta kill."

"But you obviously killed this one?" I had to shake my head, envisioning Tallis in combat with such a horrible-looking thing. Seeing how scary its skull was, I couldn't begin to imagine what it must've looked like in the flesh. And, furthermore, I hoped I'd never find out.

"Aye."

"So why the hell are you wearin' it like it's a freakin' Gucci jacket, yo?" Bill demanded from ten feet away.

When Tallis answered, he faced me. "'Tis mah proof that Ah am nae someone to confront," he said simply, taking a few steps toward the gates as an indication that the conversation was over. For my part, I neither needed nor wanted to know anymore. As long as I didn't have to walk behind Tallis and deal with the demon skull smiling at me, I'd be okay.

When Tallis was a mere few feet from the gate, he fished inside his sporran and produced what looked like a skeleton key that spanned the length of his entire hand.

"Do you have one of those?" I whispered to Bill, worried about how we'd make our way back into this hideous place when Tallis was no longer escorting us.

"A freakin' goat demon skull?" Bill asked, spearing me with an expression of disbelief that told me my question was pretty stupid.

"No!" I snapped in response. "A key to the gate!" Then I pointed at Tallis who was busily ramming the key into the lock while twisting and turning it left, then right.

"Oh," Bill said distractedly as he watched Tallis wrestling with the lock. Facing me, he shook his head. "Skeletor failed to include a key in our goody bag. Guess we just gotta ring the doorbell." Then he shrugged with a wide grin, like he thought the whole thing was just a big joke.

"Not funny," I said, exhaling a pent-up breath of anxiety, and wondering how in the world I could get a key from Jason since he was next to impossible to contact.

One step at a time, Lily Harper, I reminded myself. *Finish this mission first before you start worrying about the next one.*

Satisfied with my point, I set aside my worry. My attention returned to Tallis as he pulled the key from the lock and pushed the gate open. It groaned, sounding cranky at being pushed open, but opened all the same. I felt an icy jolt of unease as I realized what this meant—I was about to enter the Underground City, a place where I could very well die.

"Angel, ye will walk behind the lass at all times," Tallis barked at Bill.

"Dude, didn't your mom teach you to say 'please'?" Bill responded, frowning at me as he shook his head. "Manners are a lost art form, I swear."

All I could do was raise my eyebrows at him because I wasn't in the mood to point out that he, the pot, was absolutely calling Tallis, the kettle, black.

"An' dinnae break formation," Tallis continued, spearing Bill with his narrowed gaze before his eyes settled on me. "Besom, ye will be mah shadow, do ye oonderstand?" He took a few steps closer to me until I could feel his breath against my forehead. Consequently, his close proximity forced me to swallow down a big lump. I wondered if Tallis insisted on intruding on my personal space because he knew it made me uncomfortable, or if the ancient Druids didn't believe in keeping their distance.

"Y ... yes," I stammered as I looked up at him.

His eyes were hard, and his lips just as unforgiving. "Ah want ye one step behind me."

I nodded, swallowing down the lump of angst that was occupying my throat. Tallis looked at Bill, extending his hand as he backed up a few steps and I was able to breathe again. "Gimme the map."

"What map?" Bill asked.

"He means your phone," I translated.

Bill didn't say anything as he handed his phone to Tallis who checked it one last time, before placing it into his sporran.

"Don't get any ideas, yo," Bill started. "I want that phone back." He narrowed his eyes on the enormous Scotsman. "Got lotsa chick's digits, ya know?"

"An so ye shall have it," Tallis responded. "As soon as this mission is over." Then, without another word, he started forward, pushing through the gate, with me right behind him and Bill right behind me.

As soon as my foot touched the asphalt road of the Underground City, my stomach felt as if it were trying to turn inside out. It was so sudden, and the pain so immeasurable that I couldn't move, breathe or even think for at least a few seconds. Then it felt like someone dropped a hundred-pound sack on top of my shoulders, even though no one had. My knees buckled in response and I collapsed onto the freezing ground. Despair, the likes of which I'd never known, completely overcame me. A deluge of tears fell from my eyes and my chest heaved with sobs.

"Lily!" Bill yelled, throwing his arms around me and trying to lift me.

My body was so weak, I could only flop around in his arms like a dying fish. But I wasn't fully aware of anything, really, except fear, which radiated through me. The pain became so fierce, I couldn't think of anything else, much less comprehend what was going on around me.

I suddenly saw nothing but darkness. I could hear Bill's and Tallis's voices, but couldn't make out what they were saying. Someone shook me and when my eyes popped open, I realized it was Tallis. He was holding me, and gripping my cheeks to hold my head up as he forced my mouth open. The agony inside me continued to rage. It felt as if my blood was on fire, along with my organs and skin. I was barely aware of Tallis's thumb over my mouth until I saw drops of red sailing through the air and felt them landing on my tongue. I frowned at the salty taste, which was instantly replaced by a searing pain that overcame my entire body.

"Hold her!" Tallis shouted at Bill.

Faced with darkness again, I could feel Tallis's large hand around my upper arm as he shook me, and forced my eyes open. I felt thick fingers around my neck, and I flopped my head back, only to see Bill, who was holding me in place. My bleary vision returned to Tallis who appeared rather angry above me, using his free hand and squeezing his thumb until blood gushed up. He rotated his thumb, holding it above my mouth, while using his other hand to part my lips and ensure my mouth was open. I felt the drops fall on my teeth. Tallis squeezed my lower jaw between his thumb and index finger, forcing my mouth open wider. Then many more drops of blood landed on my tongue.

"Swallow!" he yelled at me.

My throat was swollen shut and the blood that landed on my tongue simply pooled in the back of my mouth. I was so overcome by whatever was destroying me that I didn't even buck at the realization that Tallis was feeding me his blood.

"Swallow, damn ye!" he roared again and at the fury in his eyes, I felt a bite of fear which urged me to open my throat, if only slightly. I threw my head forward, and tried desperately to swallow. Tallis thumped me hard on the back, causing my throat to open for the briefest moment, and I swallowed a mouthful of his blood.

I had no idea how much time passed until I could inhale deeply. It could have been a mere few seconds or a whole minute. As soon as the icy air filled my lungs, I exhaled it and inhaled again. With every breath came renewed relief. The fire devouring my insides began to subside and I could now breathe and swallow with much more ease.

"Are you all right, babydoll?" Bill whispered, his wide, concerned eyes on me.

I felt winded and unable to form words so I just glanced up at him and tried to nod. Bill looked at Tallis, still standing above me, with a frown. "What happened to her?"

Tallis sighed and studied me for another few moments, while I took notice of my surroundings. I was resting against Tallis's immense chest and I felt his muscular thigh beneath my back as he knelt. I continued to inhale and exhale deeply, as my vision began to clear.

"Innocence cannae exist in this place," Tallis said softly, his eyes on me, and a haunted expression on his face.

"What does that mean?" I ground out, in a rough voice. I tried to lift my head, but Tallis held me in place, firmly shaking his head.

"Take yer time, Besom." He took a deep breath. "Yer innocence was bein' strangled, taken from ye."

"But your blood?" I started before he interrupted me.

"'Tis the blood of someone devoid of innocence. Ah polluted ye with it, ta save ye."

Reaching forward, he lifted me underneath my arms, and pulled me to my feet at the same time that he stood up. My body felt light, pins and needles numbing my extremities. He started to release me, but when my knees began to buckle again, he reestablished his grip.

"Shake yer foot out," he commanded.

Obeying his order, I felt the warm flush of blood returning to my toes, stinging like a blazing fire. I shook my hands and felt each of my fingers come alive again, thanks to Tallis's blood. "I think I'm okay," I said softly.

Tallis released me, and this time, despite being a bit unsteady, I managed to remain on my feet. I took a step, feeling stronger with every second that passed.

"Are ye right?" Tallis asked, studying me with his piercing midnight eyes.

I took a deep breath, surprised to feel like I was mostly back to myself. "Thank you," I whispered.

He just nodded, evidently uncomfortable with my show of gratitude. He simply turned around and resumed his stance ahead of me. The awful demon skull continued glaring down at me from its position against his back. Bill stepped behind me as we started forward again, walking single file, into the city.

My first impression of the city, from this side of the gate, was that it was pretty much like any other city. Skyscrapers reached the clouds while a few paved roads wove between the buildings. The only difference I could make out between this city and any other was its utter lack of foliage. There were no trees, bushes or vegetation of any kind. In every direction, nothing but asphalt and concrete were visible. The sky, too, lacked any life. No birds or insects, only ugly, monolithic buildings. The air was remarkably chilly, and smelled like the inside of an old freezer.

Tallis's stride was long and purposeful as we started down the street. With Bill just behind me and Tallis right in front of me, I felt some level of protection. I gripped my sword as tightly as I could, scared to death at what awaited us, although I had to admit that, so far, the city didn't appear that threatening—unless you considered urban sprawl threatening. 'Course, I *had* nearly died as soon as I touched foot in the place … but I didn't want to think about that. Not now. Not when I needed to pay attention to my surroundings, and remain on the alert.

We moved at a fast clip. As soon as we passed the first skyscraper, the clouds in the sky eclipsed the moon, leaving us in near darkness. My eyes widened as I glanced around and saw we weren't alone. I wasn't sure why I hadn't seen them before, or maybe we were too close to the entrance of the city for them to freely walk around; but now we were surrounded by what appeared to be business men. They wore suits as they shuffled this way and that, all rushing about in a hurry.

"Ew, someone got walloped with the ugly stick," Bill whispered as one of the "business men" crossed Tallis's path.

I gasped when my eyes fell on the ... creature. Its body looked like a man's, but its face had lines so deep, it almost looked like a mummy. It had no hair, but a round, grayish head with what looked like spaghetti weaving across it. Its face was a salmon pink, while its nose and mouth appeared almost orange. Sheets of taut skin formed the bridge of its nose and walled in its eyes, making them look as if they were small and deeply set. The lower region of its face was charcoal black. Four teeth peeked out of the narrow drain of its striated mouth. It glanced over at us with a hostile expression, pausing for a second or two when it saw Tallis. Then it retreated and we continued forward, the moon's illumination reflecting the sheen of its sports coat.

"What was it?" I breathed down Tallis's neck.

"Ah watcher," he answered with little interest. We turned to the right once the street T-boned into another. "They keep an eye on things, reportin' back to the master."

"Who is the master?"

"The keeper of the Oonderground City."

Another watcher crossed our path, and gave each of us the once-over. Even though this one also continued on his way, just like the other one had, I definitely sensed that neither one was exactly happy to see us. "Will they report our whereabouts?" I asked.

"Aye, they already have."

"How?" I demanded, frowning as I wondered how that could be since none of them carried cell phones or walkie-talkies, or anything else of that nature.

"They are the master's eyes," Tallis responded. "What they see, he sees."

"Then the master knows we're here?" I continued, gripping my sword so tightly, my knuckles turned white.

"Aye."

"Is he going to come after us?" I asked, unable to mask my fear.

"Ah doona know," Tallis answered, his tone of voice level, precise. "Boot it doesna matter. Ye have ah right ta be hare, as ye are employed by AfterLife Enterprises."

"Then there's nothing anyone can do about us being here?" I asked immediately, feeling slightly relieved at the mere idea.

"Just because ye have ah right ta be here doesna mean anyone has ta like it. An' most dinnae like us bein' here."

The watchers continued coming and going, some stopping and staring at us while others showed less interest. I stayed quiet, almost afraid to attract attention or distract my own attention away from constant awareness of our surroundings.

"Shit, you weren't kiddin', Conan," Bill piped up as he pointed to the end of the street.

In slow motion, I turned my head and swallowed hard. There, in red, glowing fluorescent lights, was a sign that spelled out: *Freak Show.*

> "I came into a place mute of all light, which
> bellows as the sea does in a tempest, if by
> opposing winds 't is combated."
> — Dante's *Inferno*

FOURTEEN

Luckily for me, my new body was healthy and fit, otherwise I might have had a heart attack or a stroke because my heart was beating so quickly. I was intensely reluctant to even consider crossing the threshold of the amusement park, *Freak Show*, the first level of the Underground City.

Reluctant or not, however, we started forward and passed through the turnstiles which separated the amusement park from the rest of the city. I immediately focused on the brilliant lights of the numerous rides and attractions surrounding me. The garishly colorful lights almost blinded me against the backdrop of the pitch-black sky. What was even more uncanny was that we appeared to be the only ones here, as far as I could tell anyway. Even though the rides were lit up and some were even moving, there wasn't a soul in sight. It was as if every patron had simply disappeared.

"What does Dante say about this level?" I demanded of Bill, not daring to glance over my shoulder to look at him. Nope, instead I kept strict attention on everything in front and beside me.

"I don't frickin' know," Bill answered, sounding put out.

"Well, look!" I railed at him, not meaning to sound so angry, but I was beyond scared, and my fear was doing a number on my nerves. "You're the one with the book!"

I could hear Bill grunting as he reached into his back pocket. Seconds later, I recognized the sounds of him rustling through the pages of the *Inferno*. I yanked my foot forward when I felt him stepping on my heel and clipping me.

"Sorry," he muttered. "Not exactly easy to read and walk."

"It's okay, just get to the part about this level." I needed some sort of warning as to what we would encounter next, and even though Tallis was less than impressed with Dante's travel guide, I was desperate for the information.

"Chitty-chitty-bang-bang, we love you," Bill started singing beneath his breath as he continued rustling through the pages. "Oh yeah, chitty-chitty-bang-bang, where the fuck is level one?"

More sounds of pages turning as he fumbled through them. "Found it!" he called jubilantly before clearing his throat. "Um, Dante says this is the level of the lustful." He was quiet for a second or two. "Damn right, maybe we're gonna see some tig ol' bitties."

I rolled my eyes and shook my head at the same time that Tallis slightly turned his head in my direction. "What is he goin' on aboot?"

"Boobs. He's talking about boobs," I muttered, wishing I had the peace of mind to be thinking about male body parts instead of my impending fate.

"Why?" Tallis continued. I could see his furrowed brow in his profile.

"Because he's Bill," I answered, rather snidely. Tallis just shrugged and faced forward again, the demon skull grinning down at me while I tried to ignore it.

"This shit don't look very sexy to me," Bill grumbled.

"No, it doesn't," I agreed. Glancing over my right shoulder, I took in an awful carnie ride just beside me. It appeared to be a haunted house or something of that nature. At the entrance and, coincidentally, hanging just above me was a green monster prop. It had a skull for a head, and its bright, blinking lavender eyes were making me nauseous. Red and yellow lights danced in the background beyond it, their flashes enough to give someone a seizure. I moved my eyes from the green monster to another prop beside it—a skull with small horns protruding from its forehead and cheekbones, with a whole lot of blood just below its chin. Its infernal, yellow eyes glowed from their gaping eye sockets as its mouth chomped up and down.

Continuing forward, the sudden sounds of carnie music began to roll through hidden speakers, the music sounding tinny and old. A roller coaster revved to life beside us, and the sound of its cars skidding on the tracks was the perfect macabre soundtrack to my overwrought mind. My heart was pounding so fiercely, I felt winded and almost dizzy. Recordings of screams and shrieks pierced the black sky, lending the grisly paintings on the side of a fun house a more extreme level of realness. One painting was of a demon with shark teeth wielding a sword, and another was of a moon with a vampire face. The word *Thriller* lit up the entryway to the fun house, the white lights giving way to red, as if the letters themselves were bleeding.

"Well, this just killed anymore circuses for me," Bill ground out with a humph.

"This isn't a circus," I corrected him, my voice faltering. "It's an amusement park."

"Whatever it is, it's givin' me the fright shits."

"At least you can't be killed," I muttered, feeling sorry for myself again. I was the only one of us to whom this place could do permanent damage. Apparently, I also seemed to be the only one concerned about it.

Tallis continued down the asphalt, never turning his head in either direction. Instead, he paid strict attention to wherever we were going. And he wasn't just strolling either; he was walking at such a fast pace, Bill and I had a hard time keeping up with him. 'Course, given the fact that we were in the bowels of hell, I couldn't really blame him—getting in and getting out did seem to be the best plan.

Tallis took a right when the street dead-ended in front of us; and after another few paces, he stopped dead in his tracks. Before us was an area of the amusement park which appeared to be shut down. There were no lights in this section; just an unused roller coaster, an abandoned Ferris wheel, and a body piercing station that appeared to be long forgotten. A large, resin clown's face leaned against the wall. Its black-and-orange-striped hat nearly reached the shop's sign overhead. The clown's eyes were open, and aside from the thick layer of dust, it appeared to be in decently good condition.

Another large sign overhead read: *Welcome to Fun Town*. The letters and the bottom of the sign were also made to look like blood was dripping off them, but the paint was peeling and, as such, was less than convincing. No sooner did I drop my attention from the sign than the Ferris wheel suddenly came to life, erupting into a brilliant display of green and blue lights. The seats swung to and fro, as the wheel circled through the black air, even though no one was riding in them and no one was operating the ride.

"They know we are here," Tallis said softly. "Be ready."

At his words, a spike of fear shot straight down my spine. I didn't know just what I needed to be ready for but I clutched my sword as tightly as I could and stood stock still, right behind Tallis. I waited for him to take another step.

"Ah am on AfterLife Enterprises business, an' wilna be denied!" Tallis yelled, although I wasn't sure to whom he was yelling, since there was no one in sight. There was no response. But a slight whisper of wind suddenly kicked up and threw itself full-force against us. Then, from the shadows on our right, I heard the sound of labored, heavy breathing, like a smoker with asthma who'd just tried to run a marathon. Even though the breathing started as a faint sound, it got louder and louder until it seemed to fill my entire head. It was the definite sound of someone breathing, no, panting in my ears. I cranked my head to the left and right, but saw nothing, only darkness.

"The bladessssmith!" The serpent hiss came from right beside Tallis. In a split second, something materialized from thin air, within inches of him. To Tallis's credit, he didn't flinch. He didn't even move.

I screamed and jumped, I couldn't help it. As soon as I did, though, the creature turned its hideous face in my direction and I found myself staring into the soulless eyes of the most menacing, ferocious ... clown I'd ever seen. Its head was bald, with two tufts of fire-engine red hair sticking out of the sides right above its ears, like Bozo. It wore a white, Elizabethan collar that framed its hideous face. Frankenstein-like stitches attached its skin to its head. Its face was painted white, and its nose red, while black paint circled its eyes and Joker-like mouth. Blood oozed from the stitches that held its upper and lower eyelids open. It seemed to have a perpetual grimace, the corners of its lips pulling up all the way to its temples and revealing two sets of savage-looking, pointed teeth. Its eyes glowed a fierce red.

I gulped so hard, I was afraid I'd swallowed my tongue.

"And who isss thissss?" the thing asked while cocking its head to such a degree that a human neck would have broken. Its voice reminded me of a talking snake—it accentuated its esses.

"Nae one ye need ta bother yerself with, Ragur," Tallis answered in a steely voice, not even an ounce of fear in his tone. "We have come for the soul an' so we shall retrieve it."

But Ragur, the obscenely ugly clown, didn't hear Tallis or, more probably, just didn't care. Instead, it stared at me, its head arcing in each direction as it examined everything about me with an expression of complete fascination. I swallowed down my own utter revulsion and fear, refusing to drop my gaze from the blood-red of its eyes, refusing to notice how it smiled even more broadly to reveal its myriad razor-sharp teeth.

The only sound to fill the air was the creature's labored heavy breathing, the same sound that had been echoing through my head only moments earlier.

"Hey, Darth Breather, move along. Ain't nothin' more ta look at here," Bill announced from behind me.

"Angel," the clown hissed. It turned its head and glared at Bill right before it spat a loogie beside Bill's feet. Its spit, the color of lemonade and the consistency of Jell-O, immediately fizzed against the concrete, burning a hole into it.

"Son of a bitch!" Bill yelled as he hopped back like a frightened rabbit.

My heart climbed up into my throat as I clenched my sword tightly, wondering if I'd need to use it. A second or so later, Ragur simply stepped aside. Tallis, never one to waste time, proceeded forward, with Bill and me right behind him, like baby ducks in a row.

"What the hell was that messed up shit?" Bill roared. "Flippin' Stephen King just nearly took ma damn toes off!" he continued once we were out of earshot from Ragur. That is, of course, unless the clown also possessed incredible hearing—something I didn't want to find out. "Frickin' thing nearly turned me into handiman!" Jabbing me in the back, he asked, "You see that shit, nips?"

"Yes, Bill, I saw it."

"'Twas ah demon," Tallis answered nonchalantly as he reached into his sporran, and pulled out Bill's phone. He glanced down at it for a moment or two before putting it back, and saying, "This way."

We walked down a long and dark walkway, a thick black tarp obscuring the top of the walkway and falling down on either side of us, so that we were completely enclosed by it. I felt beyond claustrophobic. Upon reaching the end of the walkway, I realized we were on a boardwalk that led into a black and white tent, similar to what you'd see in a circus. The entrance to the tent was a simple flap, which was pulled to one side and fastened.

Tallis had to duck under the flap; Bill and I were right behind him. As soon as I entered the tent, I felt innumerable large, fat drops of rain as they shot down from the tent's canopy. The rain came down so hard, it was deafening and I had a hard time keeping my eyes open. I ran my sleeve across my face, clearing my bleary vision, only to have my eyes flooded with more rain.

"What is this place?" I had to shout against the torrential downpour. Wiping my arm across my eyes again, I tried to identify what I was looking at. A whirlwind of lights, circling round and round in a hurricane suddenly appeared in the center of the tent. Surrounding the hurricane was nothing but darkness—so dark that I couldn't even see the tent's walls. It was as if we'd walked inside the tent, only to end up outside during a severe storm.

The driving rain splashed right past the revolving lights which changed direction, whenever a gale of freezing wind pushed through them. The lights began to change color from a grayish-white to a blazing yellow-green, and then to an aqua blue. They moved so quickly, they were no more than a mere blur.

"Souls," Tallis answered as he plodded forward, forging a path against the wind, and taking us ever closer to the tempest in the center of the tent.

"Souls?" I repeated as I peered at the whirling lights more closely. "It just looks like a bunch of swirling lights."

"Aye, that's because they are movin' so quickly."

Tallis held his arm out against the blasting wind and continued pushing forward until we were only feet away from the vacillating lights.

"Are you going into it?" I screamed out against the blast of wind that nearly knocked me off my feet.

"Aye!" Tallis yelled back. Finding courage from somewhere, I dropped my face to shield it from the pouring rain. Then, with Bill at my heels, I entered the surging tempest. As soon as we were in it, the wind increased tenfold. I felt like any second would be my last before I was pulled off my feet and whipped into the maelstrom. The rain seemed less of a problem inside the wind tunnel, probably because the wind blew the rain right out. I took a deep breath and forced my face upward, ready to inspect my surroundings.

Before I could so much as blink, a face suddenly appeared in the circling wind. It was that of a woman who appeared to be screaming, even though no sound came from her mouth. I wasn't sure if that was because the wind swallowed her voice, or she simply didn't have one. Large and small holes appeared in her skin, as if the wind was blowing right through her face and tearing her skin apart. A split second later, she vanished back into the spinning lights.

"We must push through to the other side!" Tallis yelled out. Now that we were directly in the eye of the storm, it was easier to hear him. The wind and rain still raged, but they weren't as strong as when we were in the walls of the storm. Another face emerged from the circling lights; this one a man's. His face was easier to identify, more delineated. I could clearly see his open mouth, also mid-scream, even though he didn't make a sound either. He held his hands to his face, and I watched the skin of his hands eaten away by the wind.

"Holy crapanoly!" Bill roared out behind me. "Did you see that dude's hands?"

I didn't respond, but shielded my face against the wind as Tallis held his arm in front of him and forged his way through the blasting wind. I wondered why he didn't just use his shield but then figured maybe it would be more of a hindrance in the wind. I started forward again, prepared to fight my way through the other side of the hurricane in order to get beyond it. As soon as we entered the opposite wall of the hurricane of souls, I felt my hair blasted away from my face as an onslaught of freezing rain peppered my skin. The drops were so large and coming down so hard, I half wondered if we were being pelted with hail. I gripped my sword as hard as I could, afraid the gusts of wind might snatch it from me. I tried my best to stay a step behind Tallis, which proved progressively more difficult the further we went. The demon skull blew a few feet off his back but he must have done a good job tying it down because it never broke free.

You're almost there! I said to myself, wishing and hoping it was the truth. I couldn't really see anything because Tallis's body completely obstructed my view. The rain and wind that relentlessly attacked me from all sides made it difficult to keep my eyes open long enough to get a good idea of where we were.

I took another step forward and got blasted by a gust of wind that came from directly in front of me which was odd, considering Tallis was standing there and should have blocked its force. I tried to open my eyes, but found it impossible as long as the wind kept beating against me. I held my hands up to ward off the elements and tried to peek through my fingers, only to find no one shielding me at all.

"Tallis!" I screamed out, my heart dropping to my feet.

The lights on the wind continued to encircle me, and when I glanced behind me, to make sure Bill was still there, I was dumbfounded and petrified to find he wasn't.

"Bill!" I yelled, now terrified to find I was standing alone in the middle of the soul storm. The wind and the rain continued assaulting me as the lights of souls flew past my body. Every now and then, a face popped out of the storm in mid-scream, but again, made no sound.

"Tallis!" I repeated, feeling the bitter sting of rain on my face as I half wondered if maybe the rain was really my tears instead. I searched around, trying to find out if maybe Bill and Tallis had somehow gotten sucked up into the maelstrom. But the merciless assault of rain and wind prevented me from seeing anything. I could barely even open my eyes.

I suddenly felt a hand around my arm at the same time that I was yanked forward. I gasped and tried to pull away from it, not knowing who it was, or what was happening.

The wind continued blasting against my face with renewed intensity, as if trying to keep me within its confines. The hand on my arm tightened and pulled me even harder until I was yanked right out of the wind funnel. Finally managing to open my eyes, I found Tallis facing me impatiently, with a frown etched on his face.

"Didnae ye hear me?" he demanded, shaking his head with obvious disapproval.

"Hear you? You just disappeared!" I protested, glancing first at Tallis and then at Bill who stood beside him. "Both of you did! I thought you both got sucked up into the whirlwind!"

"Um, honey loaves, you were the one who pulled the Bermuda Triangle," Bill said, frowning at me. "Not us."

"Nevermind," Tallis interjected. "We need ta focus on findin' the soul." His expression was stern. "It should be here," he finished. By the way he was searching around himself, it looked like he had no idea where the missing soul was. He reached inside his sporran and produced Bill's phone, glancing down at it and shaking his head in what appeared to be confusion. Then he took stock of our surroundings again, shrugging before facing the hurricane of souls.

"You think our soul is in there?!" Bill asked, in a tone of disbelief, his eyes wide.

"Ah hope not," Tallis answered succinctly even though his lingering gaze on the hurricane suggested that he thought that was exactly where we'd find the missing soul.

"Talk about a needle in a haystack, yo!" Bill yelled, throwing his arms up in the air as he shook his head. "We'd have better luck tryin' ta find your sense of humor!"

"Looking for something?" The voice came from another clown who simply materialized in front of Tallis, just as the first one had. "Or should I say, looking for someone?" the thing smiled up at Tallis with an expression of absolute lunacy in its eyes.

This clown wasn't quite as frightening as Ragur, but was a close second. Its head was hairless, and completely white, its skin puckered in places. Seeing a wide arc of blue around its eyes, I couldn't tell if the blue was natural or painted. Its mouth was red, filled with yellowed human teeth and blood stained its chin. Its eyes were completely black, and the white surrounding the irises was severely bloodshot.

"Ye know why Ah am here, Kipor," Tallis shouted at the thing. The creature darted this way and that, around all of us, appearing and disappearing as if the air sucked it in and spat it out again.

"Of course I know," it replied in a voice that sounded very different to Ragur's. Instead of a constant hissing sound, this creature's voice kept echoing. "A misplaced soul, ah the tragedy!" It clapped its hands together before its eyes fell on me. When it moved a few steps closer, I had to force myself to hold my ground. Just like Ragur, this creature's face immediately took on an expression of complete captivation, as if having never seen a human before. It walked around me to inspect me from the other side. All the while, I gripped my sword and stared straight ahead.

"What being have you captured, bladesmith?" it asked, never pulling its eyes from me.

"Doona make this more trouble than it needs ta be," Tallis spat back, turning slightly so the clown could feast its eyes on the demon skull he wore on his back. At the sight of the skull, the creature backed up and seemed in less of a daze somehow. It studied the skull for a few moments, resting its hand beneath its chin before glancing up at Tallis with a frown.

"Betret, is it?" the creature asked. It showed no indication of being upset by the death of Betret or not.

"Aye," Tallis nodded. "He gave me trouble an' Ah doona think ye would want ta do the same."

The clown tsked and shook its head. "I would never think to give *you* trouble, bladesmith," it said as it laughed a horrible, tinny sound.

"Then do as Ah say," Tallis insisted.

The clown, in opposition to Tallis's demand, didn't do anything for a few seconds. Instead, it stared at Tallis, as if deciding whether or not to obey or give him a hard time. Finally it brought its hand forward and rotated it so its palm faced upward. It opened its hand, revealing a tiny glowing ball, maybe the size of a quarter, in its palm. The ball was a pure white and bounced around the clown's hand, looking like a Mexican jumping bean, only on fire.

Tallis immediately reached for the glowing ball, but the clown closed its fingers around it, pulling its hand out of Tallis's reach. Its smile would haunt my dreams for years to come.

"I have so enjoyed keeping her as my pet," the creature whispered. It looked down at its hand again, and opened its long, skinny, white fingers to observe the ball of light.

"Hand it over, now," Tallis ground out, his eyebrows knitting in the middle as his jaw tightened. He reached inside his sporran and produced what looked like a purple vial with a corked cap. He pulled the cork out of the vial and held the open end toward the clown. "Ah doona want ta fight ye, boot Ah will if Ah must."

The clown pouted as it brought its palm toward Tallis. When Tallis lowered the vial over the glowing orb, the thing eagerly moved into the vial. Tallis quickly recapped the vial and placed it directly into his sporran again. He glanced at me and motioned for me to stand behind him, which I did. Bill immediately fell into line behind me. We started forward, away from the hurricane of souls and toward the rear of the tent, the wall of which was now visible again.

"We miss you, bladesmith," the clown called out behind Tallis's retreating back. "You should visit us more often!"

I thought it a strange thing for the creature to say, but was even more floored that both clowns had not only recognized Tallis, but also knew the nature of his business, that he was a bladesmith. It was a level of intimacy I didn't imagine Tallis sharing with creatures of the Underground City...

"So was that glowing ball the soul?" I asked, once we emerged from the tent.

"Aye," Tallis answered dismissively.

"Amen to that!" Bill called out behind me. "Now we can get the hell outta this shithole!"

Looking around myself, I didn't know where we were. Although I could say we were definitely still in the amusement park, judging by the flickering neon lights of the various hideous attractions; but we sure hadn't come in this way. I could only hope that Tallis knew where he was going.

No sooner did the thought cross my mind than someone or something dropped from the ledge of a building right in front of us. She landed on her toes, and in the next instant, held the blade of her long sword at Tallis's throat. He stopped short and I nearly walked headlong into him, but caught myself just in time. Bill, on the other hand, walked straight into my butt.

"Frickin' walk blocker!" he yelled into my ear. "Don't just stop walkin' when I'm right behind you!" Any further arguments died on his tongue as soon as he realized we weren't alone.

"Tallis Black," the woman purred, the lilt in her voice a direct contradiction to the sword she held at Tallis's throat. "Bet you aren't too happy to see me."

In the reflection of the brilliant lights, I could just make out her features. She looked like she was in her late twenties, maybe. She was tall, probably my height of five feet eight inches, and appeared quite slender in her dark blue jeans and zipped up leather jacket. Her skin and hair were the same shade of dark chocolate, and her large, round eyes and full lips made her very pretty. Her lips parted into the semblance of a smile as she beheld Tallis. Even with the smile, I couldn't tell if she was happy to see him or not.

As for Tallis, I could only wonder what his reaction might be to having her sword parked precariously over his throat. I waited in heated anticipation for him to say or do something. When he chuckled and shook his head, I was more than a little surprised.

"Ah admit Ah am nae happy ta see ye, lass," he said with genuine amusement.

The woman's smile fell and she frowned instead, cocking a well-manicured eyebrow with obvious irritation. "Well, when you steal other people's belongings, it's best to lay low."

"Steal?" I heard myself ask out loud.

The woman turned her attention from Tallis to me and nodded. "That's right." Then she glanced back at Tallis. "You want to tell your friends the story? Or shall I?"

"Be mah guest," Tallis said, with the same lilt of amusement in his tone.

The woman nodded and faced me. "First off, introductions, I'm Sherita Eaton, and I'm also the unlucky SOB who fell victim to this jerk." She inclined her head in Tallis's direction.

"That isna fair," Tallis said, shaking his head and, apparently, finally standing up for himself. "We both happened ta be after the same soul. It could have happened ta anyone."

"No," Sherita snapped at him, shaking her head as her eyes boiled with anger. "I was on AfterLife Enterprises business, and it was my mission to rescue that soul! Furthermore, you knew it then just as you know it now." She took a breath and continued to glare at him. "You were just going after an easy win."

"You're a Retriever?" I asked, surprised.

Sherita nodded. "That I am and a damned good one."

"Ah can attest ta that," Tallis offered, still chuckling.

"Compliments aren't going to get you anywhere," Sherita said. She held her sword a bit higher so that it rested at the base of his chin. "You know what I want, Black."

Tallis said nothing, but reached inside his sporran and produced the vial with the glowing soul inside it, handing it to her.

"You're just going to give it to her?" I blurted out incredulously. Anger welled up inside me at the very thought that I was risking my own life in the bowels of this godforsaken place to save a soul that he'd just handed over to a stranger! It was bad enough that I'd allowed Tallis to take the credit for the mission!

"Aye, she's right. Ah owe her one."

Sherita held her palm out and Tallis dropped the vial into it. Snapping her hand back, she placed the vial in her jacket pocket, being extra careful to zip it up.

"Mah debt is paid," Tallis announced to her. She just nodded and removed her blade from his chin. In the same moment, Ragur the clown popped out from behind a nearby wall and threw himself on her.

> "... I swooned away as if I had been dying, and fell, even as a dead body falls."
> — Dante's *Inferno*

FIFTEEN

First, I screamed, then Bill screamed. That was all I remained conscious of for at least the time between two heartbeats. I suddenly snapped back into reality and watched Tallis hoist his blade above his head. He screamed something indecipherable before launching himself forward. First, he kicked the clown off Sherita, who crab-crawled backwards towards the wall. Although she gasped for air and the shocked expression of fear was still very much in her eyes, she didn't look too much the worse for wear.

"Are you all right?" I yelled to her.

Bringing her wide eyes to mine, she simply nodded. Clearly, she was still caught in the web of surprise. After shaking herself off, she glanced down at her body, as if taking stock to make sure she wasn't wounded. As far as I could see, she wasn't bleeding, so I assumed Ragur hadn't hurt her. A split second later, she was on her feet, standing alongside Tallis, her sword above her head.

Tallis and Ragur faced off, each waiting for the other to make the first move. Tallis's back was towards me so I couldn't see his expression, but Ragur wore an obscene smile. The blood from its stitches dripped into its mouth, making its grin all the more sinister. Ragur wasn't armed as far as weaponry, although it *was* armed with incredible speed and the ability to materialize and dematerialize at will. Tallis made the first move and wielded his blade at his opponent, but Ragur simply disappeared into the ether, only to reappear a few feet away.

Sherita took the opportunity to throw herself forward, thrusting her sword directly in front of her, where Ragur stood. She lost her grip on the sword, however, when it merely penetrated the air and, consequently, dropped into the dirt. The sound of Ragur's hissing laugh haunted my ears as the hideous clown materialized just five steps away. Sherita was quick to regain her balance and grabbed her sword, thrusting it forward again. But Ragur vanished just as quickly.

"Bastard!" she yelled out in frustration, looking at Tallis, her face filled with exasperation.

"Keep ah watch on him!" he reprimanded her.

She immediately faced forward again as Ragur materialized behind Tallis. The bladesmith was unnaturally swift on his feet as he spun and plunged his sword at Ragur. Again, only the air suffered the blow.

It soon became obvious that Ragur was doing this little game of cat and mouse on purpose—to tire Tallis and Sherita out. Once exhausted, they would be much less of a threat. It was a good strategy, but I guessed Tallis was already onto it. I mean, he *was* possessed by that warrior, Donald (or someone), right? So that had to mean he was gifted when it came to combat ... right?

Thinking it wouldn't do anyone any good for me to just stand on the sidelines and watch, I lifted my sword, along with my courage, and took a step forward.

"Oh, fuck to the hell's no! You aren't goin' out there!" Bill chided me as he gripped my collar, firmly yanking me backwards. "You die the second time around on my watch an' I'll prolly end up cleanin' toilets."

I frowned at him, saying nothing because it was more than obvious that I couldn't add much to the fight. I'd probably just end up getting in the way. So, instead, I stood by and watched Ragur continue its disappearing act while Sherita and Tallis tried to take the clown out. After another few seconds, during which time neither Tallis nor Sherita could get the upper hand, I felt my heart climb up into my throat.

What if one or both of them get injured or killed? Or worse, what if other creatures in this awful place get wind of this battle and come en masse, to fight us? The thought of Shade suddenly flashed into my mind and I had to consciously banish it.

"What if Tallis and Sherita don't win?" I whispered to Bill, never pulling my attention from the two in question. "What happens if Ragur wins?"

Bill's eyebrows reached for the night sky as he shrugged. "You better pray Conan and Conette win."

Gulping down the acidic taste of panic, I faced the three of them again. As Ragur pulled another invisibility stunt, Tallis took a few steps back and rested the blade of his sword on the dirt. Sherita immediately frowned at him, shrugging her shoulders in an enactment of "what the hell are you thinking?" His simple nod hinted that he had a plan. She exhaled a deep breath and shook her head, but the small smile at the ends of her lips intimated her trust in him. I could only hope her intentions were right on.

Sherita faced Ragur again, who materialized directly in front of her. As she heaved her sword and leveled the blade, the clown again dematerialized. Tallis, meanwhile, closed his eyes and dropped down to one knee. Gripping his sword with both hands, he seemed to be in some sort of trance. The seconds ticked by like hours as my heart pounded through me. I couldn't understand why Tallis would risk so much by closing his eyes. It just seemed like an open invitation for Ragur to attack him. Biting my lip, I suppressed the need to either yell at him, or throw myself into the fight. Instead, I merely watched. Tallis opened his eyes and reached over to his right side, pulling his sword back against his outer thigh. He immediately drove it forward, into thin air.

The sound of a grunt followed before a few flashes of what looked like lightning traveled up Tallis's sword. The flashes of lightning made a popping sound as they danced along the steel. Ragur appeared again, only this time at the end of Tallis's blade, the look of sheer surprise visible in its red eyes. Tallis stood up, lifting his foot and placing it against the clown's thigh. Using Ragur's body for leverage, he pulled his sword free. A black, oily goo bled from the enormous wound in Ragur's stomach as the awful creature fell backwards onto the ground. Then its body began to spasm, as if in the midst of a seizure.

Tallis approached the dying abomination, the expression on his face revealing nothing. Aside from the beads of sweat along his hairline, he didn't even look like he'd just been in mortal combat. Without a word, Tallis raised his sword above his head and narrowed his eyes on the clown. He swiftly sliced Ragur's neck, severing the clown's head from its body in one quick, clean stroke. A spray of inky, gooey blood issued from Ragur's headless corpse, which started to twitch. Ragur's head, meanwhile, rolled away from its body, its eyes still wide open with surprise. The debris on the ground got caught in its stitches and the sticky fresh blood at the corners of its mouth. The head came to a rest in front of Bill, who glared down at it.

"Snap!" he yelled at the head, doing some sort of little hop-jump thing before breaking into a reverse lunge, while thrusting his palm out. It was a move that I imagined was supposed to look like something from the martial arts. Losing his balance, however, he had to pull his leg forward again to narrowly avoid toppling over. With his hands on his hips, he stared down at Ragur's head. "How you like them apples, you ugly, motherfuc ..."

Ragur's mouth suddenly opened and exhaled a dying hiss. With an exceptionally shrill, girly scream, Bill doubled over on himself trying to get away from it. When he was far enough away from the repugnant thing that it could no longer be considered a threat, he turned his stricken expression to Tallis. "Dude! What the hell? Isn't it dead yet?"

Tallis crossed his arms against his chest, shaking his head while chuckling. I wasn't sure whether it was Bill's lack of coordination or his girl scream which Tallis found so amusing. "Aye, 'tis dead."

"Finally!" Bill exhaled, appearing annoyed. "Can we get the hell outta Dodge now, please?" he continued, shaking his head, running a beefy hand through his hair. "I've had enough of this crazy ass shit!" He yelled the last bit and reached for my hand to lead me around Ragur's head. He glanced down at it and sighed. "Frickin' clowns ... this shit's gonna start makin' me wet the bed again."

"Interesting friends you've got there, Black," Sherita said. Her eyebrows furrowed in the middle as she motioned to Bill.

"Aye, ah know," Tallis replied, smiling at her. When his eyes found mine, he smiled more broadly. Feeling fairly sure his response wasn't meant as a compliment, I just frowned at him.

The smile fell completely off his face a split second later, just as I felt an arm across my chest. I was yanked backwards so suddenly and quickly, all the air was emptied from my lungs. I faced Bill, who first gaped at me and then at whoever was holding me. The sickening scent of rotted meat suddenly turned my stomach as I felt a bony hand closing around my throat.

My heart pounded so intensely, it felt like a jackhammer behind my eyes. But the headache wasn't my biggest problem. Nope, the only thought to occupy my mind was whether or not I still held onto my sword. I couldn't look down, since whatever had me by the throat wouldn't allow it. Instead, I flexed both of my hands, and felt the welcome grip of my sword in my right one.

"An eye for an eye, bladesmith," Kipur, the other clown we'd encountered at the amusement park, yelled right next to my ear. Its words echoed so much, it sounded like it was at the bottom of a well. "A tooth for a tooth."

"Nae," Tallis said, shaking his head and taking a step forward. Kipur immediately tightened its hold on my neck, prohibiting Tallis from moving any closer. Tallis's eyes narrowed as he focused on the hideous creature, whose smell would have made me gag if its hand weren't constricting my throat so much I couldn't inhale. Its bony fingers felt like a chain wrapped around my neck.

"Ragur attacked us," Tallis continued, his expression completely unreadable. Was he nervous? Angry? Or relieved to be done with me? I couldn't tell. "We had naethin' ta do with it."

"Your word against his," Kipur snapped back, pointing to Ragur's head where it lay on the ground with its tongue hanging out of its mouth. "And, unfortunately for him, he's dead and can't defend himself."

"Don't go there, Kipur," Sherita said in an icy tone. "You know we're here on AfterLife Enterprises business and you don't want management looking into this, do you?"

Kipur didn't say anything for a second or two, but the frigidity of its skeletal fingers still threatened my neck. "I don't give a shit about management!" it suddenly burst out. "You attacked one of ours so we attack one of yours." Kipur thrust me forward a few steps and I could feel its other bony hand running through my hair.

"You hurt one hair on her head, you fugly ass bitch, and I'll ..." Bill started, but Kipur's mocking laugh interrupted him.

"You'll do what, angel?" Kipur demanded, snickering again. Apparently, the clown was well educated as to Bill's shortcomings when it came to protecting me in the Underground City.

"You'll have ta answer ta me," Tallis finished for Bill. With his arms crossed against his chest and his sword resting against his thigh, the Scotsman appeared quite intimidating. The deadly look in his eyes, though, took him far beyond intimidating, more like completely terrifying. For as scary as

Ragur and Kipur were in their horrific goriness, Tallis was easily more daunting.

"Answering to you is nothing new, bladesmith!" Kipur spat out as I wondered what the comment meant. The clown's grip around my neck tightened again, and it started pulling its fingers through my hair, yanking out the tangles until the strands of hair broke free and my scalp stung.

"Ah am losin' mah patience," Tallis ground out.

"I've weighed my options, bladesmith, and I've decided I'd rather take my chances with management …" The creature paused for a moment or two. I could tell it was examining me, studying me. "So I can dig my fingernails into her throat and rip out her windpipe."

A scream began growing inside me at the same time as Kipur's sharp fingernails threatened to pierce my skin. A split second later, Tallis's eyes burned into mine, somehow flooding me with the urge to loosen the grip on my sword. I released it slightly, until I was only holding it with my fingertips. Then I felt the sword shifting beneath me, moving, although I wasn't the one maneuvering it.

That was when I understood. Looking up at Tallis, I found his eyes fixed on my sword. I felt the sword rise maybe a foot or so, while my hand simply rested on it. In a flash, it buried itself into Kipur's toes. With a bellow, the clown immediately released me. I darted a few steps away from the loathsome creature as Tallis yelled: "Dinnae let go!"

I figured he must have meant not to let go of my sword. I gripped the hilt more firmly and felt my sword freeing itself from Kipur's toes. Raising itself up into the air, the sword pulled my arm along with it. In a second, it slashed Kipur from its right shoulder to the left of its waist. Black goo, just like what came out of Ragur, rained down on top of my sword and me.

In an instant, Tallis was beside me, wielding his sword against Kipur's neck, severing the clown's head in the same way as Ragur's. Kipur's body collapsed into a solid heap.

There was so much black blood, it looked as if we were standing in the midst of an oil spill. I felt myself panting as my sword dropped onto the ground. Whatever magic possessed it for that instant was now gone. I picked my sword up and held it close to me, realizing it had just saved my life.

No, Tallis saved your life.

I looked up into Tallis's eyes, only to find they were already leveled on me.

"Collect the heads," he called from the corner of his mouth, his eyes still firmly planted on mine. Whether he addressed Bill or Sherita, I had no clue. He continued to hold my gaze, but said nothing.

"I think I just shat myself, yoze!" Bill called out from behind me.

***

We left the Underground City without further ado. The watchers continued walking this way and that, some studying us while others showed less interest. It was pretty safe to say that the "master" would soon find out he was down two employees.

Once we passed the double gates to the city and were deeply ensconced in the skeleton-tree forest, I figured it was safe to talk. "What's going to happen with Ragur and Kipur?" I asked Tallis, who walked in front of Bill and me, with Sherita at his side.

"Ah doona know." He didn't slow his pace, but answered over his shoulder.

"Well, isn't this 'master' you were talking about going to find out that Ragur and Kipur are dead?" I persisted.

"Aye."

Sherita glanced back at me. "The master of the Underground City's name is Alaire. He will take it up with AfterLife Enterprises, so don't be surprised if they contact you. They'll want to write everything up, get your side of the story … you know how it goes."

"Like filing an accident report?" I asked.

Bill chuckled. "Yeah, something like: Hiya, Skeletor, so on our trip to the Underground City, which coincidentally, is a great vacation spot—I'd like to raise my kids there—Conan accidentally dismembered two ugly-as-fuck clowns. But, wait, it gets better! Then he decided to keep their heads for souvenirs."

Sherita laughed at the same time that she nodded with a sigh. "Yep, something like that."

"Will you get into trouble, Tallis?" I asked, suddenly concerned that maybe AfterLife Enterprises wouldn't take kindly to the situation.

Tallis shook his head. "Ah doona care."

Silence descended again as we made our way through the burnt-out forest. I walked directly behind Tallis, still trying to ignore the demon skull smiling down at me. Instead, I rested my gaze on Sherita's tall, willow-like form. I didn't really know what to make of her. It was obvious that Tallis and she had some sort of relationship. I didn't know that I would have called it a friendship, but as we continued to work our way through the forest, they seemed rather chummy.

After walking another three hours or so, my legs, calves and butt well beyond sore, we made camp in a large clearing. Tallis busily removed his backpack and shield. He'd put the heads of Ragur and Kipur inside the pack and now pulled them out, carefully placing one on the west side of our clearing, and one on the east. Then he set the grinning demon skull at the southernmost point.

"Is this your idea of decorating, Conan?" Bill asked, while eyeing the heads with obvious unease. "'Cause if it is, it's pretty much totally messed up. I mean, none of us wants to stare at either of those clown's mugs, especially that one." Frowning, he pointed at Ragur's head, the tongue of which still hung limply from its mouth.

Leveling a raised brow at Bill, Tallis shook his head. "Protection," he answered simply.

"What is it with you?" Bill continued, throwing his hands into the air as if in exasperation. "Does it cost you money every time you say a word or something?"

Sherita laughed and faced Bill from where she collected kindling. "The bladesmith is a man of very few words."

"You're tellin' me, shit," Bill muttered. "'Course, whenever he says anything more than 'aye' or 'nae,' I can't flippin' understand him anyway, so maybe it's a good thing."

"There is that," Sherita agreed with an armful of kindling that she set beside me. Tallis pulled out my fireboard from his pack and handed it to me. I hadn't even realized he'd kept it, but was grateful since we wouldn't have to make another one. I tried to ignore the black stains on one side of the board, which had to be from one or both of the bloody heads.

"Okay, so what's a hot babe like you doin' with Mr. I Have A Shitty Personality, anyway?" Bill demanded as he approached Sherita and watched her collect branches.

"If you're going to pick up on me, the least you can do is help," she said, motioning to the mound of branches she'd collected while hiding a little smirk.

"Oh, sorry," Bill said, almost sputtering. He bent down to retrieve a nearby stick that looked as if it had rolled away from her pile. He replaced it on the top of the pile before taking a seat, and making cow eyes at Sherita as she continued her task. "So tell me about you and Conan," he continued.

"Thanks for the generous contribution," she said, frowning at the small branch he'd placed on top of her pile.

"Don't mention it," Bill said, apparently unaware of her sarcasm.

When Sherita glanced at me, I just shrugged. Then she looked over at Tallis, who pretended like he wasn't paying any attention to our conversation. Who knew? Maybe he wasn't.

"Black and I go way back," she started. She dropped the last branch on top of another pile beside me.

"Thanks," I said. "That's enough."

She nodded, wiping the dirt and dust off her hands and onto her jeans before facing Bill again. "I met 'Conan' when I started working as a Retriever, years ago."

"How long have you been a Retriever?" I asked, taking a break from my fire-making duties.

She shrugged. "I think it's probably going on twelve years now."

"How did you become one?" I continued, so relieved to finally have found someone who might shed some light on my new career path.

"I was killed in combat," she started.

"Combat?" Bill repeated, sidling closer to her as she frowned at him. He was so ridiculously obvious! Yep, he and I would definitely have a conversation once we were safely back in Edinburgh. Bill needed schooling on how to treat a woman.

"I was a Marine," she continued. "I was deployed to Afghanistan and happened to be in the wrong place at the wrong time when our tank blew." She sighed as she remembered the particulars. "So, I died; and the next thing I knew, I was sitting in an office, facing Jason Streethorn." She glanced at me and shrugged. "That was my introduction to AfterLife Enterprises."

"So you met Jason too?" I asked, surprised.

"We all get ta meet the arch douche," Bill interrupted, no doubt trying to impress Sherita with his lingo, as he called it.

"All Retrievers do," she answered me. "He's the only one who decides whether or not to give us the option of becoming Retrievers."

I thought about asking her if she chose a new body and all that stuff, but then decided maybe I shouldn't. It could have been that she was touchy about that sort of thing. For myself, I still hadn't really accepted the body I'd chosen. Even though I was becoming more comfortable with the new me as the days went by, 'I' still felt foreign. It was an incredible relief, though, to discover that Sherita, too, had undergone something very similar to what happened to me, and that I wasn't alone. I could only wonder at what she used to look like.

"So why did Jason offer you the chance to become a Retriever?" Sherita asked me. It was plainly clear she saw a huge disconnect somewhere because I obviously couldn't fight.

"Because I wasn't supposed to die when I did," I said, careful not to glance at Bill. I figured I should let bygones be bygones and forgive him for the past. There was really no use harping on it. Plus, I had to admit it seemed like Bill was really trying to do a better job of guarding me now.

Forgiveness is the virtue of the brave, I repeated Gandhi's words to myself, pleased that I could find virtue and bravery in myself.

"So to Jason, offering you the chance to become a Retriever was just a consolation prize?" Sherita asked, her eyebrows raised.

"I guess so," I answered with a shrug.

"Hmm, doesn't sound like much of a prize to me," Sherita continued, shaking her head. "Sometimes I think I should have just let things happen the way they did." I figured that meant she should have been allowed to die. I didn't really know what to say to that so I didn't say anything at all.

***

After another two hours, Sherita and Tallis managed to kill something in the forest. Not only did I not know the species of said kill, I also didn't want to find out. We barbequed it over the open flame of the fire I'd built. After everyone ate their fill, Tallis announced we should get some sleep. He took it upon himself to assume the role of first watch.

We all huddled around the fire for a few minutes until Bill's loud snoring sounded through the night sky. I sighed and rolled from my right side to my left, still uncomfortable. I couldn't fall asleep even though I was well beyond exhausted. I looked at Sherita, to find her in a fetal position, facing the fire with her hands neatly folded beneath her cheek. She appeared to be happily in repose. I rolled onto my back and sighed again.

"Lass, ye are makin' me uneasy," Tallis said in a soft voice.

I sat up and huffed out in frustration. "I just can't sleep."

He nodded as if he weren't surprised. "So talk ta me."

I was taken aback and raised my eyebrows in disbelief. "Um, what do you want to talk about?"

Tallis smiled at me; why? I wasn't sure. "Kipur gave ye ah scare?"

I nodded, not wanting to remember exactly how close I came to having my windpipe ripped out. "Yeah, you could say that." I took a deep breath when something crossed my mind. "My sword," I started.

"Aye?"

"It moved on its own like you … like you were controlling it."

He nodded smugly. "Aye, Ah was."

"Because it had your blood on it?"

He laughed. "Ye are quick, lass, Ah'll give ye that."

"Tallis, thank you," I said immediately. I knew full well that my gratitude was meaningless to him, but I had to let him understand how appreciative I was all the same. "Without you, I would have died."

The smile dropped off his lips, but he held my gaze. "You're welcome, Besom."

"I will pay you the money I owe you as soon as I get back to my apartment in Edinburgh," I continued. I certainly didn't want him to think I'd skip out on my promises. "I still need to figure out the particulars with my bank account."

"Ah am nae in ah rush, lass," he said. "Take yer time."

"One other thing," I started, watching his lips curl up with a slight smile. Suddenly, it struck me that in the past few days, he'd smiled way more than he had in the first few days of our acquaintance. Could it be that Bill and I were growing on him?

"Aye?"

"Um, could you maybe give me the final tally of what I owe you?" I asked with a laugh. "I sort of lost track."

He nodded, chuckling. "Aye, if ye give me yer address, Ah'll send ye an invoice."

I studied him for a second or two before I realized he was joking. "Good one."

"... silent is the wind, as it is now."
— Dante's *Inferno*

SIXTEEN
TWO WEEKS LATER

"What about these, Lil?" Bill asked. He pulled out two pillows from a cardboard box, one of many boxes that had just been delivered. Both the pillows were covered with plastic wrap. I'd ordered the pillows as well as the contents of my entire house from a nearby furniture store and today happened to be the delivery day.

"Um, both of those go on the couch," I said, admiring the floral pattern on the brown pillows.

"'Kay," Bill said, throwing them onto the sofa. Opening the next box, he fished inside, extracting four sepia-toned prints of flowers, framed in off-white frames. "What about this super girlie ass shit?"

I laughed, pointing to the bathroom just off the master bedroom, my bedroom. "Those go over the tub, but we'll have to hang them later. You can just lean them against the wall for now." I watched him nod and disappear into the bathroom, re-emerging empty-handed.

"They kinda go with the brown wall we painted," he commented. "Excuse me, the brown wall *I* painted."

"You mean the brown wall *you* painted and the same brown wall *I* repainted?"

Bill grinned from ear to ear, looking like a little kid. "Yep, that one!"

We'd spent the entire last week painting the inside of the apartment, no easy feat considering it was a sprawling two-bedroom, two-bathroom, plus an office. And when I say sprawling, I mean sprawling! The living room alone was bigger than my entire apartment back in Colorado Springs. And the U-shaped kitchen was large enough to encompass an extra wide island. Bill and I painted most of the rooms in earth tones, although Bill did insist we paint the guest bedroom bright red. He had a vested interest in it.

"Where the hell is all the shit I ordered?" Bill asked impatiently, throwing his arms up into the air in disappointment. He'd just unpacked another box that contained two wheat-colored chairs I'd selected for the area at the foot of my bed, just in front of the windows that overlooked the meadows below.

"Just keep unpacking," I answered, glancing around at the myriad boxes now littering the entire living room and kitchen. "Your stuff is in there somewhere."

Yes, Bill was moving in. Even though we only broached the subject a few weeks ago, during our first meeting, and both of us abhorred the idea at the time, now the comfort of having a roommate was growing on me. After returning from the Underground City, Bill and I had to stay in a hotel while awaiting the delivery of our new furniture. During our entire stay at the hotel, I was tormented by nightmares. At the time, I realized the last thing I wanted, much less needed, was to live alone. I asked Bill what he thought about becoming roomies ... at least temporarily, and his immediate consent gave me a sneaking suspicion that I wasn't the only one suffering night terrors.

So, here we were, organizing our new home and both genuinely grateful for the other's company.

"Dude, the neighbor's dog left another yard bomb on our side," Bill complained as he peered through the living room window at our plot of garden in the backyard.

"Bill, we have more important things to worry about," I reprimanded him. "Like unpacking all of this stuff. Can you empty that box right there?" I asked, pointing to a large one beside him.

He sighed, using a box cutter to open it and exhaled much more dramatically when the open box revealed a wooden entertainment center I'd ordered for my bedroom. "Seriously, Lil, I think they forgot all my shit!"

I sighed and nodded. "Maybe you're right. Maybe they sold it to the next customer who walked in, just to tick you off."

Bill narrowed his eyes and began chewing on his lower lip. "You think?" he asked me seriously.

I broke into a laugh and shook my head, busying myself with putting the sheets I'd just unpacked on the table beside me, where I was piling the rest of the bedroom stuff so I could make one trip of it.

Shifting another big box next to him, Bill glanced down at his bicep and smiled at it, flexing a few times before turning to show me. "Check this out, Angel Billy's got some mean ol' biceps goin'."

"Nice, Bill," I answered absentmindedly. Truth be told, I couldn't see even the hint of a bicep muscle in his fleshy arm.

"'Course, maybe it's not from lifting all this shit," he continued, more to himself than me, as he frowned at his arm. "Could just be masturbatone."

"God, Bill!" I exclaimed, throwing my hands on my hips as I gave him an irritated expression. "Why do you have to be so gross!"

"Okay, okay ... Sheesh." He held his hands up in surrender. "Excuse the hell outta me for bein' born." Then he rubbed his stomach as it noisily growled. "I gotta eat somethin'. How 'bout I go and pick us up some takeout?"

I nodded, considering it would get him out of my hair for a little while so I could actually concentrate on unloading all the boxes. "Sounds good."

"'Kay, butter nipples," Bill said as he started for the door. Upon exiting, he reached over to turn on the radio-CD player that we'd set up over an hour ago. "I'll bee bock," he finished in a terrible rendition of Arnold Schwarzenegger, before opening and closing the door behind him.

"I Love It" by Icona Pop filled my living room and I found myself immediately swaying to the beat as I pulled a full-length mirror out of its cardboard box, accidentally spilling Styrofoam peanuts all over the floor. I leaned the mirror against the wall and caught my reflection.

I couldn't help my smile as I beheld the beautiful image staring back at me. Dressed in hip-hugger jeans and a white singlet, my body was everything I ever wished my old one could have been. And even though my dark red hair was pulled up into an untidy ponytail, my face was in a word—lovely.

"I'm beautiful," I whispered to my reflection as I ran my hands down my cheeks, staring at the girl looking back at me. Two words I'd never dared say before, and two words which felt amazing to say.

I don't care! I love it! Hearing the words spilling out of the radio, I was suddenly overcome with absolute happiness. There was just so much to be grateful for—surviving the Underground City, moving into this beautiful apartment, Bill … yes, I had to admit I was thankful for my basically incompetent guardian angel. Bill just had a way about him that allowed me to forget all my worries and concerns whenever I was around him.

Feeling a burst of joy light up within me, I laughed out loud and jumped up and down to the beat of the music, swaying my hips as I held up my fist, using it as a microphone to sing along.

"I'm beautiful!" I said again, and then yelled it a third time. "No, I'm fucking beautiful!" I sang out, enjoying the feel of the word "fuck" as it fell off my tongue.

"That's right!" Bill's voice sounded from behind me. I turned to smile at him, feeling only slightly embarrassed that he'd caught me lauding myself so obviously.

Bill, however, barely noticed my embarrassment, if he did at all. He was already too busy doing what looked like the twist while singing: "Who da bomb?" Then he pointed dramatically at me. "You da bomb!" He started doing extremely suggestive pelvic thrusts and singing at the top of his lungs: "I don't care!" Then he added to the song, mimicking the same melody: "I forgot my wallet on the counter in the kitchen so I couldn't get us no food, but I don't care! I love it!" Dancing his way over to the counter, he put his wallet into his pocket before dancing his way back over to me.

Reaching for my hands, he twirled me around a few times until I started to get dizzy. Then, holding my hands up over my head, we both continued to dance terribly. I jumped up and down while Bill did some pathetically strange grinding move, and both of us sang off-key to the music.

"Hello?" I heard Tallis's loud baritone at the same time that a sharp knock sounded against the wall.

I stopped jumping immediately and felt a wash of hot embarrassment pass through me. Glancing over, I realized Bill had left the door open. Now, the bladesmith stood in the doorway, staring at both of us with an expression of amusement and surprise in his beautiful midnight gaze.

"T ... Tallis?" I asked, being caught totally unawares and not really knowing what else to say. I hadn't heard from Tallis since we'd left him at his cabin in the Haunted Wood over two weeks ago. Sherita had traveled with us for the first two days of our voyage through the skeleton-tree forest, before she'd made her exit through a portal in one of the clearings. She'd returned back to Washington DC with the soul Tallis had retrieved. I still wasn't sure how I felt about the whole Tallis-willingly-allowing-Sherita-to-take-the-soul thing but figuring the credit wasn't mine to collect anyway, I chalked the whole thing up to a learning experience.

As to Tallis, I'd expected to receive a letter from him, itemizing the expenses I owed him (I had, after all, given him my address), but I definitely never thought he'd make a personal appearance.

"Ah hope Ah'm nae interrupting," he continued, glancing around the apartment with interest. He nodded a few times, as if he approved of the place.

My voice totally failed me because seeing Tallis Black standing in the doorway of my apartment, dressed in dark blue jeans and a dark black sweater, was the last thing I anticipated. Aside from his immense height and the scar that bisected his face, he looked ... normal. Well, he looked hot, if I wanted to be honest with myself.

"No, no, you're not interrupting," I said as I walked across the room and straight into a box, the corner of which imprinted itself into my knee. I wasn't sure which was worse—the intense humiliation or the stabbing pain shooting straight up my thigh.

"Smooth, Lil," Bill said and laughed.

"Are ye okay?" Tallis asked, obviously trying to hide a smile behind his expression of compassion.

"I'm fine," I answered hastily and turned off the radio before smoothing my hands down the front of my jeans nervously. After trying to discourage myself from thinking about Tallis Black for the last two weeks, I was nothing less than stunned to find him standing on my doorstep. I half wondered if maybe I was just dreaming the whole thing.

Bill started for the door, frowning at Tallis as he asked me, "Is Conan staying for dinner?"

I gave Tallis a questioning expression, answering, "Um, I don't know?" Then the reason why Tallis had come in the first place suddenly occurred to me and I felt stupid for imagining it might have been anything else. "Oh, you came to collect the money I owe you." I couldn't hide the disappointment in my tone.

But Tallis shook his head. "Nae." He quickly glanced at Bill before returning his attention to me. "If ye dinnae mind, Ah would like ta join ye for supper."

"Um, yeah, sure," I stammered, unable to hide my smile. "I mean, under the circumstances, it's the least we can do."

"What the fuck you wanna eat?" Bill grumbled, addressing Tallis with raised brows as if to infer he had places to go and food to order.

"Whatever the lass is havin'."

"Whatevs," Bill said as he started for the door. Then, thinking better of it, he leaned back in as he said to me, "Lil, cover your virgin ears."

"What?" I asked with a frown. But his attention was already on Tallis.

"Just 'cause I'm playin' errand boy, don't think you're gonna have Conan's sexfest 2013 with nerdlet, namsay?"

Tallis shook his head, chuckling. "Aye, naamsay."

"No, dude," Bill said, shaking his head in dramatic exasperation. "You don't say 'namsay' ta me. You say, 'Yeah, I,' meaning you, 'namsay.' Otherwise, it's like you just said: Yeah, know what I'm saying?" He nodded and immediately shook his head. "Yeah, no. See? Dude, that makes like zero sense!"

"Bill," I warned him, getting annoyed at his long-winded explanation that was more confusing than it was enlightening. Then I turned my attention to Tallis. "Um, can I ask why you're here now?"

Tallis just shrugged like the answer should be obvious. "Did ye forget yer trainin'?"

"Training?" I repeated, clearly at a loss.

Tallis nodded, offering me a boyish smile. "Och aye, ye said yerself ye werenae fit ta travel inta the Oonderground." Then he paused, his eyebrows raised. "How were ye plannin' on preparin' for the next time?"

I shook my head since I had no answer.

"Good thing Ah was thinkin' aboot it for ye," he finished with a little chuckle.

"Hey, Conan," Bill started, his eyebrows meeting in the middle of his forehead as if he were in deep, meditative thought. "About our next trip to the Underground, I was thinkin' …"

Tallis eyed me quickly with a drawn brow before facing Bill again with an entertained grin. "Aye?"

"There're a few items we're gonna need before we willingly go back down ta that shithole."

"Such as?"

Bill took a deep breath and then flicked up his chubby index finger. "First, we need at least a week's worth of frozen burritos, so we don't have ta eat anymore o' that nasty ass shit you catch. Second ..." And his middle finger joined his index finger. "I can't deal with all that walking and materializing so much; makes me a tired SOB, so I'm gonna need some sort of motorized wheelchair like a Rascal—something with like, four-wheel drive though, so it can handle that scary ass forest. Third ... we need Ipods, dude! Then we can rock out and avoid boregasms ..." His voice trailed off as he observed the ceiling, trying to remember the rest of his list. "Oh, yeah, I could also seriously use a Conan translator, 'cause half the time, I can't understand a fucking word you say. And the Conan translator needs ta be a super hot chick. I ain't picky about age but she's gotta be a freeboober ..."

"A what?" I asked.

"No over the shoulder boulder holder," Bill informed me before turning his attention back to Tallis. "Speaking ah hot ladies, the last thing I could seriously use is the phone number of that naughty little Sherita number."

"Naughty?" I asked, frowning at Bill as I wondered what alternate universe he lived in.

"'Tis all?" Tallis asked, shaking his head with a raised brow expression and a healthy smile.

"Yeah, for now, give me a little more time, and I'm sure I can come up with some other stuff," Bill finished.

I couldn't help laughing as I looked first at Bill and then at Tallis. I suddenly felt extremely lucky to call them both my friends. Yes, my relationship with each one was quite odd, at the very least, but of one thing I was sure ... I was exceedingly fortunate that Bill and Tallis had entered my life.

Walking with a friend in the dark is better than walking alone in the light, I said to myself, remembering Helen Keller's famous quote.

Yep, Helen, you definitely got that one right.

To Be Continued...

Also Available From HP Mallory:

FIRE BURN AND CAULDRON BUBBLE

HP MALLORY

ONE

It's not every day you see a ghost.

On this particular day, I'd been minding my own business, tidying up the shop for the night while listening to *Girls Just Wanna Have Fun* (guilty as charged). It was late—maybe 9:00 p.m. A light bulb had burnt out in my tarot reading room a few days ago, and I still hadn't changed it. I have a tendency to overlook the menial details of life. Now, a small red bulb fought against the otherwise pitch darkness of the room, lending it a certain macabre feel.

In search of a replacement bulb, I attempted to sort through my "if it doesn't have a home, put it in here" box when I heard the front door open. Odd—I could've sworn I'd locked it.

"We're closed," I yelled.

I didn't hear the door closing, so I put Cyndi Lauper on mute and strolled out to inquire. The streetlamps reflected through the shop windows, the glare so intense, I had to remind myself they were just lights and not some alien spacecraft come to whisk me away.

The room was empty.

Considering the possibility that someone might be hiding, I swallowed the dread climbing up my throat. Glancing around, I searched for something to protect myself with in case said breaker-and-enterer decided to attack. My eyes rested on a solitary broom standing in the corner of the Spartan room. The broom was maybe two steps from me. That might not sound like much, but my fear had me by the ankles and wouldn't let go.

Jolie, get the damned broom.

Thank God for that little internal voice of sensibility that always seems to visit at just the right time.

Freeing my feet from the fear tar, I grabbed the broom and neared my desk. It was a good place for someone to hide—well, really, the only place to hide. When it comes to furnishings, I'm a minimalist.

I jammed the broom under the desk and swept vigorously.

Nothing. The hairs on my neck stood to attention as a shiver of unease coursed through me. I couldn't shake the feeling and after deciding no one was in the room, I persuaded myself it must've been kids. But kids or not, I would've heard the door close.

I didn't discard the broom.

Like a breath from the arctic, a chill crept up the back of my neck.

I glanced up and there he was, floating a foot or so above me. Stunned, I took a step back, my heart beating like a frantic bird in a small cage.

"Holy crap."

The ghost drifted toward me until he and I were eye level. My mind was such a muddle, I wasn't sure if I wanted to run or bat at him with the broom. Fear cemented me in place, and I did neither, just stood gaping at him.

Thinking the Mexican standoff couldn't last forever, I replayed every fact I'd ever learned about ghosts: they have unfinished business, they're stuck on a different plane of existence, they're here to tell us something, and most importantly, they're just energy.

Energy couldn't hurt me.

My heartbeat started regulating, and I returned my gaze to the ectoplasm before me. There was no emotion on his face; he just watched me as if waiting for me to come to my senses.

"Hello," I said, thinking how stupid I sounded—treating him like every Tom, Dick, or Harry who ventured through my door. Then I felt stupid that I felt stupid—what was wrong with greeting a ghost? Even the dead deserve standard propriety.

He wavered a bit, as if someone had turned a blow dryer on him, but didn't say anything. He was young, maybe

FIRE BURN AND CAULDRON BUBBLE
HP MALLORY

in his twenties. His double-breasted suit looked like it was right out of *The Untouchables*, from the 1930s if I had to guess.

His hair was on the blond side, sort of an ash blond. It was hard to tell because he was standing, er floating, in front of a wooden door that showed through him. Wooden door or not, his face was broad and he had a crooked nose—maybe it'd been broken in a fight. He was a good-looking ghost as ghosts go.

"Can you speak?" I asked, still in disbelief that I was attempting to converse with the dead. Well, I'd never thought I could, and I guess the day had come to prove me wrong. Still he said nothing, so I decided to continue my line of questioning.

"Do you have a message from someone?"

He shook his head. "No."

His voice sounded like someone talking underwater.

Hmm. Well, I imagined he wasn't here to get his future told—seeing as how he didn't have a future. Maybe he was passing through? Going toward the light? Come to haunt my shop?

"Are you on your way somewhere?" I had so many questions for this spirit but didn't know where to start, so all the stupid ones came out first.

"I was sent here," he managed, and in his ghostly way, I think he smiled. Yeah, not a bad looking ghost.

"Who sent you?" It seemed the logical thing to ask.

He said nothing and like that, vanished, leaving me to wonder if I'd had something bad to eat at lunch.

Indigestion can be a bitch.

~

"So no more encounters?" Christa, my best friend and only employee, asked while leaning against the desk in our front office.

FIRE BURN AND CAULDRON BUBBLE

HP MALLORY

I shook my head and pooled into a chair by the door. "Maybe if you hadn't left early to go on your date, I wouldn't have had a visit at all."

"Well, one of us needs to be dating," she said, knowing full well I hadn't had any dates for the past six months. An image of my last date fell into my head like a bomb. Let's just say I'd never try the Internet dating route again. It wasn't that the guy had been bad looking—he'd looked like his photo, but what I hadn't been betting on was that he'd get wasted and proceed to tell me how he was separated from his wife and had three kids. Not even divorced! Yeah, that hadn't been on his *match.com* profile.

"Let's not get into this again ..."

"Jolie, you need to get out. You're almost thirty ..."

"Two years from it, thank you very much."

"Whatever ... you're going to end up old and alone. You're way too pretty, and you have such a great personality, you can't end up like that. Don't let one bad date ruin it." Her voice reached a crescendo. Christa has a tendency towards the dramatic.

"I've had a string of bad dates, Chris." I didn't know what else to say—I was terminally single. It came down to the fact that I'd rather spend time with my cat or Christa rather than face another stream of losers.

As for being attractive, Christa insisted I was pretty, but I wasn't convinced. It's one thing when your best friend says you're pretty, but it's entirely different when a man says it.

And I couldn't remember the last time a man had said it.

I caught my reflection in the glass of the desk and studied myself while Christa rambled on about all the reasons I should be dating. I supposed my face was pleasant enough—a pert nose, cornflower blue eyes and plump lips. A spattering of freckles across the bridge of my nose interrupts an otherwise pale landscape of skin, and my shoulder length blond hair always finds itself drawn into a ponytail.

Head-turning doubtful, girl-next-door probable.

As for Christa, she doesn't look like me at all. For one thing, she's pretty tall and leggy, about five-eight, and four inches taller than I am. She has dark hair the color of mahogany, green eyes, and pinkish cheeks. She's classically pretty—like cameo pretty. She's rail skinny and has no boobs. I have a tendency to gain weight if I eat too much, I have a definite butt, and the twins are pretty ample as well. Maybe that made me sound like I'm fat—I'm not fat, but I could stand to lose five pounds.

"Are you even listening to me?" Christa asked.

Shaking my head, I entered the reading room, thinking I'd left my glasses there.

I heard the door open.

"Well, hello to you," Christa said in a high-pitched, sickening-sweet and non-Christa voice.

"Afternoon." The deep timbre of his voice echoed through the room, my ears mistaking his baritone for music.

"I'm here for a reading, but I don't have an appointment ..."

"Oh, that's cool," Christa interrupted and from the saccharin tone of her voice, it was pretty apparent this guy had to be eye candy.

Giving up on finding my reading glasses, I headed out in order to introduce myself to our stranger. Upon seeing him, I couldn't contain the gasp that escaped my throat. It wasn't his Greek God, Sean-Connery-would-be-envious good looks that grabbed me first or his considerable height.

It was his aura.

I've been able to see auras since before I can remember, but I'd never seen anything like his. It radiated out of him as if it had a life of its own and the color! Usually auras are pinkish or violet in healthy people, yellowish or orange in those unhealthy. His was the most vibrant blue

FIRE BURN AND CAULDRON BUBBLE

HP MALLORY

I've ever seen—the color of the sky after a storm when the sun's rays bask everything in glory.

It emanated out of him like electricity.

"Hi, I'm Jolie," I said, remembering myself.

"How do you do?" And to make me drool even more than I already was, he had an accent, a British one. Ergh.

I glanced at Christa as I invited him into the reading room. Her mouth dropped open like a fish.

My sentiments exactly.

His navy blue sweater stretched to its capacity while attempting to span a pair of broad shoulders and a wide chest. The broad shoulders and spacious chest in question tapered to a trim waist and finished in a finale of long legs. The white shirt peeking from underneath his sweater contrasted against his tanned complexion and made me consider my own fair skin with dismay.

The stillness of the room did nothing to allay my nerves. I took a seat, shuffled the tarot cards, and handed him the deck. "Please choose five cards and lay them face up on the table."

He took a seat across from me, stretching his legs and rested his hands on his thighs. I chanced a look at him and took in his chocolate hair and darker eyes. His face was angular, and his Roman nose lent him a certain Paul Newman-esque quality. The beginnings of shadow did nothing to hide the definite cleft in his strong chin.

He didn't take the cards and instead, just smiled, revealing pearly whites and a set of grade A dimples.

"You did come for a reading?" I asked.

He nodded and covered my hand with his own. What felt like lightning ricocheted up my arm, and I swear my heart stopped for a second. The lone red bulb blinked a few times then continued to grow brighter until I thought it might explode. My gaze moved from his hand, up his arm and settled on his dark brown eyes. With the red light reflecting against him, he looked like the devil come to barter for my soul.

FIRE BURN AND CAULDRON BUBBLE
HP MALLORY

"I came for a reading, yes, but not with the cards. I'd like you to read … me." His rumbling baritone was hypnotic, and I fought the need to pull my hand from his warm grip.

I set the stack of cards aside, focusing on him again. I was so nervous I doubted if any of my visions would come. They were about as reliable as the weather anchors you see on TV.

After several long uncomfortable moments, I gave up. "I can't read you, I'm sorry," I said, my voice breaking. I shifted the eucalyptus-scented incense I'd lit to the farthest corner of the table, and waved my hands in front of my face, dispersing the smoke that seemed intent on wafting directly into my eyes. It swirled and danced in the air, as if indifferent to the fact that I couldn't help this stranger.

He removed his hand but stayed seated. I thought he'd leave, but he made no motion to do anything of the sort.

"Take your time."

Take my time? I was a nervous wreck and had no visions whatsoever. I just wanted this handsome stranger to leave, so my habitual life could return to normal.

But it appeared that was not in the cards.

The silence pounded against the walls, echoing the pulse of blood in my veins. Still, my companion said nothing. I'd had enough. "I don't know what to tell you."

He smiled again. "What do you see when you look at me?"

Adonis.

No, I couldn't say that. Maybe he'd like to hear about his aura? I didn't have any other cards up my sleeve … "I can see your aura," I almost whispered, fearing his ridicule.

His brows drew together. "What does it look like?"

"It isn't like anyone's I've ever seen before. It's bright blue, and it flares out of you … almost like electricity."

His smile disappeared, and he leaned forward. "Can you see everyone's auras?"

FIRE BURN AND CAULDRON BUBBLE

HP MALLORY

The incense dared to assault my eyes again, so I put it out and dumped it in the trashcan.

"Yes. Most people have much fainter glows to them—more often than not in the pink or orange family. I've never seen blue."

He chewed on that for a moment. "What do you suppose it is you're looking at—someone's soul?"

I shook my head. "I don't know. I do know, though, if someone's ailing, I can see it. Their aura goes a bit yellow." He nodded, and I added, "You're healthy."

He laughed, and I felt silly for saying it. He stood up, his imposing height making me feel all of three inches tall. Not enjoying the feel of him staring down at me, I stood and watched him pull out his wallet. I guess he'd heard enough and thought I was full of it. He set a one hundred dollar bill on the table in front of me. My hourly rate was fifty dollars, and we'd been maybe twenty minutes.

"I'd like to come see you for the next three Tuesdays at 4:00 p.m. Please don't schedule anyone after me. I'll compensate you for the entire afternoon."

I was shocked—what in the world would he want to come back for?

"Jolie, it was a pleasure meeting you, and I look forward to our next session." He turned to walk out of the room when I remembered myself.

"Wait, what name should I put in the appointment book?"

He turned and faced me. "Rand."

Then he walked out of the shop.

~

By the time Tuesday rolled around, I hadn't had much of a busy week. No more visits from ghosts, spirits, or whatever the PC term is for them. I'd had a few walk-ins, but that was about it. It was strange. October in Los Angeles was normally a busy time.

FIRE BURN AND CAULDRON BUBBLE

HP MALLORY

"Ten minutes to four," Christa said with a smile, leaning against the front desk and looking up from a stack of photos—her latest bout into photography.

"I wonder if he'll come," I mumbled.

Taking the top four photos off the stack, she arranged them against the desk as if they were puzzle pieces. I walked up behind her, only too pleased to find an outlet for my anxiety, my nerves skittish with the pending arrival of one very handsome man.

The photo in the middle caught my attention first. It was a landscape of the Malibu coastline, the intense blue of the ocean mirrored by the sky and interrupted only by the green of the hillside.

"Wow, that's a great one, Chris." I picked the photo up. "Can you frame it? I'd love to hang it in the store."

"Sure." She nodded and continued inspecting her photos, as if trying to find a fault in the angle or maybe the subject. Christa had aspirations of being a photographer and she had the eye for it. I admired her artistic ability—I, myself, hadn't been in line when God was handing out creativity.

She glanced at the clock again. "Five minutes to four."

I shrugged, feigning an indifference I didn't feel. "I'm just glad you're here. Rand strikes me as weird. Something's off …"

She laughed. "Oh, Jules, you don't trust your own mother."

I snorted at the comment and collapsed into the chair behind her, propping my feet on the corner of our mesh waste bin. So I didn't trust people—I think I had a better understanding of the human condition than most people did. That reminded me, I hadn't called my mom in at least a week. Note to self: be a better daughter.

The cuckoo clock on the wall announced it was 4:00 p.m. with a tinny rendition of Edelweiss while the two resident wooden figures did a polka. I'd never much liked the clock, but Christa wouldn't let me get rid of it.

FIRE BURN AND CAULDRON BUBBLE

HP MALLORY

The door opened, and I jumped to my feet, my heart jack hammering. I wasn't sure why I was so flustered, but as soon as I met the heat of Rand's dark eyes, it all made sense. He was here again even though I couldn't tell him anything important last time, and did I fail to mention he was gorgeous? His looks were enough to play with any girl's heartstrings.

"Good afternoon," he said, giving me a brisk nod.

He was dressed in black—black slacks, black collared shirt, and a black suit jacket. He looked like he'd just come from a funeral, but somehow I didn't think such was the case.

"Hi, Rand," Christa said, her gaze raking his statuesque body.

"How has your day been?" he answered as his eyes rested on me.

"Sorta slow," Christa responded before I could. He didn't even turn to notice her, and she frowned, obviously miffed. I smiled to myself and headed for the reading room, Rand on my heels.

I closed the door, and by the time I turned around, he'd already seated himself at the table. As I took my seat across from him, a heady scent of something unfamiliar hit me. It had notes of mint and cinnamon or maybe cardamom. The foreign scent was so captivating, I fought to refocus my attention.

"You fixed the light," he said with a smirk. "Much better."

I nodded and focused on my lap. "I didn't get a chance last time to ask you why you wanted to come back." I figured it was best to get it out in the open. I didn't think I'd do any better reading him this time.

"Well, I'm here for the same reason anyone else is."

I lifted my gaze and watched him lean back in the chair. He regarded me with amusement—raised eyebrows and a slight smirk pulling at his full lips.

FIRE BURN AND CAULDRON BUBBLE

HP MALLORY

I shook my head. "You aren't interested in a card reading, and I couldn't tell you anything ... substantial in our last meeting ..."

His throaty chuckle interrupted me. "You aren't much of a businesswoman, Jolie; it sounds like you're trying to get rid of me and my cold, hard cash."

Enough was enough. I'm not the type of person to beat around the bush, and he owed me an explanation. "So are you here to get a date with Christa?" I forced my gaze to hold his. He seemed taken aback, cocking his head while his shoulders bounced with surprise.

"Lovely though you both are, I'm afraid my visit leans more toward business than pleasure."

"I don't understand." I hoped my cheeks weren't as red as I imagined them. I guess I deserved it for being so bold.

He leaned forward, and I pulled back. "All in good time. Now, why don't you try to read me again?"

I motioned for his hands—sometimes touching the person in question helps generate my visions. As it had last time, his touch sent a jolt of electricity through me, and I had to fight not to lose my composure. There was something odd about this man.

I closed my eyes and exhaled, trying to focus while millions of bees warred with each other in my stomach. After driving my thoughts from all the questions I had regarding Rand, I was more comfortable.

At first nothing came.

I opened my eyes to find Rand staring at me. Just as I closed them again, a vision came—one that was piecemeal and none too clear.

"A man," I said, and my voice sounded like a foghorn in the quiet room. "He has dark hair and blue eyes, and there's something different about him. I can't quite pinpoint it ... it seems he's hired you for something ..."

My voice started to trail as the vision grew blurry. I tried to weave through the images, but they were too inconsistent. Once I got a hold of one, it wafted out of my grasp, and another indistinct one took its place.

"Go on," Rand prodded.

The vision was gone at this point, but I was still receiving emotional feedback. Sometimes I'll just get a vision and other times a vision with feelings. "The job's dangerous. I don't think you should take it."

And just like that, the feeling disappeared. I knew it was all I was going to get and I was frustrated, as it hadn't been my best work. Most of the time my feelings and visions are much clearer, but these were more like fragments— almost like short dream vignettes you can't interpret.

I let go of Rand's hands, and my own felt cold. I put them in my lap, hoping to warm them up again, but somehow my warmth didn't quite compare to his.

Rand seemed to be weighing what I'd told him—he strummed his fingers against his chin and chewed on his lip. "Can you tell me more about this man?"

"I couldn't see him in comparison to anyone else, so as far as height goes, I don't know. Dark hair and blue eyes, the hair was a little bit longish, maybe not a stylish haircut. He's white with no facial hair. That's about all I could see. He had something otherworldly about him. Maybe he was a psychic? I'm not sure."

"Dark hair and blue eyes you say?"

"Yes. He's a handsome man. I feel as if he's very old though he looked young. Maybe in his early thirties." I shrugged. "Sometimes my visions don't make much sense." Hey, I was just the middleman. It was up to him to interpret the message.

"You like the tall, dark, and handsome types then?"

Taken aback, I didn't know how to respond. "He had a nice face."

"You aren't receiving anything else?"

I shook my head. "I'm afraid not."

He stood. "Very good. I'm content with our meeting today. Do you have me scheduled for next week?"

FIRE BURN AND CAULDRON BUBBLE

HP MALLORY

I nodded and stood. The silence in the room pounded against me, and I fought to find something to say, but Rand beat me to it.

"Jolie, you need to have more confidence."

The closeness of the comment irritated me—who was this man who thought he could waltz into my shop and tell me I needed more confidence? Granted, he had a point, but damn it all if I were to tell him that!

Now, I was even more embarrassed, and I'm sure my face was the color of a bad sunburn. "I don't think you're here to discuss me."

"As a matter of fact, that's precisely the reason I'm …"

Rand didn't get a chance to finish when Christa came bounding through the door.

Christa hasn't quite grasped the whole customer service thing.

"Sorry to interrupt, but there was a car accident right outside the shop! This one car totally just plowed into the other one. I think everyone's alright, but how crazy is that?"

My attention found Rand's as Christa continued to describe the accident in minute detail. I couldn't help but wonder what he'd been about to say. It had sounded like he was here to discuss me … something that settled in my stomach like a big rock.

When Christa finished her accident report, Rand made his way to the door. I was on the verge of demanding he finish what he'd been about to say, but I couldn't summon the nerve.

"Cheers," he said and walked out.

AVAILABLE NOW!

Also Available From HP Mallory:

TO KILL A WARLOCK HP MALLORY

ONE

There was no way in hell I was looking in the mirror.

I knew it was bad when I glanced down. My stomach, if that's what you wanted to call it, was five times its usual size and exploded around me in a mass of jelly-like fat. To make matters worse, it was the color of overcooked peas—that certain jaundiced yellow.

"Wow, Dulce, you look like crap," Sam said.

I tried to give her my best "don't piss me off" look, but I wasn't sure my face complied because I had no clue what my face looked like. If it was anything like my stomach, it had to be canned-pea green and covered with raised bumps. The bumps in question weren't small like what you'd see on a toad—more like the size of dinner plates. Inside each bump, my skin was a darker green. And the texture … it was like running your finger across the tops of your teeth—jagged with valleys and mountains.

"Can you fix it?" I asked, my voice coming out monster-deep. I shouldn't have been surprised—I was a good seven feet tall now. And with the substantial body mass, my voice could only be deep.

"Yeah, I think I can." Sam's voice didn't waver which was a good sign.

I turned to avoid the sun's rays as they broke through the window, the sunlight not feeling too great against my boils.

I glanced at Sam's perfect sitting room, complete with a sofa, love seat and two armchairs all in a soothing beige, the de facto color for inoffensive furniture. Better Homes and Gardens sat unattended on Sam's coffee table—opened at an article about how beautiful drought resistant plants can be.

"You have nine eyes," Sam said.

At least they focused as one. I couldn't imagine having them all space cadetting out. Talk about a headache.

TO KILL A WARLOCK — HP MALLORY

Turning my attention from her happy sitting room, I forced my nine eyes on her, hoping the extra seven would be all the more penetrating. "Can you focus please?" I snapped.

Sam held her hands up. "Okay, okay. Sheesh, I guess getting changed into a gigantic booger put you into a crappy mood."

"Gee, you think?" My legs ached with the weight of my body. I had no idea if I had two legs or more or maybe a stump—my stomach covered them completely. I groaned and leaned against the wall, waiting for Sam to put on her glasses and figure out how to reverse the spell.

Sam was a witch and a pretty damned good one at that. I'd give her twenty minutes—then I'd be back to my old self. "Was it Fabian who boogered you?" she asked.

The mention of the little bastard set my anger ablaze. I had to count to five before the rage simmered out of me like a water balloon with a leak. I peeled myself off the wall and noticed a long spindle of green slime still stuck to the plaster; it reached out as if afraid to part with me.

"Ew!" Sam said, taking a step back from me. "You are so cleaning that wall."

"Fine. Just get me back to normal. I'm going to murder Fabian when I see him again."

Fabian was a warlock, a master of witchcraft. The little cretin hadn't taken it well when I'd come to his dark arts store to observe his latest truckload delivery. I knew the little rat was importing illegal potions (love potions, revenge potions, lust potions ... the list went on) and it was my job to stop it. I'm a Regulator, someone who monitors the creatures of the Netherworld to ensure they're not breaking any rules. Think law enforcement. And Fabian clearly was breaking some rule. Otherwise, he wouldn't have turned me into a walking phlegm pile.

Sam turned and faced a sheet of chocolate chip cookie mounds. "Hold on a second, I gotta put these in the oven."

She sashayed to the kitchen and I couldn't help but think what an odd picture we made: Sam, looking like the quintessential housewife with her apron, paisley dress and

TO KILL A WARLOCK   HP MALLORY

Stepford withe smile, and me, looking like an alien there to abduct her.

She slid the cookies in, shut the oven door and offered me a cheery grin. "Now, where was I? Ah yes, let me just whip something together."

Kneeling down, she opened a cupboard door beneath the kitchen island and grabbed two clay bowls, three glass jars and a metal whisk. One jar was filled with a pink powder, the next with a liquid that looked like molasses, and the third with a sugary-type powder.

"Sam, I don't have time to watch you make more cookies."

"Stop being so cranky! I'm stirring a potion to figure out how the heck I'm going to help you. I have no idea what spell that little creep put on you."

I frowned, or thought I did.

Sam opened a jar and took a pinch of the pink powder between her fingers. She dropped it in the bowl and whisked. Then she spooned one tablespoon of the molasses-looking stuff into the bowl and whisked again. Dumping half the white powder in with the rest, she paused and then dumped in the remainder.

Then she studied me, biting her lip. It was a look I knew too well—one that wouldn't lead to anything good.

"What?" I demanded.

"I need some part of your body. But it doesn't look like you have any hair. Hmm, do you have fingernails?"

I went to move my arm and four came up. But even with four arms, I didn't have a single fingernail—just webbed hands that looked like duck feet. I bet I was a good swimmer.

"Sorry, no fingernails."

"Well, this might hurt then."

She turned around and pulled a butcher knife from the knife block before approaching me like a stealthy cat. Even with my enormous body, I was up and out of her way instantly.

"Hold on a second! Keep that thing away from me!"

TO KILL A WARLOCK — HP MALLORY

"I need something from your body to make the potion work right. I won't take much, just a tiny piece of flesh."

I felt like adding "and not a drop of blood," but was too pre-occupied with protecting myself. I glanced at the wall and eyed the snotty globule, still attached to the plaster as if it had a right to be there. "What about that stuff?"

Sam grimaced but stopped advancing. "I'm not touching that."

"Okay, fine. How about some spit then?"

"Yeah, that might do."

My entire body breathed a sigh of relief which, given the size of me, was a pretty big breath. She put the knife back, and I made my way over to her slowly—not convinced she wasn't going to Sweeney Todd on me again.

She held out the bowl. "Spit."

I wasn't sure if my body was capable of spitting, but I leaned over and gave it a shot. Something slid up my throat, and I watched a blob of yellow land in her bowl.

It was moving. Gross.

It continued to vacillate as it interacted with the mixture, sprawling this way and that like it was having a seizure.

"Yuck," Sam said, holding the bowl as far away from her as possible. She returned it to the counter as the timer went off. Facing the oven, she grabbed a mitt that said "Kiss me, I'm Wiccan," pulled open the oven door and grabbed hold of the cookie sheet, placing them on the counter.

My stomach growled, sounding like an angry wolf, and unable to stop myself, I lumbered toward the cookies. I grabbed the sheet, not feeling the heat of the tin on my webbed hand. Sam watched me, her mouth hanging open as I lifted the sheet of cookies and emptied every last one into my mouth, swallowing them whole.

Sam's brows furrowed with anger, giving her normally angelic face a little attitude. "I was saving those to bring to work on Monday, thank you very much!"

TO KILL A WARLOCK   HP MALLORY

Sam didn't wear angry well. She was too pretty—dark brown shoulder length hair, perfect skin, perfect teeth, and big brown eyes.

"Come on, Sam," I pleaded, my mouth brimming with gooey chocolate. "You know I didn't do it on purpose. I don't even like sweets."

Something slimy and pink escaped my mouth and ran itself over my lips. It took me a second to realize it was my tongue. Rather than curling back into my mouth, it hesitated on my lip as I focused on a stray chocolate chip lounging against the counter. Instantly, my tongue lurched out and grabbed hold of the chip, recoiling into my mouth like a spent cobra.

Sam quirked a less-than-amused brow and ran her palms down her paisley apron, as though composing herself. I have to count to ten, twenty sometimes. Otherwise, my temper is an ugly son of a bitch.

"Besides, none of the guys at work deserve them anyway." I knew because I worked with Sam.

She appeared to be in the process of forgiving me, a slight smile playing with the ends of her lips. I turned to the potion sitting in the bowl. The yellow ball of spit was still shivering. I nearly gagged when Sam stabbed it with the whisk and continued stirring.

I peered over her shoulder and watched the potion change colors—going from a pale brown to red then deepening into flame orange. "What's it doing?"

Sam nodded as if she were watching a movie, knew the ending, and was just dying to tell someone what happens. "Ah, of course, I should've known. The little devil put a *Hemmen* on you."

"A what?"

"It's a short-term shape-shifting charm. You'll be back to normal in about five hours or so."

"Five hours? Look at me! Can't you get rid of it sooner?"

Sam shook her head. "Would take lots of herbs and potions I don't have. I'd probably have to get them at

TO KILL A WARLOCK — HP MALLORY

Fabian's." She laughed. "How ironic is that? Just hang tight. It'll go away, I promise."

It figures the little bastard would've put a short-term spell on me. Currently, there weren't any laws against turning someone into a hideous creature if it would wear off after a day. And even if he had turned me into this creature long term, he'd probably only get a slap on the wrists. The Netherworld wasn't exactly good with doling out punishments.

I was working on making it better.

"You're sure?" I asked.

She nodded. "One hundred percent. Let's just watch a couple movies to keep your mind off it."

She hurried to her entertainment center and scanned through the numerous titles, using her index finger to guide her. "Dirty Dancing? Bridget Jones?"

"The first or second Bridget?"

"I have both," she said with a triumphant smile.

"I like the first one better."

With a nod of agreement, Sam pulled the DVD out and gingerly placed it into the player.

I wasn't really sure what to do with myself. I couldn't fit on her couch, and with my slime ball still suspended on the wall, sitting was out.

Sam pointed a finger in my general direction. "How did Fabian catch you unaware enough to change you into … that?"

I sighed—which came out as a grunt.

"Well?" she asked while skipping into the kitchen to microwave a packet of popcorn.

I couldn't quite meet her eyes and, instead, focused on drawing slimy lines on her counter top with one of my eight index fingers.

This was the part of the story I was least excited about. Fabian never should've caught me with my guard down. I'm a fairy. We're renowned for being extremely quick, and we've got more magic in our little finger … well, you get it.

TO KILL A WARLOCK — HP MALLORY

"My back was to him," I mumbled. "I know, I know … super dumb."

Sam's eyebrows reached for the ceiling. "That doesn't sound like you at all, Dulce. Why was your back to him?"

If I wasn't excited about that last part of the story, this part excited me even less. "There was someone in his shop—a guy I've never seen before."

Sam laughed and quirked a knowing brow. "So let me make sure I've got this right."

She plopped her hands on her hips and paused for a good three seconds. Maybe she was getting me back for the cookies. "You, one of the strongest fairies around, turned your back on a known dark arts practitioner because he had a hot guy in his store?"

"No, it wasn't that at all. I'd never seen him before, and I couldn't figure out what he was."

As a fairy, I have the innate ability to decipher a creature as soon as I see one. I can tell a warlock from a vampire from a gorgon in seconds. I don't get paid the big bucks for nothing.

Sam's face took on a definite look of surprise, her eyes wide, her lips twitching. "You couldn't tell what he was? Wow, that's a first."

I nodded my bulbous head. "Exactly. And if he's here permanently, he never checked in with me or Headquarters."

Any new creature who hoped to settle in Splendor, California, needed to contact Headquarters, otherwise known as the A.N.C (Association for Netherworld Creatures). And more pointedly, they had to register with me. This new stranger had done neither. Maybe he'd gotten lost when coming over. It wasn't rare for a creature to come through the passage from the Netherworld to Earth and somehow get lost along the way. You'll find the directionally challenged everywhere.

"Maybe you should talk to Bram," Sam said. "He always seems to know what's going on."

It wasn't a bad idea, actually. Bram was a vampire (I know, how cliché …) who ran a nightclub called No

TO KILL A WARLOCK   HP MALLORY

Regrets. No Regrets was in the middle of the city and was the biggest hangout for creatures of the Netherworld. If something was going down, Bram was always among the first to know.

"Yeah, not a bad idea," I said.

First things first, I'd pay a visit to Fabian and let him know how much I didn't appreciate his little prank. Then, if he couldn't give me any info on his strange visitor, I'd try Bram. My third choice was Dagan, a demon who ran an S&M club called Payne that wasn't far from No Regrets. Dagan was always my last resort—I hated going to Payne. I'd seen things there that had scarred me for life.

So it looked like my plans for the weekend were shot. Not like I had much planned—just editing chapters of my romance novel, *Captain Slade's Bounty*. I'd been looking forward to a quiet weekend, so I could focus on Captain Slade and his ladylove, Clementine. Now, it looked like I'd be working the streets of Splendor instead.

Big goddammit.

###

Six hours later, and with Bridget Jones one and two, Dirty Dancing and four bowls of popcorn under my belt, I was home and back to myself. I felt like hell considering I'd eaten more in one evening than I usually ate in a day.

I headed through my sparse living room and straight to my bathroom. I threw off the clothes Sam had lent me (the mass I'd been turned into had shredded my outfit) and turned on the shower full force. I was back to myself, but still disgusting—covered in a layer of what looked like clear snot, like I'd just dropped out of God's nose.

I tested the water, waiting for it to warm. Then I turned to face myself in the mirror. I'm not a vain person but I was very happy to see my small and slender self reflected back at me. I pulled my mane of honey-gold hair from behind my back and inspected it. If I was narcissistic about anything, it was my hair. It was long—right down to my lower back and

TO KILL A WARLOCK — HP MALLORY

it looked like it had fared well in the metamorphosis. Except for the slime.

I keep my hair long because I'm not thrilled with my ears. As a fairy, my ears come to points at the tops. Think Spock. Other than that, I look like a human. And no, I don't have wings.

I checked the water again; it was warm enough. I lived in a pretty crappy apartment and the pipes in the wall screamed every time I turned the hot water on—they'd just pound if I wanted cold. I know I mentioned earlier that I make a good living, and I do. The crap apartment is due to the fact that I'm saving all my money to retire from the A.N.C. Then I can focus on my writing full time.

It might sound strange that one as magical as I would need to work nine-to-five weekdays and some weekends, but there it is. There are strict laws that disallow those of us who can, to create money out of thin air. I guess the powers that be thought about it and realized all creatures who can create something from nothing—fairies, witches and warlocks, just to name a few—certainly would be at the top of the food chain ... something bad for the less fortunate creatures and humans, too.

That, and money created from magic turns to dust after a few days anyway.

So I have to work. I've accepted it.

I stepped under the less-than-strong flow of water, which was more like a little boy peeing on my head, and grabbed my gardenia-scented soap, lathering my entire body. I repeated the process four more times before I could actually say I felt any semblance of clean.

After toweling myself off, I plodded into the living room with a towel wrapped around my head and body. Then I noticed the blinking red light on the answering machine beckoning to me. I had three new messages.

I hit play. Bram's alto voice, the pitch reminiscent of his English roots, filled my living room.

"Ah, I've missed you, Sweet. Come by the club. I have information for you."

TO KILL A WARLOCK — HP MALLORY

The arrogant bastard—he never bothered saying, "It's Bram." As to the information he had ... that could be meaningless. Bram had been trying to get into my pants since I became a Regulator—about two years ago. And just because he had my home phone number didn't mean he'd succeeded—I used to be listed in the phone book.

I deleted the message. I'd have to pay him a visit tomorrow. The next message was from my dry cleaners—my clothes were ready to be picked up. The third message was from my boss.

"Dulce, it's Quillan, Sam told me what Fabian did to you. Just calling to make sure you're okay. Give me a call when you get in."

I hit delete. Quillan was a good boss; he was the big wig of Headquarters, and an elf.

Elves are nothing like you're imagining them, although they are magical. Whereas I have the innate ability to create something from nothing (all it takes is a little fairy dust), Quillan is magical in his own way. He can cast spells, control his own aging and he's got the strength of a giant. Fairies and elves are like distant cousins—sprung from the same magical family tree but separated by lots of branches.

Quillan is tallish—maybe five-ten or so, slim, and has a certain regality to him. He's got a head of curly blond hair that would make Cupid envious, bronze skin, and eyes the color of amber. And he's also the muse for the hero in my romance novel. But he doesn't know that.

I wasn't in the mood to call Quillan back. I'd add him to my long list of visits for tomorrow. Even though it was Saturday, it looked like I'd be working.

Sometimes working law enforcement for the Netherworld is a real bitch.

AVAILABLE NOW!

H. P. Mallory is the author of the Jolie Wilkins series, the Dulcie O'Neil series and the Lily Harper series.

She began her writing career as a self-published author and after reaching a tremendous amount of success, decided to become a traditionally published author and hasn't looked back since.
H. P. Mallory lives in Southern California with her husband and son, where she is at work on her next book.
If you are interested in receiving emails when she releases new books, please sign up for her email distribution list by visiting her website and clicking the "contact" tab:
www.hpmallory.com

Be sure to join HP's online Facebook community where you will find pictures of the characters from both series and lots of other fun stuff including an online book club!
Facebook: https://www.facebook.com/hpmallory

Find H.P. Mallory Online:
www.hpmallory.com
http://twitter.com/hpmallory
https://www.facebook.com/hpmallory

THE JOLIE WILKINS SERIES:

Fire Burn and Cauldron Bubble
Toil and Trouble
Be Witched (Novella)
Witchful Thinking
The Witch Is Back
Something Witchy This Way Comes

Stay Tuned for the Jolie Wilkins Spinoff Series!

THE DULCIE O'NEIL SERIES:

To Kill A Warlock
A Tale Of Two Goblins
Great Hexpectations
Wuthering Frights
Malice In Wonderland
For Whom The Spell Tolls

THE LILY HARPER SERIES:

Better Off Dead

Made in the USA
San Bernardino, CA
14 July 2015